cp smith
Wallflowers
Three of a Kind

Felicia
you Rock

First Edition: November 2016

Formatting: CP Smith
Cover design: Dark Waters Covers
Cover Photograph Depositphoto Fresh lilac flowers @ daffodil

ISBN-13: 978-1540442864

ISBN-10: 1540442861

Information address: cpsmith74135@gmail.com

Titles by CP Smith

Acknowledgments

This section is for those who helped me while I wrote this book. To say it would also have to include my readers is an understatement. You stood by me while I grieved the loss of my mother, and encouraged me to keep writing even when I wanted to stop. Thank you!

To my family, who feeds me when I don't eat, tells me to go to bed when I don't sleep, and loves me even when I forget to shower, *all* of this is for you. I love you!

Julia Goda and Mayra Statham. What can I say? You're my rock in this crazy publishing world. Soul Sisters. You held my hand while I cried. Yelled at me when I needed it, and put up with my crabby ass even when you shouldn't have to. I LOVE you both. To the moon and back.

Deb Hawblitzel Schultz, you treat me like family, always have my back, and bring me tiny cans of Mountain Dew on book signings! You're the tops! Best PA out there. I love you, my hooker . . . Oh, yeah!!!!

Angela Shue, Kelly Marshall-White, Sallie Brown Davis, Michelle Reed, Allison Michaels, and Joanne Thompson. You, ladies, are the best bunch of betas out there. Thank you for taking time out of your busy day to help bring my stories to life.

Julia Goda, besides being my sister you're also the best damn editor out there. Thank you!

Tracie Douglas-Rabas, you took my hopes and dreams for this cover and made them a reality. It's stunning. Thank you!

Nikki Worrell, your knowledge about Harleys impresses me, and I'm eternally grateful for your help. Devin thanks you for not making him look like a beginner.

And to my original Dream Team. You ladies are never far from my thoughts. All of this is because of you! You encouraged me to publish, and because of your faith in me, I did! That's a debt I can never repay. Thank you!

Dedication

For my favorite Wallflower Kellyann Armstrong

cp smith

Wallflowers

Three of a Kind

One

NATHANIEL HAWTHORNE ONCE WROTE in the preface of *The Marble Faun* that *"Romance and poetry, ivy, lichens, and wallflowers, need ruin to make them grow."* Hiding behind a flowering lilac bush near my aunts' back garden, frozen in place as my new neighbor worked out in the courtyard, I stared at a single wisteria vine, reflecting on Hawthorne's words. The vine had worked its way down the side of the wooden pergola, then through the cobblestone path to break free from its prison. It had been trained carefully over time to flower in one spot, but this single branch had defied its current state, sprouting through the crumbled ruins, just as Hawthorne had written.

I envied that vine's courage. It had fought against what life had dealt it, searching for a better one outside the confines of the pergola—unlike me . . .

The doorbell ringing.

An officer speaking in hushed tones.

The wailing sound of a child screaming for her parents.

I closed my eyes against the echoes of my past and tried to block them out.

The sound of male exertion resonated throughout the courtyard, so I opened my eyes and turned my head, shaking off the memory that had held me hostage my whole life.

An unexpected spark of excitement bubbled in my chest, working its way down to settle in my gut as I watched the black-haired stranger. The sensation was foreign to me—unsettling. I'd spent so much time avoiding life that my immediate attraction for this unknown man caught me off guard. But I couldn't deny the truth. The evidence was in the racing of my heart and the moisture collecting in my palms as my mouth ran dry. All my carefully laid plans to protect my heart seemed childish now; and in that moment of sexual awareness, I wondered what it would be like to be in love.

Peeling my eyes off the stranger, I looked back at the vine growing through the crack in the path and wondered if I could take a chance like it had and change the course of my life.

I knew if I wanted a life outside my books, a life that also included a man like the one currently shirtless in my aunts' back garden, I, too, would have to break down the walls I'd hidden behind so I could grow from the rubble of my past . . . To bloom.

Just like those wallflowers.

However, as much as I wanted a different course for my life at that moment, I wondered if I could truly let someone in. Let someone scale the walls I'd built.

Looking up from the courageous root, I scanned the private flower-covered courtyard abutting my aunts' three-story building—which sat in the heart of historic Savannah, Georgia—until my eyes once again landed on the black-haired man. This courtyard was my favorite place in or out of Savannah. My aunts had spent years cultivating the area until it was an oasis from the world. Flowers of every color bordered the fence while overgrown lilac bushes scented the air. Pink and purple wisteria wound tightly around the pergola, providing shade from the Georgia heat, as a small water garden with a replica of the *Bird Girl*—a statue made famous by the book *Midnight in the Garden of Good and Evil*—sat in the center. The trickling cascade, combined with the heady scent of flowers, always relaxed me, focused my thoughts, and helped transport me into the worlds of the books I read.

Today, like every Saturday of my adult life, I'd decided to read. So I'd picked up one of my well-read copies of *Devil's Bride* by Stephanie Laurens and headed downstairs to the courtyard for a relaxing afternoon of reading before heading to a mandatory company picnic that night. But the flowers and historical romance were immediately forgotten the moment I'd walked out the back door of my aunts' store and laid eyes on my new neighbor.

Still hiding behind a flowering lilac bush, I watched each descent and ascent as the new tenant in 2B lifted his hard body with ease. I was fully captivated by the sheen of sweat coating his body, and tracked the sweat dripping down his brow in tiny droplets. This man was beautiful, and I was utterly transfixed by his graceful movements as his biceps contracted with each rise, but none more so than when he lifted his head and looked up. Eyes the color of brilliant blue topaz glowed in the morning sun, blazing with crystalline fire like a diamond yet holding the coolness of ice.

He'd moved in the day before while I was at work, and all I knew about my new neighbor was that he was a man—though the common term used to describe the opposite sex wasn't strong enough for this particular male—who liked to listen to Lynyrd Skynyrd late at night. No, he was no ordinary man; he held an air of danger that smoldered just beneath the surface—and every inch of me approved.

When he looked in my direction I inched back further to avoid detection, bumping into a familiar warm body liberally doused with Calvin Klein's *Obsession*.

"He's a fine specimen, isn't he?" I jumped at my Aunt Bernice's whispered voice and nodded slowly as I continued to stare. "And, I might add, from what I've seen of the gentleman in question, you could do a far sight worse."

"Bernice, I'm just . . . I'm not . . ." I stopped and gave up. She knew what I was doing, so it was a waste of time to argue.

"Of course, you are, butterbean. You've been livin' a half-life, barely breathin' except for your books since your family died," she whispered low. "You and I know better than most that life is a fleetin' moment in time, every moment extraordinary and priceless. So don't waste it because you're scared to let people in."

"Are you readin' my mind?" I asked back, turning to look at her.

"So you agree you've hidden from the world long enough?"

"It may have crossed my mind," I whispered, folding my arms about my chest.

"I'll bet," she snorted. "If I were you and knew I had a man like that livin' right next door, I'd take a breath and start livin' pretty darn quickly."

"I'm not sure datin' my neighbor is a good idea," I replied, jerking my head in 2B's direction.

Bernice's eyebrows shot skyward, and she laid me out with a look of pure disbelief.

"Sorry?" she replied dumbfounded. "Did you just say you don't think a man who's as gorgeous as the devil himself, seems like a Southern gentleman, and has a body that would tempt the purest of virgins isn't a good idea 'cause he lives next door?"

I snorted at my fifty-six-year-old aunt then threw my hand over my mouth and looked back at 2B to see if he'd heard.

Nope, just up and down and up and down.

Lord, that man is strong.

"Since when does bein' a Southern gentleman garner points in your book?" I asked quietly, not taking my eyes off the perfection that was 2B. "You preferred bein' single your whole life."

"Since your daddy would have wanted that for you."

I froze at the mention of my father and curled my hands into fists so hard that my nails bit into my skin.

"You know I loved my brother somethin' fierce," she continued, "so I plan to honor his wishes. He instructed us in his trust to make sure you were happy, and you're not. Don't follow in my footsteps, sugar. What I wanted for *my* life is entirely different than what you want for yourself," she lilted with a drawl, but with an edge of sophistication that would have put Scarlett O'Hara to shame. "So go on now. Take the first step." She nudged me forward, but I locked my knees and shook my head. "Lord, you're stubborn," she huffed. "Calla, if you don't introduce yourself, I'll do it for you, and you won't like it."

"I need a minute."

"Well, make it quick. There's a truck comin' soon with a load of clothes we bought at an estate sale, and we'll need your help unpacking it," she ordered before turning to leave.

I nodded again, ignoring her parting comment. My focus was on 2B's hair. It was longer than most men wore, and the bangs had fallen into his eyes, creating a frame around the brilliant blue.

"Calla Lily!" Bernice shouted out my given name. I startled at the sound as 2B looked in our direction. Jumping back further so he wouldn't see me gawking through the lilacs, I turned to find Bernice standing at the back door of Frock You, the vintage clothing store she and her sister Eunice had owned since 1984.

"Ma'am?" 2B asked in a gravelly Southern drawl that was as smooth as molasses and just as dark and delicious. The deep timbre of his voice was like an aphrodisiac, so I turned back to soak in the sound of it.

"Don't pay me any mind, Mr. Hawthorne. I was just tellin' my dear sister we needed more Calla Lilies in the garden. You just keep workin' those fine muscles of yours as if I weren't here."

He'd paused mid-pushup and began again, grinning wickedly at my aunt as he dropped down.

Turning back, I waved her on, shushing her with a look that begged her to stay quiet, then turned back and watched who I now knew was Mr. Hawthorne finish his pushups.

Hawthorne?

The fact that I'd just been thinking about Nathaniel Hawthorne's quote seemed like a sign from above.

"Maybe I *should* introduce myself," I whispered.

I looked down at my worn-out jeans, flip-flops, and light blue, vintage peasant top I'd grabbed in the last haul my aunts had bought for their store. It wasn't an outfit that encouraged men to look once, let alone twice. I would need help with my wardrobe if I was going to venture forth into the world of dating.

Just as I had with my books, I'd used clothing to hide from men. The loss of my family in a car accident when I was six was the reason why. I'd purposely avoided the opposite sex and intimate friendships as a way to insulate myself from further heartache and loss. If I didn't put myself out there, I couldn't be hurt. At least that's what the child inside me reasoned anytime someone tried to get close. Of course, she was silent in the face of 2B's presence. Instead, she'd turned into a hormone-driven adolescent.

Mr. Hawthorne grunted low with exertion, so I peeked through the bushes again. Framed in the morning sun he stood and began stretching an arm across his chest, tugging with his other hand to loosen the muscles he'd just worked. I watched in silence as he repeated the action with the other arm then bent at the waist to stretch out his legs. He was the finest-looking man I'd encountered in my twenty-seven years. Well over six feet, his proportions were perfectly symmetrical, perfectly muscled—perfectly male. All the way down to the deep V in his lower abdomen. He was, in my mind, Devil Cynster come to life from the pages of *Devil's Bride*.

"Be bold, Cali," I whispered, moving forward a step. "It's time to start livin'."

Besides needing to take the first step toward shattering the walls I'd built and move forward into a brave new world, he was my neighbor. It was only polite to introduce myself. The fact that I'd watched his body rise and fall like a lover in the heat of passion shouldn't affect my manners in the least.

Taking another step toward revealing myself to him, determined that the ruins of my past should be felled that very instant, I stopped short when the gate that opened to the side alley swung wide, and an attractive blonde dressed to the nines walked into the courtyard. I watched as my Devil come to life turned, leveled a sinister smile at her, and then wrapped her in a hug that spoke of affection and love for the woman.

"Well?" Bernice asked with humor laced in her voice. "Are you gonna take the plunge and talk to the man or let another woman have first dibs?"

Frozen like a statue, I watched as Mr. Hawthorne and the blonde conversed with each other, completely absorbed and unaware of my presence.

Too late.

Turning away from the couple, I marched toward Bernice, brushing past her, and kept walking through the back door of Frock You.

"There are other fish in the sea," I mumbled as I passed.

"True enough, sugar. But I'm not sure the other fish would taste as good as Devin does."

I stopped in my tracks and looked back at her. "Devin?"

"Devin Hawthorne," she confirmed. "Former Atlanta police detective. He's hangin' up his badge to become a private investigator and moved to Savannah for a change of pace. He *also* rented the office space next to the store, so I imagine we'll be seein' plenty of him," she explained. "You sure you don't wanna go back out there and introduce yourself, butterbean?"

The twinkle in her eyes as she relayed this information was as infuriating as a mosquito in search of blood.

"I'll pass. I'm not so desperate for a man as to make a ninny of myself."

"Spoken like a true Southern lady. A gentleman should always do the pursuin' anyhow."

I rolled my eyes. "Bernice, since when do you hold to the ways of the South?" I asked while heading for the store's kitchen and a cup of coffee and biscone. "You fought Granddaddy at every turn when it came to me bein' raised by him and Grandmother so I wouldn't turn into some snooty debutante."

"True, but my daddy raised a lady to begin with, butterbean. I may have thumbed my nose at borin' cotillions and charity events, but that doesn't mean I don't hold to the ways of the South when it comes to my dearest niece and men. I raised you, wanted what was best for you just like any mother would, because you, my dear sweet girl, are magnificent. You deserve a man who knows how to treat her." She ran her fingers gently across my cheek as her eyes softened. "So don't jump at the first chance you have with any ole man. Hold out for a true gentleman, hold out for someone like Mr. Hawthorne."

"Bernie," I whispered, grabbing hold of her hand as it cupped my cheek.

"No tears, sugar. We're Armstrongs, not bleedin' heart liberals. Suck it up," Bernice admonished with a wink.

As I tried to hold back the tears, my Aunt Eunice came rushing in with a look of sheer delight plastered across her face, dragging her longtime *friend* Odis Lee Wilder in her wake.

My aunts were two years apart in age. Eunice was the older of the two. Both were Southern beauties with shoulder length, blonde hair—they kept it that way thanks to Miss Clairol—with bright blue eyes and peaches and cream complexions.

They were rebels from what I liked to refer to as 'The Madonna Generation.' My aunts believed in doing whatever the hell they wanted whenever they wanted. And they'd done it with gusto for years until it all came to a screeching halt when my family died and they took me in.

Much to my grandparents' chagrin, both were named as my guardians. Because of this, they'd stopped their wild ways and settled down to raise me for their beloved older brother.

At the time of my parents' death, Frock You had been more of a hobby for them, but when they found themselves with a child to raise, they settled into the store and turned it into an upscale boutique the rich and famous frequently visited.

It was situated at street level of the three-story building fronting the Savannah River on River Street. They'd bought the old building with the inheritance they'd received when their grandfather died, back when historic Savannah didn't have the price tag it does now. They renovated the top floor into a spacious three-bedroom apartment and converted the office spaces on the second floor into two one-bedroom apartments. I lived on the second floor, right next door to 2B.

This old building with its aged brown brick, private flower-covered courtyard and cobblestone-paved street was the only home I remembered, and I loved every inch of it.

"Sister, it finally happened!" Eunice exploded as she entered the kitchen.

"Calm yourself, Neecy," Odis Lee chuckled with a gleam in his eyes. "Mornin', Calla Lily. Mornin', Bernie."

Odis Lee was a cross between Colonel Sanders and Sonny Crockett. His dark blond hair was speckled with gray, which he wore too long and slicked back. His moustache ran long and thick down the sides of his mouth, and he paired it with a petite goatee on his chin. Odis also dressed like he had just stepped off a plane from Miami, Florida, during the 1980s. Light blue linen pants showed off tan loafers worn without socks, topped off with a white T-shirt and a tan linen jacket. His entire ensemble had been put together by Aunt

9

Eunice with vintage pieces they'd purchased for the store.

Like Bernice, Eunice—or Neecy as she liked to be called—never married. Unlike Bernice, Eunice still entertained gentlemen when she felt like it. Odis Lee has held the position of *friend* for the past fifteen years.

"Hush, Odis Lee. This is far too good not to be excited about," Eunice scolded.

"For goodness sake, Neecy. I don't want to hear about you and Odis Lee's sex life," Bernice said, holding up her hands in protest.

Eunice gasped, and I rolled my lips between my teeth to keep from laughing.

"Don't be crass, Bernie," Eunice admonished. "I'm *talkin'* about Billy Ray Stutter."

"All right, I'll bite. What's that horse's patootie done now?"

"That jackass has finally left his shrew of a wife, and she is dumpin' everythin' of his on the front lawn in a hissy fit to end all hissy fits. Odis and I saw it with our own two eyes."

"Wouldn't that be your own four eyes, Aunt Neecy?"

Bernice turned and looked at me, grinning. "Smartass becomes you, butterbean," she chuckled and grabbed her purse off the counter.

"We'll get coffee to go at Blends," Bernice announced as she brushed past Eunice and Odis Lee. "Do we still have the foldaway chairs in the back of the Wagoneer? The way that woman carries on, it could take her hours before she's done makin' a spectacle of herself; and if the park benches are all taken by rubberneckers, I don't wanna stand all day long.

"Y'all are horrible, vile snoops," I shouted as they made their way to the front of the store. "I heard Billy Ray hasn't been seen in days. What if somethin's happened to him?"

"Nonsense, Calla Lily," Aunt Eunice hollered back. "Only the good die young. Just ask Billy Joel. Billy Ray Stutter has been a blight on Savannah since he was a teen. The man is a no-good scoundrel. I guarantee he's off whorin' around up near Atlanta and he'll haul his sorry ass back when he's done. Then we'll have another show to watch when he finds out all his stuff is gone."

Bernice ripped open the door at that announcement, hooting with excitement.

Clearly, she was looking forward to that showdown as well.

"Call Shelly and have her mind the store while we're gone," Eunice shouted as the door closed behind them, leaving behind a perfumed haze of Calvin Klein's *Obsession*.

I'd followed them to the door, so I watched out the side window as they turned the corner and climbed into Eunice's Jeep, then drove up the cobblestone ramp that led to Bay Street.

It must be noted that all three had varying degrees of giddiness on their faces.

Giggling in amusement, I checked the clock and saw that I had a few hours to kill before Poe Publishing's company picnic, so I called Shelly and went to the stock room to grab a ladder and the outfit I'd put aside to dress the front of the store.

The oversized picture window where I created the vignettes was enclosed with walls like the high-end boutiques so we could change out the clothes to go with the seasons. Since it was springtime now and summer was fast approaching, I wanted to create a beach theme with straw bags and beach balls.

Unlocking the door, I pulled it open and started to walk in, but paused before entering when I heard footsteps upstairs in apartment 2B. Moaning in frustration, I grabbed the ladder I'd set aside and walked into the staging area hell-bent on forgetting about my new neighbor.

Savannah could be hotter than Hades, and the huge picture window brought in the sun, heating the small space like an oven. Sweat dampened my skin within minutes, making my hands slippery as I replaced clothing on the mannequin. Twinkle lights needed to be taken down and replaced with raffia, so I climbed the ladder and began disassembling each section. With slick hands and arms full of lights, I threw loose strands around my neck so I could reach the last section. I was leaning too far to the right when the front door opened, causing the bell to ring loudly in my ear. Startled, I jumped and lost my grip, squeaking out, "Oh shit," as the ladder came out from underneath me.

Squeezing my eyes shut as I fell, I landed hard on the ground with a thud as the twinkle lights scattered and tangled in my hair.

"Calla?"

I opened my eyes at the sound of Bobby Jones' amused voice and groaned. Bobby was an old friend of the family who worked for my grandfather, one who'd like to be more than just a friend. But the chemistry had never been there on my end. That, and the fact that I'd always kept my distance from entanglements, meant I treated him more like an annoying older brother than relationship material. Which also meant Bobby catching me with my proverbial drawers around my ankles pissed me off.

"Help me up, will you?"

He leaned over and grabbed me under the arms, hauling me from the floor. Then, per usual, he pulled me into a hug once he had me on my feet, holding me a little longer than was comfortable.

"You can let me go now," I sighed.

"Where's the fun in that, sugar?"

I tried to push him back, but he didn't budge.

"Bobby, we are standin' in the window. All of Savannah can see us. Please, let go."

A deep chuckle rolled through his chest as he let go and stepped back. When I turned to pick up the ladder, I found Devin Hawthorne standing in front of the window with his girlfriend. He'd changed his clothes and was now wearing a tight white T-shirt, equally tight jeans that accentuated his powerful legs, and scuffed motorcycle boots instead of the customary Ropers most men wore. He'd rendered me breathless without his shirt on, but the whole package, down to the scuffed boots, left me speechless and unmoving as a scarecrow guarding corn.

I locked eyes with his and my reaction was immediate. My body hummed with attraction and my nipples hardened in response. Devin's gaze dropped to my body as my face flushed with embarrassment, scanning me slowly from head to toe.

"You're a mess, sugar," Bobby chuckled from behind me.

When Devin's girlfriend looked at him and laughed, I came unstuck and stepped back, crashing into Bobby, scooting around him as I rushed out of the window.

Kill. Me. Now.

I'd just made an utter ninny of myself in front of 2B.

Grabbing hold of my arm as I made my escape, Bobby crooned, "Hold still while I get the lights out of your hair."

I paused reluctantly.

I heard Devin open and close his office door, then a low murmur of voices reached through the wall.

"Did your aunts rent the office space next door?"

"Mmm," I answered, distracted as I tried to hear through the walls what was being said.

"I came by to take you to lunch," Bobby announced once he'd removed the lights from my hair. When he put his hands on both my shoulders and squeezed, I stepped forward out of his reach.

I may not have grown up in high society like most of the young women born into wealthy families, thanks to my aunts, but that didn't stop some of their eligible sons from pursuing me from time to time. They'd like nothing more than to tie their family to mine since an Armstrong had been in Savannah since, well, forever. There was no doubt in my mind that having one as your wife would be a crowning achievement for anyone who cared about keeping Savannah's bloodlines pure. Unfortunately for Bobby and the other eligible founding sons, I would rather eat mud than marry one of them. My aunts and I didn't care about bloodlines. If I got married, it would be for love. Nothing more, nothing less. Be it with a farmer, a mechanic, or a police officer turned private investigator. But definitely not to someone like Bobby Jones.

With blond hair and squinty, green eyes to go along with an unimpressive chin, Bobby wasn't as stuck-up as some of the other men of supposed good breeding in town, but he was boring as hell in that upper crust, entitled way some prominent families could be. He wasn't bad looking, but he lacked that certain something that set him apart from other men. He also got weekly manicures and played golf entirely too much for my taste. Bobby was, quite literally, the prototypical antagonist in a romance novel, not the muscle-bound hero to the damsel in distress. And though I looked like a Georgia peach with blonde hair and ivory skin, my taste in men ran darker, maybe even a little dangerous.

Female laughter sounded through the walls and tweaked my last nerve. Closing my eyes for patience, I envisioned Devin and his girlfriend as he showed off his new office space. His touch would be whisper soft as he led her through the rooms, heightening her awareness of him. He'd also smile that wicked smile of his as she flirted and giggled in her *increasingly* irritating tone.

When the low rumble of a male voice filtered through the wall, causing my heart to accelerate, my eyes popped open as a revelation broke to the surface. *He'd eat me alive and leave me in a puddle of unrequited love.*

Devin Hawthorne may have been the prototypical protagonist in my personal romance novel. But I knew with certainty, as I listened to his sexy timber through the walls, I was not experienced enough to handle a man like that.

"Did you hear me, sugar? I said I came to take you to lunch."

Turning to reply to Bobby's invitation, I shook my head. "I have to wait for a shipment, then I have to attend a company picnic later in the day."

Bobby's mouth pulled into a half-assed grin. "Sugar, if you'd just marry me, you could stop editin' books for a livin' and spend your days shoppin' to your heart's content."

Do nothing but shop? The thought caused a shiver.

"Temptin', Bobby, but I have bigger dreams for my life than spendin' it shoppin' for the perfect outfit."

He raised a surprised brow I had no doubt had been manscaped and tsked at me. "Calla Lily, you're an Armstrong. You were born to shop."

"Don't call me Calla Lily," I bit out. "As for the '*born to shop*,' that particular gene must have skipped a generation. Now, run along, Bobby. Go find yourself a perfect princess who doesn't mind spendin' her days in high heels, 'cause you and I both know you're only interested in me for my money."

Bobby threw a hand over his heart dramatically and stumbled back as if he'd been shot. "You wound me, Calla. I'm not *just* after your money. I would dearly love to get inside your pretty panties, too."

"Scoundrel! Reprobate," I gasped, laughing. "Out!" Then I pointed toward the door.

He bowed elegantly, grinning at my mock outrage, then sneaked a quick kiss on my cheek before leaving.

"Spend my days shoppin'? No, thank you," I grumbled as I watched him turn the corner to the alley and slide into his Mercedes coupé. "I'd rather roll around in the mud."

At that moment, Devin walked past the window with his girlfriend in tow as I watched Bobby drive away. When they climbed onto the back of a black Harley parked at the curb, I bit my lip to keep from groaning.

The dreams I'd had over the years about that very scenario could fill a book.

Baby steps, you ninny. Learn to walk before you run for your life.

"You know, Devin, when you said you were movin' to Savannah, I didn't think you'd do it. You've always been an adrenaline junkie, so I figured the slower pace here wouldn't appeal to you," Megan teased as she climbed off his bike.

"Just because I dove from cliffs when we were kids doesn't mean I'm an adrenaline junkie," Devin chuckled low.

Megan Hawthorne Pierce turned back, looked at his Harley, and raised a brow. "You, dear cousin, are the epitome of an adrenaline junkie. Fast cars in high school. Faster bikes as an adult. Not to mention carryin' a gun and huntin' bad guys for a livin'," she chuckled. "Though, that bein' said, I don't think you're prepared for what's about to hit you. For once in your life, you may not be able to handle what's comin' your way."

Climbing off his Harley, Devin leaned against his cousin's car and crossed his arms as a slow, devilish grin pulled across his mouth.

"All right, I'll bite. Tell me what's comin' my way that you don't think I can handle."

"Oh, no. I think it will be more entertainin' to watch it unfold."

Shaking his head slowly, Devin pushed off her Lexus. "I think after ten years on the force, four of those as a homicide detective, I can handle whatever Savannah throws my way."

Born and raised in a small town just outside of Atlanta, Devin was a typical Southern man who played hard and lived his life on his own terms. Those terms included taking risks that some wouldn't.

Growing up poor, Devin's parents counted pennies to keep food on the table for their kids. He knew if he wanted more out of his life than a job at the tire factory like his father, he needed a degree. So he'd concentrated on his studies instead of chasing girls and was awarded a scholarship to the University of Georgia, where he earned a degree in criminal justice. But after years of dealing with bureaucratic red tape and watching criminals walk free, Devin had had enough and turned in his badge, opting for another way to help people find justice.

He'd chosen Savannah to start over for two reasons. One, his best friend from college and his cousin lived here. And two, he could make a healthy living as a PI. Atlanta may have their rich and famous, but Savannah had their old money and secrets. Secrets they wanted to keep buried. And uncovering secrets was his specialty. So, after careful consideration, he'd decided Savannah was the perfect compromise to Atlanta.

"Oh, I'm sure you can handle the criminals, but they've got nothin' on the women of Savannah when a handsome man comes to town."

Devin's blue eyes lit up with laughter, and he rolled his teeth between his lips.

"Laugh it up, but you'll be callin' me for advice soon enough."

"I appreciate the offer to run interference. But I've got it covered."

"Hmm, maybe so," she replied, tilting her head and eyeing him thoroughly. "Correct me if I'm wrong, but I'm thinkin' from the way you reacted to the blonde in the boutique window, the women of Savannah are too late."

Devin feigned innocence with a shrug. "I'm not lookin' for a woman right now," he replied in deflection. "My life is in upheaval, and the last thing I need is one complicatin' it more," he lied. He wasn't about to admit anything to his cousin, because she'd keep at him like a bloodhound after a rabbit. But she wasn't wrong. When they'd rounded the corner and he'd seen the blonde balanced awkwardly on a ladder, something about her seemed familiar. He'd paused, intrigued by the beauty as a man entered the store, then watched with concern as shop girl lost her balance and fell. His immediate reaction had been to rush in, but her man had stepped in before he could move, pulling her into his arms.

Then she turned around.

When their eyes locked and held, a subtle current of attraction passed between them before her cat-like, blue eyes shied away from his in surprise. Unable to stop himself, he'd scanned her body from head to toe, biting his lip to keep from swearing in frustration. She was an adorable, sexy mess in faded jeans and flip-flops. The kind of mess that would have sent him straight into the store if she weren't already taken by another man.

"Earth to Devin."

Megan's laughter-filled voice broke through his thoughts, and he asked, "What?"

"I said, how about lettin' me decorate your new office?"

"I'll think about it. But it's the least of my worries right now."

"I already know exactly what it needs," Megan carried on, ignoring him.

Devin grabbed hold of her driver's side door handle and opened it while she rattled on about leather chairs and antique oak desks. He kept his opinions to himself as she slid into her leather seat and buckled up. When she opened her mouth to continue, he'd heard enough. Pointing a finger at her, he ordered, "No antique desk."

"But they're all the rage right now."

"I don't give a rat's ass. Do I look like a man who would sit behind one?"

"Devin, this is Savannah. We embrace that which is old."

"Jesus, Meg. What did I say?"

Sighing, her lips twitched before she conceded. "I suppose Harley posters *are* more your style."

He grinned slowly with just a hint of cocky mixed in. "Now you're talkin'."

"You're impossible," she chuckled as she closed her door then rolled down her window before leaving. "Will you be at Nate's later in the day? I'll bring Greg by to say hi if you are."

Nate Jacobs had been his best friend in college, and they'd stayed close after graduating. Like Devin, Nate also had had a drive to make something more out of his life after growing up on the wrong side of the tracks in Savannah. They'd hit it off immediately.

While Devin had studied criminal justice with a minor in forensics, Nate had studied business management with dreams of converting one of the old historic buildings into a gambling hall once the State of Georgia legalized the sport. Devin had made detective within six years of joining the Atlanta PD, and Nate had his investors lined up and ready, waiting for gambling to be legalized. But for now, while he bided his time, he owned a sports bar.

Jacobs' Ladder sat in the heart of River Street, just down the block from his new office and apartment. The close locale to Nate was one of the reasons Devin had chosen the location.

"I plan on it," Devin answered. "I haven't met Gertrude yet."

"Oh, Dev, you'll adore her. She's just the right mix of bull and princess," Megan laughed as she started her car and shifted into reverse. "See you later."

Megan blew him a kiss before pulling out of her parking spot, her fingers wiggling an excited good-bye as she left.

Devin looked down the hill at the old brick building that was now his home and place of business. It was time to get on with the next chapter of his life. The first thirty years had been in or near Atlanta; so he was curious to see what Savannah brought to the table.

Office first, he thought, climbing back on his bike and driving the short distance back down the ramp toward River Street. After securing his Harley in the alley, he made his way around to the crowded street and took in the river. The location of his office was perfect. In the heart of the historic district, he'd get plenty of foot traffic passing by. Free advertising was a boon for a man on a budget. And there were worse views. He could be stuck in an alley staring at a brick wall. Instead, he had a waterfront view with steamboats and cargo ships passing by on their way out to sea.

Directing his attention down the street, he stopped in his tracks before he could take another step. In front of Frock You was the woman from the window. Shop girl was bent at the waist, digging through boxes next to a delivery truck with her ass on display.

Jesus.

Peeling his eyes off temptation, he moved to his office and unlocked the door, but looked back one last time before he entered to catch her turned at the waist, watching him. Jerking his head in greeting, he pushed through the door and shut it firmly behind him.

Then he bit out, "Fuckin' hell."

She had the face of an angel, the lips of a seductress, but an innocent quality that called to his baser needs. His needs to pursue, to claim—to fucking protect.

And she was taken by another man.

Two

Three of a Kind

WANDERING LAZILY TOWARD THE company picnic, I took in my surroundings. The bright Georgia sun couldn't hold back the beauty of Forsyth Park. The deep-green color of live oaks, dripping in a blanket of sage-colored Spanish moss, still captivated me no matter how many times I laid eyes on them. Their huge diameter and broad-reaching limbs created a tunnel of intertwined branches that transported me back in time, harkening back to the days of sugar plantations and cotton fields. In contrast, billowing pink, white, and red azalea bushes were now in bloom, casting vibrant color into the darker foliage and scenting the air with floral perfume. This park was one of my favorite places in Savannah. I could spend hours here reading beneath an oak tree or people watching as tourists gathered at the fountain to take pictures.

I'd arrived on time for Poe Publishing's annual employee picnic rather than dragging my feet per usual. I couldn't avoid the picnic since it was mandatory, per Poe's Grand Dame: unless you were in labor or had a severed limb, she expected you to be there with your game face on for an evening of hot dogs, camaraderie, and baseball.

Normally, any activity that required me to stand in front of a speeding ball wasn't my cup of tea, and in previous years I was content to cheer on my department rather than play. However, this year, I decided I would take Bernice's advice and try to live my life rather than hide from it.

Since the revelation that I'd like to have more in my life besides my job and books, which included friends as well as love, I figured putting forth effort into relationships at work might be a better first step. Men could wait; friendships could not.

I'd hired on with Poe after graduating from Emory with a BS in English Literature, minoring in Editing. I'd started out as a fact-checker then slowly worked my way up the ladder, keeping to myself and proving my worth one book at a time.

I'd recently been promoted to content editor, working under a seasoned senior editor who'd produced hundreds of bestsellers for Poe Publishing. Jolene Cartwright was a no-nonsense, take-the-bull-by-the-horns forty-year-old who turned overly dramatic novels into works of art. She was tireless, vivacious, and amazing to work with. I knew after my first day working under her I'd be lucky to be half as good as she is by the end of my career.

My love for the written word was the reason I'd chosen to be an editor. I didn't have the imagination required to be a writer. But I knew I could help craft tension, find plot holes, and cut fat where it was needed, taking a rough draft full of errors to a shining diamond readers could immerse themselves in for years to come. I had the education to correct dangling modifiers or verb tense reversals, but my love for a beautifully emotional, well-written romance drove me. It fueled my fire in a way that copy editing never could.

Scanning the crowd, I smiled brightly at anyone who looked in my direction. After one pass, I didn't see anyone I'd consider possible friendship material, so I took in the men. Even though I was nervous about dating, and fraternization was against company policy, I studied the men for research purposes. Most were either too old or too weak-looking for my taste.

An image of Devin Hawthorne floated to the surface as I took in one of the only men my age in the company. His name was Alex, and where Devin was tall, muscled, and intimidatingly rugged, Alex was lean, short, and a little too polished. He was definitely the opposite of intimidating, like most of the men of my acquaintance.

"Rugged, muscled men are overrated," I lied to myself.

"Rugged, muscled men are never overrated," Jolene chuckled beside me. "Who are you referrin' to, Cali? I don't see anyone in this crowd worthy of that title. Nothin' but a bunch of fancy peacocks in their designer shirts."

I side-eyed Jolene, then giggled. She was right, of course. We were surrounded by a bunch of peacocks.

"I was just makin' an observation, that's all."

"Well, you're good at observin'," Jolene replied. "If you do see rugged and muscled, send them my way. I'm long overdue for an illicit affair."

Jolene towered over my five foot three inch frame. Lithe and glamorous with honey-blonde hair and olive green eyes, she had a quick wit and smart mouth that men found irresistible.

Maybe I should take lessons from her?

"Did you see the manuscript I left on your desk?" Jolene inquired.

"The one with family connections to Poe?"

"That's the one." She exhaled dramatically. "You know I've always been a firm believer that everyone has at least one book inside them. I may have to rethink my stance after skimmin' . . . What was the title again?"

"*The Way to a Man's Heart is Through His Dick,*" I answered with a cringe.

"Yeeees," she replied, drawing out the 'yes' on a long slow hiss. "Simply charmin'. I do hate layin' that on your shoulders, sugar. However, bein' the senior editor does have its perks."

I had no doubt she was thrilled not to have to deal with a 'family connection.' One with questionable taste in, and I use this term loosely, literature.

"Tell me," she continued. "How many blow jobs were there in the first two chapters?"

"I didn't count."

She raised a brow. "The hell you didn't," she scoffed.

I sighed before stating, "Ten." She raised her other brow, and I sighed again. "Or twenty. I lost track."

"Darlin', you should encourage her to write a non-fiction manual instead of a romance novel. That or have the protagonist die of lockjaw."

I choked on a laugh, but lost my battle. Throwing my head back, I let out a hoot of laughter that turned heads.

"Cali Armstrong, laughter looks good on you. You should do it more often," Jolene drawled, stroking my shoulder gently with her hand before walking away to speak with someone else.

Wiping tears from under my eyes, I turned toward the baseball field to see how soon the game would begin.

I'll admit I've never played baseball. But I'm athletic enough, and the new and improved Cali was up for new experiences.

As I made my way past the tables filled with hot dogs and chips, I looked to the right to my favorite oak tree and caught sight of Poppy Gentry, one of the graphic artists with Poe Publishing, heading in the direction of the shade tree. Poppy was new to the publishing house, and I'd only met her once. She was a stunning dark-haired woman about my age with jade-green eyes that seemed guarded. Guarded like the ones that stared back at me daily in the mirror.

On a hunch, I changed course and headed in her direction.

I smiled as I watched her sit with a book in hand beneath the same tree I would have chosen just a day ago.

I always carried a book in my bag, so I pulled mine out. It was *Devil's Bride*. I'd brought the copy I'd been holding when I realized I'd been stuck in neutral for far too long as a reminder to let down my guard. To let fate guide my path instead of hiding from the world.

Poppy looked up as I approached and smiled openly.

That's encouraging.

"Care if I join you?"

"No, of course not," she answered genuinely.

Definitely encouraging.

I dropped my bag and then squatted to my haunches before I plopped to the ground. Once I was settled with my back against the tree, I turned my head and reintroduced myself.

"Cali Armstrong," I said, putting out my hand. "We met last month at Elle Reynold's book launch."

"I remember. You were wearing the cutest vintage halter dress with polka dots."

Smiling because I couldn't remember what I wore yesterday, I snickered and replied, "That old thing?"

"Exactly. It's my experience that that which is old is far superior to anything the world has to offer nowadays. Books included," she answered, raising a well-read copy of a paperback.

"May I?" I asked, pointing to her book.

She turned it over, and I saw that it too, was a historical romance, one written by Loretta Chase titled *Lord of the Scoundrels.*

"Nice. Sebastian Ballister is one of the best anti-heroes ever written."

"It's fiction. Men like him don't really change their stripes. *My* favorite part is when Jessica shoots him," Poppy said with a sly grin.

"I'm sensing some animosity," I chuckled. "Is that your opinion based on experience?"

Instead of answering, she leaned forward and grabbed my book. "*Devil's Bride?* They don't make men like that either."

"Don't they?" I watched her mouth pull tighter as she shook her head. "I wouldn't know. I've been too busy with my career to find time," I lied.

"It's not been my experience," she finally answered. "Save yourself some time and stick with books and a sturdy vibrator. Men will only complicate your life and leave you cryin' in your beer."

My excitement at the idea of pursuing love came to a screeching halt. "I'll bear that in mind," I answered, looking down at my copy of *Devil's Bride*, running a finger across Devil's profile.

"I do miss the excitement of a relationship, though."

I turned my head and looked at her. She was staring off into the distance, her face relaxed and wistful.

"Excitement?"

"Yeah. The way it feels when they call for a second date. The butterflies you get in your stomach when they enter a room. Or the heat that pools between your legs when they pin you against a wall and kiss you so thoroughly you don't ever wanna come up for air."

I shifted a little and cleared my throat. The images she described left me restless. Definitely wanting. That's what I dreamed about when I thought about love. What I now hoped to find.

"Maybe you've just dated the wrong type of men?"

Poppy thought for a moment, then nodded "Probably. But as my sweet momma used to say, 'You can't live with them, and you can't skin them alive and feed them to the gators.'"

"What was your father like? Surely she didn't include him in that philosophy?"

"No idea. I never met him."

"Never?" I asked, surprised.

Shrugging, she opened her book and turned the pages until she found her bookmark. "Nope. He left before I was born. He didn't want anything to do with Momma or me."

I opened my mouth to respond, not entirely sure what to say in the face of her father's desertion, but a shout distracted me. Looking toward the baseball field, I saw Sienna Miller— personal assistant to the CEO of Poe Publishing, not the actress—waving as she headed in our direction. Poppy put down her book and waved back, smiling. I'd dealt with Sienna on several occasions, but only in the capacity of forwarding emails and manuscripts for the Grand Dame of Poe Publishing to approve.

I didn't envy her job. Alexandra Poe could be ruthless and short with her employees, yet fair at the same time. At seventy, she was a legend in the publishing world. Born and raised in Savannah, she was the daughter of a newspaperman who started Poe Publishing for his daughter so she could publish her romance novels. When Alexandra's books didn't sell, her daddy said, "Acquire some authors and run the damn thing yourself." So she did. Alexandra had an eye for talent, a nose for bullshit, and a mind for numbers. She had as much of her daddy in her as she did a romantic side, and soon Poe was competing with New York and Chicago.

When Sienna was close enough, I waved as well.

"What's up?" Poppy asked.

"Alexandra saw you sittin' over here and sent me to tell you to get your firm, young asses off the ground and play baseball."

Sienna was a few inches taller than me with light-blonde hair and espresso-colored eyes she hid behind Wayfarer sunglasses. She was highly efficient as an assistant but seemed quiet. And she was stunning. Heads turned when she entered a room, but I doubted she noticed.

"Oh, come on. I don't want fast-moving balls thrown at me," Poppy complained.

I snickered. That was my opinion as well.

"You think I do?"

"Why don't you tell Alexandra to play if she has a death wish?"

"She is. Now get up, they've already started."

Poppy and I both gasped at that announcement and jumped to our feet. No way was I missing Queen Alexandra play ball.

"Can you play ball, Cali?" Sienna asked as we headed to the field.

"Define play."

She looked down at my book and grinned. "I guess not. You do have your nose in a book anytime I see you."

"It's what I'm paid to do."

"No, I meant around town. I've seen you on your days off, and even then you have your nose in a book."

The sharp crack of a bat broke through the air, and someone yelled, "Catch it." I looked up and saw a baseball on a trajectory for the three of us, so I dropped my book and raised my hands. Unfortunately, for me, the ball passed through my fingers, bounced off my palm, and clocked me on the cheek.

I grabbed my face and dropped to my knees as pain exploded across it. It wasn't a direct hit, more of glancing blow I'd feel in the morning and the one after that, but it still hurt like hell.

"Jesus," Poppy shouted. "Are you okay?"

"She got knocked in the head with a ball, do you think she's okay? How many fingers am I holdin' up?" Sienna asked, waving her hand in front of my face.

"I'm fine. Nothin' a little ice won't cure."

I could hear voices shouting as my co-workers came running toward us. My cheek was killing me, but I needed a beer and to escape from the heat more than I needed ice.

I glanced around the field looking for a way to leave. My attention landed on Sienna and Poppy, and I studied them. I liked them. A lot. They were friendly, smart, and exactly what I needed in my life right now.

Since I was looking for friends, and these two fit the bill perfectly, I made a split-second decision and prayed I wasn't making a mistake.

"I think I need both of you to take me to the doctor."

"What? How bad is it?" Poppy asked, trying to look over Sienna's shoulder.

"I need you to take me to see Dr. Budweiser." I smirked and then winked.

A sly grin pulled across Sienna's mouth and she nodded.

"Poppy, get some ice. We're goin' to see a man about a bruise."

❁ ❁ ❁

Turning in her seat, Poppy blurted out, "Okay, spill," as I held a bag of ice to my cheek. Since I'd ridden my bike the mile to Forsyth Park, we'd thrown it in the back of Sienna's car and climbed in to go see a hypothetical doctor for my bruised face.

"Spill?" I asked, confused.

"Yeah. I've seen you at Poe, but you keep to yourself. And Sienna here says you've both worked there for years, yet you don't know each other. So spill. What's your story?"

"Hold that thought. First, where do you live?" Sienna jumped in before I could answer.

"Oh, um, River Street. But I don't need to go home. My cheek burns, but it's not bad."

"Are you near Jacobs' Ladder?"

"Yeah. It's a few blocks from my apartment."

"Perfect. Poppy, hold the question and answer session until we get there. She's more likely to open up with alcohol in her system."

"Open up?" I chuckled.

"Well, duh. You're this hotshot editor who no one knows diddly about. Sienna and I have been curious about you for a while."

I looked back and forth between them as Sienna navigated the mile to River Street. "You've been curious about me?"

"Oh yeah. Normally, you've got this look about you that screams *back off, keep your distance*," she explained. "I can tell by lookin' at you that there's a story behind those walls."

"And here I thought I'd hid it so well."

"I knew it." Poppy smiled.

Ten minutes later, Sienna pulled in behind the bar off River Street and threw the car into park. We all piled out and made our way down the side of the old brick building, then turned onto River Street and kept going until we reached Jacobs' Ladder. I'd never been inside the bar, but I'd heard the music spilling out the door when I'd passed by. It consisted of two levels, with the upper floor open to the one below. The main bar was in the center of the lower level, facing the river. The walls were Georgia oak and covered in University of Georgia memorabilia and art. There was a huge picture of a bulldog over the bar wearing a Georgia T-shirt, but I could tell from the markings it wasn't the current mascot for the school.

Sienna pointed to a table on the second level, so we headed for the stairs. I was ready to take the first step when coal-black hair caught my attention through the crowd. With each rise of the stairs, I tried to see around the crowd standing at the bar. On the fifth tread, the man turned his head while laughing, and I paused. It *was* Devin Hawthorne, and standing next to him was his girlfriend and two other men. Peeling my eyes off his face, I continued up the stairs and followed Poppy and Sienna to a table that allowed us a view of everything below. I chose a seat so I could watch my new neighbor for no other reason than I clearly loved to torture myself.

I'd brought the bag of ice with me, but it was dripping, so I grabbed a napkin from the table and wrapped it up before I placed it back on my cheek. When our waitress came over, she raised a brow at me.

"Did you give as good as you got?" she asked.

"Pardon?"

"Your face," she answered, pointing to the ice pack.

"Oh, um, I got hit with a ball. Nothin' nefarious."

"Mhm. I've heard that one before. If nefarious shows up, let me know, and I'll set a bouncer on him."

Poppy and Sienna snickered, and I rolled my eyes. "Thanks," I answered. "If the culprit who did this shows up, I'll be sure and let you know. For now, can I get a Stella?"

"You got it, sweetie. And for you ladies?"

"I'm drivin', so I'll just have a sweet tea," Sienna said.

"Arnold Palmer," Poppy threw out, and the waitress wrote that down as well, mumbling, "Be right back," and then headed downstairs to the bar.

I followed her with my eyes, but they stopped when I caught sight of Devin raising a bottle of beer to his mouth. I watched intently as his mouth possessed the lip of the bottle.

"Earth to Cali?" I heard Sienna say, so I answered, "Hmm," as Devin's Adam's apple bobbed.

His neck was wide and muscled, but I could still see the apple move. There was something about his throat that held my attention as he tilted his head back.

An image popped into my mind as I watched, one of his neck thrown back in pleasure as an orgasm ripped through his body; and I was the one riding him in the vision. My body responded as if I were there and began to heat, wetness gathering between my legs as the visual replayed in a loop.

A knock on the table broke through my erotic haze, and I turned my head, asking, "Sorry. Did you say somethin'?"

Sienna turned in her chair and looked below, then turned back at me and asked, "Who's got your attention?"

"Nobody," I hedged, then figured what the hell. "Well, somebody. But nobody to me. We had a new tenant move in yesterday and he's here. I was just checkin' him and his girlfriend out." I'd been more than checking him out, which had never happened before. Not with any man.

"Which one?" Poppy asked.

I tried to point him out discreetly, saying, "The big one with the black hair."

"Lord, he's hot. He also looks familiar," Poppy answered.

"He looks like Devil."

"Who?" Sienna asked, but Poppy understood immediately.

"Holy hell. You're right."

I pulled out my copy of *Devil's Bride* and showed Sienna. She looked back at Devin and grinned. "Well, well, a fictional character come to life. Pity he's taken."

"Or not," Poppy mumbled.

I turned in my chair and looked at her. "You said earlier that men weren't worth the time. I'm sensin' a story there."

She shrugged, then turned and faced me. "Show me yours, and I'll show you mine. Spill. Tell us your story and why you keep to yourself."

With that question, the memory always came.

The doorbell ringing.

An officer speaking in hushed tones.

The wailing sound of a child screaming for her parents.

Shit.

I can do this.

Our waitress came back with our drinks, so I waited for her to leave before I answered. Taking a pull from my beer, I swallowed and cleared my throat. It was time to let go of the past. I figured you couldn't be friends with someone unless you showed them your true self.

"I *have* been closed off. You're right about that. When I was six, my parents and brother died in a car accident and I didn't deal well with the loss." Both Poppy and Sienna gasped, so I held up my hand. "It was a long time ago." That was lie; it felt like yesterday sometimes, but today was a new day, and a new beginning. "I wasn't in the beginnin', though. I shut down and pushed people away. It was easier that way. I avoided close relationships and rarely went out with men. And I kept doin' it until recently, to be truthful. I don't know why I pushed people away other than the fact that I'd convinced myself that by doin' so, I would shield myself from further pain. Sort of a defense mechanism. It made complete sense to me at the time, but now that I've examined my motivation, I realize I've been pretty stupid." I picked up *Devil's Bride* from the table and tapped the cover. "This is my favorite book. Wanna know why?"

"You're Honoria," Sienna stated.

I was shocked she knew the answer.

"You're a bibliophile as well?"

"When I'm not runnin' Alexandra's life, yes. I spend most of my downtime buried between the pages of a book."

"Contemporary or historical?" I asked.

"Historical. Definitely."

I turned and looked at Poppy. "What about you?"

"Same. There's somethin' about a duke that does it for me," she sighed.

I looked back and forth between these two stunning women. They were intelligent, easy to talk to, and they loved the written word as well. I'd just hit the friendship jackpot.

"Are you two dating?"

Poppy snorted. "Sienna's hot and all, but I prefer a thick sausage to a bun."

They both threw their heads back and laughed while I rolled my eyes.

"It's been a while for me, though," Sienna giggled, "I don't remember what sex is like. Maybe we should give it a go, Poppy? A night of Imax and climax or Netflix and chill?"

"Sex? I don't even remember how to spell it," Poppy groused.

Yes, I definitely hit the jackpot with these two.

"My aunts will love you two," I chuckled, looking back at Devin. He'd wrapped his arm around his girlfriend's shoulders as he laughed about something.

Baby steps, I reminded myself. Taken or not, he was more man than I could handle, so I needed to let it go.

"So you kept people at bay to protect yourself. I can understand that," Sienna finally stated, pulling me from my voyeuristic tendencies.

"Yes, but now I'm twenty-seven and I've never had a real relationship with a man."

Poppy blinked once then twice.

"Oh. My. God. You're not a virgin are you?" she gasped.

"No. I've . . . you know. I just didn't want anything from him afterwards."

"So what you're sayin' is you're every man's dream woman?" Sienna chuckled. "Sex without the emotional baggage."

"Hardly. I just, you know, experimented for a while in college."

"Cali, if you can't say the words out loud, how do you expect to, you know, experiment now?" Poppy said with a grin.

"I'm not a prude, if that's what you think. I'm just not sure what the rules are."

"The rules are, there are no rules. Anything goes when it comes to men," Sienna explained

"That doesn't help me at all. I need a crash course in datin'." I looked at Poppy and thought about what she'd said earlier. About the butterflies in her stomach and being pressed against a wall. "What's your experience?" I asked her. "You said earlier you missed datin'."

Poppy sobered, her face pulling into a blank mask for a moment. Then she picked up her drink and replied in a tight voice, "I've had a few relationships, but they all turned out the same. The minute you think you're buildin' somethin' special, they disappear."

"I'm sorry," I whispered, placing my hand on her arm. "I didn't mean to bring up painful memories."

"You should stick with your books and a good vibrator like I said before. My father didn't stick around and none of the men I've met have had an ounce of integrity."

I looked across the table at Sienna. Her face had pulled into a look of sorrow as she stared back at Poppy. Then she reached across the table and took her hand. "Don't let one man dictate the rest of your life."

"Don't let the loss of a man you never had dictate yours," Poppy snapped back.

Sienna sucked in a breath, then, after a moment, she nodded. "You're right. I need to let it go. If Chase and I were meant to be, he wouldn't have married someone else."

It was clear these two had been friends for a while. Much longer than the few weeks Poppy had been with Poe.

Maybe if I'd been paying attention, I would have noticed.

"How long have you two known each other?"

Leaning back in her seat, Poppy grabbed her drink and took a sip before answering. "We met a few years back at Chase's weddin'. I was datin' a friend of Chase's, one of those dirtbags I told you about, and Sienna here is Chase's best friend's younger sister. It was the stereotypical trope you read about. She fell for her brother's best friend, and he didn't see her as anything but his friend's little sister. I saw her throwin' back drinks as she watched Chase and his new bride. I could tell she was wallowin' in unrequited love, so I went over and talked to her. We've been friends ever since."

"Dark days." Sienna shivered. "She held my hair while I puked in the reception hall bathroom. It was friendship at first sight."

"Did he know how you felt about him?" I asked.

"Pretty sure kissin' him and tellin' him I loved him one night when I was drunk expressed it clearly."

"And he didn't feel the same, I take it?"

"He avoided bein' in the same room with me until the day he got married."

Ouch!

"I'm sorry, Sienna. I don't know what that's like, but I'm sure the right guy is out there just waitin' for you to come along."

"He's takin' his sweet time," she sighed.

I thought about what these women had endured and it hit me we were all in the same boat. None of us were happy with the present course of our lives. I wasn't sure how I was gonna change mine, but meeting them was a good first step.

Then an idea began to form.

"So I take it neither of you are datin' then?"

They both shook their heads.

"Do you ladies *want* to find someone to spend the rest of your life with?"

Sienna's eyes shot to Poppy, who raised a brow. Poppy exhaled loudly and ran her hands across her face, tangling them in her hair.

"I'll admit," she finally said, "that I would love for a man to prove me wrong. A vibrator is great for stress relief, but I miss the connection, havin' someone to rely on, and most definitely the skin on skin, dirty words and, well, everything."

"What about you, Sienna?"

"Yeah," she answered immediately. "It's been almost two years. I've let it go—to a degree. But I haven't had time to think about anyone new."

Looking down at Devin, I watched as he took another drink. My stomach fluttered as the corded column of his neck tilted back, reminding me of my daydream. I wanted someone in my life who made my stomach flutter just like he did.

Peeling my eyes from the scene below, I looked back at my new friends. "Would you be interested in findin' someone together?"

"Together?" Poppy questioned.

Hawthorne's quote floated to the surface again, and I grinned. I wasn't the only one who needed to cast off my past so my roots could grow from the ruins.

"Did I tell you that Cali is short for Calla Lily?"

They both shook their heads as grins pulled across their faces. Yeah, it was a corny name, but it was my mother's favorite flower.

"In case you missed it, we have a couple of things in common. One, we're all named after flowers. And two, we've been sittin' against the wall watchin' life pass us by. I don't know about you, but I, for one, don't want to be a Wallflower anymore. I say it's time we stood up and took a spin around the dance floor. I think it's time that we three *Wallflowers* take life by the horns and made our own destiny. . . What about you?"

✿ ✿ ✿

"Are you ready to meet Gertrude?" Nate asked Devin after they finished dinner. Grabbing his beer, Devin stood from his stool and gestured for Nate to lead the way.

Nate pulled a ball cap from his back pocket and threw the hat on backwards over his shoulder-length, light brown hair he'd tied back at his neck.

"God bless the dirty south," Devin chuckled. "It's the only place in the world a businessman would be taken seriously with hair like that."

Nate's black eyes, the color of rich hickory coffee, sparked with humor as he walked around the gleaming oak bar and grabbed a Jacobs' Ladder ball cap from behind the counter. Shoving the cap in Devin's gut as he came out from behind the bar, he mumbled, "Live a little. Women love the hair."

"As I recall," Devin said as he placed the cap on backwards, "the ladies loved other things about you as well."

"Do tell?" Megan laughed as she and her husband pulled up the rear, following Nate to his apartment.

Devin looked back at his cousin and winked. "His dimples made them swoon."

Jacobs' Ladder was built in the front half of the two-story building. Nate had taken the back half and turned it into a split-level apartment five years after he opened. The constant late nights and early mornings were a hassle driving back and forth from the country, so he'd opted for city living.

As they approached the locked door that led to his apartment, Devin could hear opera playing. "Gertrude likes opera?" he asked as Nate unlocked the door.

"I tried to persuade her to listen to Skynyrd, but she balked at it."

"Jesus, that's blasphemy," Devin chuckled low.

When he heard off-pitch singing coming from another room, he paused at the threshold. "Does she do that all day?"

"Woman!" Nate shouted. "Get your ass out here."

The pitter-patter of feet bounding at a rapid pace made Devin smile. When Gertrude came around the corner with her sights set on Nate, he stepped to the side to avoid the collision.

"Don't even think about it," Nate ordered in a deep voice.

Like any intelligent woman, Gertrude did as she pleased and ran at him, trying to take Nate to the ground so she could kiss him.

Chuckling as he took in the fifty-pound ball of muscle, Devin smiled when Gertrude danced around Nate in circles, her tongue lolling as she squirmed. She was the finest-looking English bulldog he'd seen since he left U of G. "I can't believe your bull sings opera."

"No woman is perfect," Nate answered as he rubbed her belly. "But you're damn close, aren't you, sugar?"

"Greg, if you agree with him, you're sleepin' on the couch," Megan warned her husband.

"I'm not stupid," he grinned, leaning against the doorframe. "I married you, didn't I?"

"Smooth, Pierce." Nate chuckled.

Kneeling so he could get a closer look at Gertrude, Devin mumbled, "Perfect is overrated. Give me complicated and passionate any day."

"Then you're in the perfect town for that. You won't find anything but complicated here," Nate replied as he stood. "All right, woman. Back to your bed," he ordered, pointing to a large dog bed. Gertrude whined, so Nate raised a brow. When she didn't move, he started counting. On the word 'three', she woofed low, then took off as fast as her stubby legs would carry her.

"We're gonna head out," Megan said as they stepped out of the apartment and headed back to the bar. "It's already past ten, and we have to get up early for church."

As they wound their way back to the bar, laughter from above caught Devin's attention. He looked up and Megan followed suit. Illuminated in a glow from the overhead light, he watched silently as the woman from the shop window threw her head back as she laughed with two other women. Her light blonde hair flowed loosely around her face, softening her features further as the light threw a halo around her head like an angel from above.

"Isn't that your blonde from the window?" Megan asked.

"No idea," he lied.

She turned back and looked at him, raising a brow. "You're paid to pay attention to details, and even I recognize that top. The robin's egg blue is hard to forget, and paired with that hair, she's hard to miss."

"What's your point, Megan?" Devin asked on a sigh.

She smiled and raised her hand, patting the side of his face. "You'll figure it out," she giggled, then leaned in and brushed a kiss across his cheek.

Devin scoffed in amusement as she left, then glanced once more at shop girl before turning back to the bar.

She's got a man, and you've got a life to sort out.

Nate popped the cap off another beer and slid it down the smooth wood before he grabbed Devin's empty and threw it in the recycling bin.

"I've got a client for you," Nate muttered low, leaning into the polished wood.

"What's the job?" Devin asked, raising his fresh beer to his lips.

"My housekeeper's daughter went missin' less than a week ago, and I want you to find out what happened to her."

Swallowing, Devin placed his beer down and reached for his phone. He pulled out the stylus, opened his S-notes, and began writing. "Has a missin' persons report been filed?"

"Yeah, but the police haven't done jack."

"When can I meet with her mother?"

"She's scheduled to come in Monday at ten. Just so you know, I'm payin' your fees, so don't worry about your expenses. Just find out what happened to her."

Devin looked up at Nate and narrowed his eyes. "Don't piss me off. I'm not takin' a dime from anyone."

A slow grin pulled across Nate's mouth, and he clapped Devin on the shoulder. "You always did have a soft spot for injustice. If you're not careful, though, you'll end up broke and on the streets if you work pro bono for every sob story that walks through your door."

"Consider it a family discount," Devin grumbled.

"All right. This time I'll let you. I've got a picture of Maria in my office. Let me get these customers situated, then I'll grab it."

Devin followed Nate with his eyes, remembering a time when they both had worked together to uncover the truth about a stolen chemistry test. Devin had followed the leads to an underclassman. Nate had distracted the kid while Devin searched his room. They'd worked well together, and Devin had no doubt he could count on Nate again in any situation he found himself, in the future.

Laughter from above broke through his thoughts and he looked up. Shop girl and her friends were standing, grabbing their purses to leave as one of Nate's waitresses was laughing with the women. Shop girl arched her back as she laughed, thrusting her chest out, and his body immediately reacted to the sight.

Hissing, "Fuck," Devin turned back to the bar. He didn't have time for the distraction. And even if he did, she already had a man.

Attempting to clear his head, Devin focused on his notes until a conversation between a waitress and bartender caught his attention.

"Table forty-two gave us a great tip, Jackson."

"The swans?"

"Yeah. Alcohol loosened their wallets."

"They celebratin' somethin'?"

"Hardly. One got punched by her dickhead boyfriend. They were havin' a girls' night out to cheer her up."

"Jesus, one of those swans was punched?"

"Yep. She's got a huge bruise on her cheek to prove it. She's not feelin' it, though, not after the fifth round of shots."

Slowly, the conversation filtered through Devin's brain and he looked up from his phone. He recognized the waitress immediately. Turning in his seat, he watched as shop girl and her friends descended the stairs. One looked sober, but shop girl and a dark-haired beauty were giggling and hanging on to the rails as they took each step slowly. The closer they got to the bottom, the more furious Devin became. On shop girl's left cheek he could see the beginning of a bruise, along with swelling. His fist clenched involuntarily as he envisioned wrapping his hands around the throat of the spit-shined playboy he'd seen her with earlier.

When she reached the third step from the bottom, he stood, his jaw ticking as he tried to control his anger. As if she knew he was watching her, shop girl directed her eyes at him on the last step and gasped, missing the tread completely.

Moving quickly, Devin reached out and plucked her into his arms before she fell, crushing her to his body. With her hands pinned to his chest, she looked up with glassy, searching eyes. When they finally locked with his and held, they widened in surprise.

His breathing halted when he got his first up-close look at his shop girl. Her eyes weren't light blue like he'd thought; they were a light shade of purple. A hue he'd never seen before in his life, and doubted he'd see again.

A moment passed before he pried his eyes from hers and scanned her face, focusing on the bruise forming just below the skin. "I want the name of the man who did this to you," he bit out between clenched teeth.

Her booze-soaked eyes turned confused, then they moved to his mouth. Prying her hand free from his chest, she placed a single finger on his lips, tracing the shape as she whispered, "You really are the devil himself." The air trapped in his lungs rushed out as she seemed intent on memorizing his mouth. "You're dangerous to someone like me. I think I better leave now," she explained in all seriousness.

When she tried to push away, Devin tightened his hold. Lust flooded his system when her soft curves molded to his hard lines, fighting for dominance over the anger swirling like a storm through his veins.

"Give me the name of the man who punched you," he ordered again.

"This?" she asked, raising her free hand to her cheek. Her breath was warm against his face, scented with alcohol and a hint of something sweet. "I think it was Paul who swung the bat," she finally answered, then pushed out of his arms as her friends grabbed hold of her. "See ya, Devil. Try not to play your music too loud tonight. I need my sleep."

Three

The Devil's in the Details

"MY MUSIC?" DEVIN QUESTIONED, confused. "How the hell do you know how loud I play my music?"

She shook her head as her friends took hold of her arms. Raising her finger to her mouth, she puckered her perfect lips and "Shhd" him.

Damn, but she was a cute drunk.

His mouth pulled into a grin as he watched her stumble where she stood. Then he caught sight of her bruised face again, and his grin fell.

"What's your name?" Devin asked.

An impish smile pulled across her mouth. "Oh, no," she answered, backing up further. "I'm not tellin' you my name is, is," she scowled in concentration for a moment, then said, "Calla Lily's such an embarrassin' name."

"Like a vault, this one," the taller blonde chuckled.

The dark-haired woman took a step forward and scanned Devin from head to toe.

"All you need to know is we're all Wallflowers. *We* don't trust men. They shit all over you and leave you when you're only a baby. And you," she pointed directly at Devin, narrowing her eyes, "you're Devil Cynster. But she's not Honoria, so move along, Duke of St. Ives."

Devin's brows shot to his forehead. "I'm who?"

The taller blonde slapped her hand over the woman's mouth, hissing, "Poppy, you're not supposed to repeat that."

Confused and a little entertained, Devin turned his attention to the sober beauty. He could wait until tomorrow to find this Paul who'd struck Calla, but there was no time like the present to teach a man some manners. "I want the name of the man who hit Calla."

"She wasn't hit by a man; she was hit by a baseball at our company picnic."

"It wasn't her man?" Devin questioned again.

Calla guffawed and stepped forward. "I already told you it was Paul who swung the bat," she slurred, poking him in the chest. She looked down at her finger with wide eyes and ran her hand across his pecs. "Whoa. Your muscles are bigger than they looked this mornin'." She looked up in amazement, her eyes sparkling in the muted light, and he felt himself being dragged under by their pull.

Feeling a presence beside him, Devin turned his head to break the spell she was casting. Of its own accord, his hand came up and took hold of Calla's, anchoring it to his chest to keep her close.

"You work fast," Nate chuckled, taking in the scene. Then he looked harder at Calla. "Isn't that one of the Armstrongs? You sure you should be flirtin' with your landlord's niece?"

"Niece?"

Devin looked back at Calla and knew instantly Nate was right. That's why she'd looked familiar to him. She had the same innocent beauty as Bernice and Eunice.

"You can move along, too," Poppy interrupted, pointing at Nate. "You're one of those men."

"I'm one of what men, gorgeous?" Nate chuckled.

"Oh, you know," Poppy replied, her finger drawing circles in the air around his face. "You're one of those men who promise forever with your sexy hair and dark brown eyes, but you're like all the rest."

"You don't know that, Poppy," Calla admonished. "And you promised not to judge a man by his looks from this day forward."

Confused, Nate turned to Devin. "I'm missin' somethin'."

"They're Wallflowers," Devin answered, his lips twitching as he spoke. "And I'm thinkin' not all women love your hair like you think."

"Ha. His hair says it *all*. Nothin'. But. Trouble," Poppy answered.

"Sugar, you don't know me well enough to make that assumption," Nate responded with a bite in his tone.

"Dilligaf," Poppy snorted.

"Pardon?"

"Do. I. Look. Like. I. Give. A. Fuck," she slurred, crossing her arms for emphasis, but losing her balance in the process.

The taller blonde stepped forward and grabbed her by the arm, laughing nervously. "On that note, we're gonna leave, I think. I'm Sienna, by the way. Nice to meet you both, but it's time to get these Wallflowers home."

Devin hadn't let go of Calla's hand, so when she tugged to free it, he looked down at her.

"Hold on a minute, Calla. How did you know I played my music loud?"

"Cali," she corrected snippily, causing Devin to grin.

"Calla." He drew out her name, long and slow, letting her know he didn't give a shit what she wanted him to call her. Calla fit, in his opinion. She was a strong, beautiful, yet delicate bloom. "How'd you know about my music?"

Pursing her lips together, annoyed by his defiance, she finally answered. "'Cause you're 2B, and I'm 2A."

"Are you sayin' I'm your neighbor?"

"Yes, Devil man, I am. The walls are thin and I can hear everything, and vice a, vice a, the same for you," she stumbled out, unable to come up with the right words in her drunken state. "So you and your Miss Fancy Pants girlfriend better keep it down, 'cause I like to sleep in on Sundays." With that bombshell, she tugged her hand free and stepped back into Sienna, who caught her.

All three women turned and staggered out while both men watched with varying degrees of incongruity.

"Poppy's a ballbreaker, not a Wallflower," Nate grumbled, following the beauty with his eyes. "Dilligaf, my ass."

"Fuckin' hell," was Devin's response. Temptation was on the other side of his bedroom walls. Walls that were thin, according to Calla. Thin enough to hear his music, and no doubt, thin enough for him to hear her moaning with pleasure while she made love to her man. "I've landed in hell."

A picture of a young Hispanic woman blocked his view of Calla exiting the bar. Devin focused on the picture and then took it from Nate.

"You're not in hell, Devin. You're in Savannah, where the ghosts of the past come out on Friday night. Hell is what Carmella is goin' through wonderin' what's happened to Maria."

"Where did she work?" Devin asked, Calla all but forgotten in the face of the missing woman.

"She worked as a housekeeper as well. She and her mother ran their own cleanin' service."

"You got an address or phone number on either the mother or Maria?"

Nate jerked his head toward his office, so Devin followed. After shutting the door, Nate moved to a filing cabinet and pulled out a file with Carmella's information. Grabbing a pen and paper, he copied down the information.

"As I said before, the police have done nothin'. They keep askin' Carmella if Maria may have gone home to Mexico. Considerin' she was born in the States, it's highly unlikely she would go there without tellin' her mother first. She's barely had contact with their family that stayed behind."

Devin took the sheet of paper and glanced at the information. "Did she have a man?"

"Not that Carmella knew about. Accordin' to her, Maria sent her a text sayin' to meet her at her apartment after she got off work. Carmella pressed her about why, but Maria said she'd have to show her or she wouldn't believe it. So she went to her apartment around seven p.m. and waited, but Maria never showed. The next mornin', Carmella went lookin' for her, but she wasn't home, and when she didn't show up for work, she went to the police. They told her to wait the requisite forty-eight hours before filin' a police report, which she did, but Maria hasn't called or texted since that day."

"What about other family?"

"Carmella's husband died a few years back, and her son lives up near Atlanta. He hasn't heard from Maria either."

"I'll need a list of all their customers. Specifically those she worked for the last night she texted her mother."

"Are you thinkin' she heard or saw somethin'?"

"I'm thinkin' a lot of things and none of them are good," Devin explained. "Did they try to locate her through the GPS on her phone?"

"I doubt it."

"I'll check just in case," Devin answered.

"You think they'll give you professional courtesy?"

"No idea. If they don't, I'll just get it off their system."

"Backdoor?" Nate asked, referring to the method hackers used to bypass normal authentication.

"Yep. I busted a guy who'd hacked into APD, and I had him thoroughly detail how he got in."

"Won't they be able to tell you were there?"

"They will. That's why I'll bounce it back to APD."

"How'd a homicide detective come by that skill?"

"Remember Parker?"

"From U of G?"

"Yeah, he's with the FBI. He had a case in Tulsa a year or so ago where the unsub hacked their system and bounced it back to a homicide detective."

"And he shared?" Nate asked, surprised.

Devin shrugged. "I asked, he shared, and I took notes."

"Jesus. You're gonna fit in here like a glove." Nate chuckled low, reaching for the doorknob to leave.

When they entered the bar area, Nate grabbed a plastic cup and filled it from the tap for Devin to take with him. Open container laws within Savannah were some of the laxest in the country. As long as Devin stayed in the historic district and kept his alcohol in a plastic cup, he could drink on the street without reprisal.

Nate handed off the foaming brew, and Devin took it, raising the cup in thanks. "Another pro to add to the list of reasons to move here."

"You gonna head back to your thin-walled apartment?"

"Thanks for the reminder," Devin gruffed. "I do my best thinkin' with music playin', so I'll wait an hour or so and hope she's asleep by the time I get back. In the meantime, I'm gonna try out a new listenin' device." Devin pulled out a portable unit from his back pocket and turned it on, inserting the single earbud into his right ear.

"Take notes." Nate chuckled, putting out his hand.

Grinning, Devin shook it.

"Later," he said and then turned to leave. He'd made it two steps before he turned back to Nate and asked the one question that had been bouncing around his head since Calla left. "Who the hell is the Duke of St. Ives?"

My aunts were sitting in the courtyard when I arrived home with Poppy and Sienna in tow. My head was still muddled, but the walk, along with stopping at every little shop between here and the bar, along with coffee and a hamburger, had helped to sober me. And by sober I mean I needed more coffee, but after years of playing it safe, being a wee bit tipsy and a little out of control felt exhilarating.

The twinkle lights wrapped around the pergola slats lit the area in a soft glow when we arrived. Tyler Farr's *Better in Boots* played softly through the outside speakers as my aunts lounged with what looked suspiciously like midnight mojitos. They had gotten the idea from the movie *Practical Magic*. They loved that movie, because they said it reminded them of our relationship. Minus the witchcraft, of course. However, instead of midnight margaritas like they drank in the movie, my aunts preferred mojitos.

"Calla Lily?" Bernice asked when I stumbled through the gate giggling. "Butterbean, are you tipsy?"

"I am," I replied proudly, as I walked toward them. "Aunties, meet Poppy and Sienna."

I plopped into one of the cushioned chairs next to Aunt Eunice then grabbed her glass and took a sip.

Yep, midnight mojitos.

"Our niece's manners seem to have disappeared with a few of the brain cells she killed off tonight," Eunice chuckled, snatching her glass back. "Sit a spell and tell us about—Calla Lily, is that a bruise on your face?" she blurted out in shock, concern and disbelief mixed equally in her question.

"Yep. I tried to catch a fly ball at the picnic, and all I got for my troubles was this here bruise."

Poppy fell into the chair next to me, and Sienna sat across from us. Aunt Bernice stood instantly as we settled in and went inside, mumbling, "We need another pitcher and an ice pack," as she went.

"This courtyard is da bomb," Poppy stated loudly. "I would live out here if I were you."

"She practically does," Eunice said. "So much so that Bernie and I were surprised when we got home and she wasn't out here."

"Oh!" I cried out, sitting straight up, "I forgot about Billy Ray Stutter. Did he come home while you were watchin' and throw a fit?"

"No!" Eunice groused. "We sat there 'til dark and watched her throw his entire life out the second-story window. Her antics caused a brawl, too, when his prized golf clubs went flyin' through the window."

"Mercy," Sienna chuckled. "Who would fight over golf clubs?"

Eunice put down her drink on a grin and leaned forward, her eyes gleaming in the soft light. "A judge, a senator, and the chief of police."

"No!" I shouted, then slapped my hand over my mouth at the volume.

"Sugar, Billy Ray has won the Members Only Golf Club Invitational for three years runnin'. If my daddy had been standin' there, he would have dove into the pile as well." She leaned in further then, looking at us as if she were ready to impart a national secret whispering, "Those old fools think the clubs are his lucky charm, so they were determined to have them. What they don't know is, that the ceremonial shot they take before the tournament begins, Billy Ray is drinkin' tea not bourbon. He also has an inside man put a little somethin' somethin' in their drinks so they'd feel the effects more." We all gasped as she sat back and smiled. "Basically, he won, 'cause they were impaired while he was sober."

"How do you know this?" Poppy asked.

Eunice winked at me. "'Cause my momma told me, who heard it from Missy Lockridge, who heard it from Diane Greer, who got if from Jennifer Wilkes, who was told by Diane after she saw the aforementioned 'inside man' sprinkle the powder in the drinks."

"Why didn't they tell someone if he was cheatin'?"

"And miss seein' a bunch of old coots stumblin' around while tryin' to make a three-foot putt? Hell, darlin', it's the best laugh we have all year."

Normally, a story like that would have garnered a snort and an eye roll, but in my semi-inebriated state, it caused a howl of laughter that sent me sliding out of my chair. I hit the ground with a thud, laughing harder at how ridiculous I was acting, while Poppy tried to help me up. I'd made it halfway into my chair when the back gate opened and Devin Hawthorne walked in. We all looked up at him and zipped it, biting our lips as he moved toward us, his gait loose but cocky as his big frame glided across the yard.

"It's the Duke," Poppy whispered.

"More like the Devil," I returned. A Devil with blue eyes and a body that would certainly haunt my dreams.

Aunt Bernice walked out with a tray full of glasses and a new pitcher of mojitos as he approached, so being the Southern gentleman she swore he was, he picked up his pace and took the tray from her as I blatantly checked out his ass. I wondered how many squats he had to do to get his glutes that tight just as he turned and gave me the front view. It became apparent as he moved closer that the front was just as *developed* as the back, and I may have groaned a little in approval.

"You're starin'," Poppy whispered loudly.

"Shh, he'll hear you."

"He's listenin' to music, see the earbud in his ear? He can't hear over that."

Devin looked toward Poppy and me as if we'd spoken to him and grinned, sending my heart racing. His blue eyes sparked like fire in the reduced light, and when they landed on me, he looked almost sinister the way his teeth flashed white like a demon.

"Good to see you Wallflowers got home okay." His deep, gravelly voice was laced with humor, and the effect caused my skin to pebble with goosebumps.

"You truly are the Devil," I whispered, reaching for a mojito. He grabbed one of the glasses and raised it for me, mumbling, "Sugar, I've been called worse," as I took it from his hand.

"What?" I gasped.

"You called me the Devil at the bar. No Devil, just Devin," he answered, winking before he turned to my aunts and inclined his head. "Night, ladies. I'll try and keep my music down." He turned back and looked at me and the girls, drawling, "Calla. Wallflowers," before turning and heading for the back stairs.

I grumbled, "Cali," when I was sure he was far enough away, but as if he'd heard me through telepathy, he chuckled low as he opened the door to the second floor.

It's like he can read my mind.

"Is it possible for someone to read minds?" I asked.

"He doesn't need to be a mind reader to tell you were checkin' him out," Poppy giggled.

I heard a squeaking noise and looked up. Devin had opened his living room window, so I raised my finger and shhd, pointing to the open window.

"Why did he call you Wallflowers?" Bernice whispered.

"Because we are," I answered in a hushed voice. "Aunt Bernice, meet Sienna Miller and Poppy Gentry."

"*I'll* explain the Wallflower bit since those two are a little muddle-brained," Sienna announced, ignoring my warning about the open window. "We work together at Poe if you're wonderin' where we met," she started off. "That bein' said, we'd never spent time with Cali until today. In the course of the day, we figured out all three of us have been holdin' back where men were concerned. We've been sittin' out on life, watchin' but not engagin'."

"Like a Wallflower in one of your historical novels?" Eunice questioned.

"Exactly," I blurted out. "It hit me this mornin' while I was starin' at a wisteria vine that I'd trained myself to be a certain way, and if I wanted a different life, I needed to tear down my walls and spread my proverbial roots."

"I'm pretty sure it was muscles you were starin' at," Bernice shot back.

"Those, too," I giggled.

"Cali convinced Sienna and me that we should band together," Poppy added loudly. "We're gonna help each other find the right man, one Wallflower at a time. We'll be objective for each other and let the others know when they're makin' a mistake."

"Cali's up first," Sienna jumped back in. "We're gonna go to one of those speed datin' events at the Baptist church since Cali needs more experience with men. We figured what better way for her to practice flirtin' than a night meetin' a bunch of men at once?"

"Yeah, one-stop shoppin'." I snorted. "I'm not expectin' much, though. I think fallin' in love happens by chance. Serendipity. Like you walk into a room and bam, you just know when you lay eyes on them they're the one."

"What kind of man are you lookin' for, butterbean?"

I raised my arms and ran my hands through my hair. My scalp tingled with the alcohol, so I settled back and enjoyed the freedom that came with intoxication. Thanks to the alcohol, words that were normally controlled flowed, and feelings I'd kept locked in a deep, dark place tumbled out with little restraint.

"Where love is concerned, it doesn't matter to me if he's a butcher, a baker, or—"

"A candlestick maker?" Poppy giggled.

"I was gonna say farmer," I snorted, "but you get my point. I want someone who will be a shelter from a storm, a beacon of light in a dark world. I want to feel safe, secure that what we have is as important to him as it would be to me. I want heat, passion, and friendship."

Eunice looked over her shoulder at the open window. "What about your new neighbor? You're both clearly attracted to one another, and he seems like a gentleman."

What is it with my aunts and their obsession with gentlemen?

"We call him Devil," Poppy snickered. "He reminds us of the Duke of St. Ives."

"Who?" Bernice chuckled.

"A fictional character," Sienna supplied.

I waved them off. "He's not attracted to me. It's more likely he finds it entertainin' to tease a drunk. Besides, he's got a girlfriend."

"About the woman you saw this mornin'," Bernice chuckled.

"What about her?"

Bernice smiled wider, as if she had a great secret.

"She's his cousin, Megan Pierce, not his girlfriend."

"What?" I asked, confused.

"She's married to Greg Pierce, a prominent divorce attorney. I ran into her on the street lookin' for Devin in his office, so I told her to park in the back and then went lookin' for him. That's why I came outside when I found you droolin' over the man."

I glanced at Poppy and Sienna. They were grinning from ear to ear.

Great.

"I was not droolin'," I bit out.

"Butterbean, you were. Your tongue was on the ground like a dog searchin' for water, and you know it."

I narrowed my eyes at her. "Well, you're a big fat fibber, Bernie. What was all that business about lettin' her have first dibs?"

"I was tryin' to light a fire under your stubborn ass."

Snickers ensued, and I clenched my jaw. "Fair enough," I admitted. "But it changes nothin'. It's still a bad idea."

"Neecy, did you hear her? She thinks a virile young man, who's sexy as sin, is a bad idea."

"Indeed, sister," Eunice responded. "Do you suppose the alcohol killed off the brain cells that control rational thought?"

"Hardy har har," I snipped. "You know you're both bein' a tad presumptuous in the matchmakin' department assumin' my neighbor would settle for a closed-off bookworm with deep-seated abandonment issues, instead of someone like the mayor's daughter."

Bernice turned to Poppy and Sienna shaking her head. "Do me a favor, will ya? Stand her in front of a mirror until she sees what everyone else does."

"That's not what I meant. I'm sayin' I'm me, and he's all charm and full of life, so why would he settle? Besides, I'm inexperienced with men, and he'd devour me. I'm better suited for a dusty old professor than someone so . . . male."

"Why's that a problem?" she chuckled. "Bein' devoured is the best part."

I smiled. On that point I agreed.

"Calla Lily, all the points you've made are just excuses. Not one of them is worth a hill of beans. So what's truly holdin' you back?" Eunice asked.

Leaning back in my chair, I closed my eyes, trying to gather my thoughts through the haze of alcohol running through my system. *Why exactly am I opposed to Devin?*

The doorbell ringing.

An officer speaking in hushed tones.

The wailing sound of a child screaming for her parents.

Blinking back the painful memory that never seemed to leave me, I shuddered. The scars that had formed from the loss of my family had indelibly marked me, clouding my perception in such a way that I was terrified of change. It was then I realized what scared me the most about Devin was feeling that type of loss again. Some men were easier to forget than others. Devin was a dark, passionate force that would imprint on your soul and never leave. I couldn't risk the heartache.

"Do you remember when Momma, Daddy, and Frankie died?" I choked on the words a little. The alcohol had also loosened my defenses, allowing my guard to slip, for my heartache to shine through. "Remember how I didn't speak for three months?" I looked between Bernice and Eunice and felt my chest tighten as their faces dropped with sadness. "If not for that puppy you bought me as a bribe to speak, who knows where I'd be today."

"Hard to forget, sugar," Eunice answered in a soft voice. "Sammy was a godsend in a dark time."

"Then try to understand that a man like Devin would be hard to get over when he left. I don't want to feel that type of pain again."

"Calla, the heart wants what it wants. Don't limit yourself because you're scared," Eunice said. "Take a chance on the man; you might just find he's what you've been waitin' for. He might be perfect for you. And, butterbean, if anyone deserves to be happy, it's you."

But I don't deserve to be happy, because I killed my family.

Sucking in a breath as that thought tumbled through my brain, I bit my lip to hold back the pain at what would follow.

My son would still be alive if it weren't for you.

Bitterness settled in my stomach, like always, at the memory of my grandfather's words.

My parents had taken my brother to the carnival without me, and I'd pouted even though I had strep throat. We'd waited until the last weekend to go, but I'd woken up sick. They didn't want to disappoint Frankie, so they'd left me behind with a kiss on my forehead and a promise they'd take me next year. I'd thrown a huge fit about being left behind, so they'd gone out of their way to pick up my favorite pizza on the way home to appease me. If they'd come straight back instead of trying to placate me, they wouldn't have been on the highway where a semi plowed into them; they'd have been at home with me and alive today. My rational side knew I was only a child at the time, that I shouldn't blame myself, but the irrational side, the one that wished every day I hadn't made a fuss, believed it.

When I was twelve, after years of punishing myself, I sought out my grandparents and confessed my sin. I was tired of the guilt and needed absolution from them, needed them to tell me I was only a child, that it wasn't my fault their only son was dead, but they'd said nothing. They'd just stared at me for a moment, then my grandfather took my grandmother's arm and walked out of the room. An hour later, they sent me home to my aunts without as much as a good-bye. We never spoke of it again, and they began to distance themselves from me. Eight visits a year turned to Christmas and Easter only, and on the occasions when my grandfather needed the future heir of the Armstrong family to make an appearance.

Then one day when I was in high school, during a heated argument about studying Business as opposed to English Literature in college, my grandfather lashed out when I refused. He'd roared he wouldn't need me to take over the helm of Armstrong Shipping if his son were still alive, and that's when he'd delivered the knockout blow. I ran from the house, gutted by his condemnation. After that, Christmas and Easter visits ended and the only time I saw my grandparents was when they summoned me.

Sitting up, I grabbed my drink and downed it to shake off my mood, then I turned to Eunice. "You're right. I know that, of course. And in a perfect world, that's what I'd do. In a perfect world, my family would still be alive, and I'd be confident enough for a man like Devin; gettin' to sit on the back of his Harley with the wind whippin' through my hair. But it's not a perfect world, is it, Eunice? Perfection doesn't exist."

Sweet Home Alabama shook the walls as Devin's fists kept time with the beat. Sweat glistened on his skin like oil as he pushed his biceps, breaking down the muscle until his arms were fatigued. Two faces filled his headspace as he attempted to pulverize the bag. One had coffee-colored eyes and a bright smile as she threw an arm around her mother's shoulders, happy and content with her life. The other had lavender-colored eyes that reached into his soul and squeezed tight until he couldn't take a breath.

Thinking Calla was taken by another man, Devin had tried to push his attraction aside, but his curious nature had won out, and he eavesdropped. He'd heard more than he expected when he'd raised his window, and in the course of a few short minutes, he knew two things: she was single, and if he hadn't already been attracted to the woman, he would have wanted her the moment she opened her mouth and touched his soul.

There was no pretense to her, nothing fake like so many women he'd met in his life. She was strong, yet soft at the same time. And what she was looking for out of life matched his own desires. Her passion matched his own—and he'd wanted her even more by the time she'd stopped talking.

But he'd also heard fragility in her voice. She'd suffered a loss at an early age and held back, built walls, protected herself to avoid additional heartache, and believed she needed a man who was safe. Boring.

He wasn't either of those.

Increasing his pace until his arms screamed for relief, Devin threw a final punch at the bag before he stepped back, his lungs heaving with exertion. He glanced at the wall that stood between him and Calla then switched gears to the brown-eyed woman.

Once Calla had said good night to the Wallflowers and headed upstairs to bed, Devin had settled into the task of tracking Maria Espinoza.

She'd fallen off the grid the Tuesday prior after finishing a job for Fang Yoo, a recent transplant to Savannah. She owned a chain of dry cleaning stores and paid her taxes religiously before they were due. That in and of itself didn't mean anything. But Devin's experience told him that anyone who kept their nose that clean had something to hide. Because of that, he planned to dig deeper into Yoo's background.

Moving to his zero gravity boots, Devin strapped them on and hung himself upside down. Curling at the waist, grunting low as he pulled his upper body toward his knees, he continued to mull over Maria's disappearance. He expected Nate to call back with her home address at any time, so he could see for himself that she hadn't packed up her belongings and left town on her own accord. Every minute counted with a missing person, so he didn't want to wait until Monday to check out her apartment.

On his third set of twenty crunches, pounding on his front door drew a smile.

She lasted longer than I thought she would.

"Door's open," he shouted over the music, then continued his set.

His door swung open then closed loudly. Tiny feet with polished pink toes attached to silky legs came into his line of sight. They traveled to his desk and didn't move again until his music stopped, then they made their way over to him. When he looked up on a decline, he found angry lavender eyes staring back at him.

Calla's hair was disheveled, her eye makeup smudged, and she was wearing nothing but an oversized T-shirt.

Devin sucked air deep into his lungs to control his body at the sight—it didn't help. His attraction to this Southern beauty was off the charts.

He knew he should steer clear of her, but he wouldn't. He'd never be boring. The safe man she thought she needed—not in his line of work. But he wouldn't let her fears stop him. She was perfect for him, and he was *exactly* what she needed. No, he wouldn't let her stop him, because where he came from, when you saw something you wanted, you went after it. And he'd wanted Calla Armstrong from the moment he laid eyes on her in the shop window.

"Pardon the interruption," she mumbled even though she was angry. Devin couldn't help but grin at her impeccable manners. "Mr. Hawthorne, last night may be a bit fuzzy, but I'm fairly sure I asked you not to play your music so loudly."

Devin ignored her and rose up, unhooking the zero gravity boots and lowering himself to the ground. Determined to keep her off-balance in order to lower her defenses, he turned until he faced her. Resting his hands on the gravity bar, he leaned down further until he was inches from her face, he grinned. When she sucked in a breath at his closeness, his grin turned devilish and predatory.

Take down the wall brick by brick.

"I don't remember agreein' to keep it down," he drawled slowly; his tone was smooth as bourbon. When her eyes glazed over, he leaned in further and dropped the level of his voice to a smoky whisper. "I thought all Southern girls liked Skynyrd."

She didn't answer him. Her eyes were locked on his lips.

Releasing the bar, he took a step closer to Calla. When she backed up to keep her distance, his lip twitched.

She blinked several times then shored up her backbone finally and crossed her arms, narrowing her eyes at him.

Stubborn and strong-willed. I'm gonna enjoy this.

"Mr. Hawthorne, I distinctly remember you tellin' my aunts that you'd try to keep your music down."

A slow grin pulled across his lips as he took in Calla's bravado. She was still a sexy mess in that oversized T-shirt. A shirt that, if he didn't already know she was single, he'd be inclined to think belonged to a man, and her sexy mop of hair a result of being thoroughly ravaged. But he knew differently; and he planned to keep it that way until he could wear her down and be the only man in her bed.

"Call me Devin," he returned, taking another step forward. "Or Devil works, too." Her eyes grew wider at the suggestion, and he knew he'd scored a hit.

While he'd been researching Maria's disappearance he'd also googled Duke of St. Ives. After hearing Devil was a fictional character, one that reminded Calla of him, he decided to check out the book. Poppy had said that Devin was Devil, but Calla was not his Honoria. She was wrong. He'd discovered as he'd scanned the book that the Duke and he were molded from the same cloth. They both went after what they wanted, they both wouldn't take no for an answer, and they both wanted stubborn women who didn't know what was best for them.

He'd liked the Duke immediately.

"Mr.—" She swallowed hard then began again. "Mr. Hawthorne, I think it's best if—"

His cell phone rang, interrupting her. Raising his finger to stall her, he moved to his phone hoping it was Nate.

"This is Devin."

"I have Maria's address. I'm textin' it now," Nate replied.

"How far is it from River Street?"

"A fair distance."

"Which direction?"

"I take it you don't have GPS on that bike of yours?"

"Nope," Devin replied, then turned and looked at Calla. "But I know someone who can help me find it."

"I'm guessin' by your reaction last night it's that Wallflower who lives next door."

"You'd guess right."

"You work fast." Nate chuckled.

"Time is of the essence."

"Another man?"

"Not if I can help it. I'll fill you in when I get back," he informed Nate. "Later."

Hanging up, Devin turned and closed the distance between him and Calla. He needed to check out Maria's apartment, but he also needed time with Calla so she'd relax around him. Going with his gut, he decided to enlist her help.

"I need a favor. My friend, Nate, the one who owns Jacobs' Ladder, a friend of his has gone missin'. A young woman. I need to check out her apartment, but I'm unfamiliar with Savannah. Will you come with me and show me the lay of the land?"

"Missin'?" she gasped, her eyes growing wider.

"Yeah, babe. Missin' since last Tuesday, and her mother's worried sick."

Calla didn't hesitate. She nodded immediately then looked down at her clothes. "I'll just be five minutes."

Stubborn, strong-willed, *and* kind-hearted. He would definitely enjoy breaking down her walls.

"Take ten," he answered, pulling off his shirt. "I need to shower off the sweat."

Her gaze shifted to his chest, and she licked her lips.

"Meet me at my bike?"

She paused her inspection of his body and looked up. "We're goin' on your bike?"

Oh yeah, they were definitely going on his bike. Hearing she'd had fantasies about being on the back with him was just the leverage he needed to chip away at her shield.

"Sugar, it's what I drive."

"Right. Right." When she didn't move and then bit her lip in indecision, he went on the offensive before she changed her mind. Grabbing her arm, Devin walked her to the door and opened it, ordering, "Change clothes and meet me in ten," before pushing her out and shutting the door in her face.

The stubborn part of her personality looked less appealing at that moment.

"Jesus. I must be nuts," he mumbled as he headed for the shower. New job, new town, and now he was taking on the monumental task of breaching the fortress of one Calla Lily Armstrong. "I should have my head examined."

He grinned all the way to the shower.

Four

The Devil went down to Georgia . . .
Riding a Harley

SHIT. SHIT. SHIT!

"Pick up, pick up, pick up!" I whined into my cell phone.

On the fourth ring, Sienna answered. I needed reinforcements, and since Sienna wasn't drunk the night before she was the best candidate.

"Hello?" she mumbled in a sleep-deprived voice.

"I have to get on the back of a Harley with Devin," I semi-shouted.

"Cali?"

"How am I supposed to guard my heart and keep from fallin' for the man if I have to get on the back of his bike?"

"Slow down." Sienna yawned. "Tell me what's goin' on."

"Devin is a private investigator, and some poor woman has gone missin'. He doesn't know Savannah yet, so he asked me to show him around. I can't say no, because there's a woman missin', for God's sake, and her mother is worried sick, but I have to ride on the back of his bike."

"So ride on the back of his bike," was her oh-so-helpful advice.

"Were you not listenin' to me last night? I told you I have a weakness for Harleys, and he's the Devil who'd be my undoin'. It's like leadin' a lamb to the slaughter!"

"Jesus, Cali. It's just a bike, and he's just a man. He isn't gonna cast some kind of voodoo spell on you."

"Don't be so sure," I grumbled. "The man goes shirtless more than Henry Cavill, and his voice . . . Let's just say he shouldn't be allowed to utter a sound near pre-teen girls, women with heart conditions, or gay men who haven't come out of the closet."

She giggled. "Then wear an amulet to ward off his voodoo."

Now we're talking!

"Do they make one to ward off men or is it just the ones that turn people into frogs?"

"Don't be ridiculous. There's no such things as voodoo charms," she yawned.

"I'm thinkin' you're not takin' this seriously," I bit out.

"I'm thinkin' you're makin' a mountain out of a molehill," she returned.

I do not think so!

"I should have called Poppy," I grumbled. "She hates all men and would have figured out an escape."

I could hear Sienna moving in her bed, sighing as she adjusted her position. "Poppy has daddy issues. She doesn't hate *all* men. As for figurin' out an escape, just drive yourself and have him follow you."

". . . That's actually perfect. Why didn't I think of that?"

"His voodoo scrambled your brains?"

"Exactly." I looked at the clock and saw I had six minutes to get ready. "Gotta run. I have six minutes to change and get downstairs."

"Wear somethin' cute!" Sienna shouted as I hung up the phone.

Not in this lifetime!

I ran into the bathroom and grabbed my toothbrush. When I looked into the mirror, I gasped. I had makeup smeared under my eyes and blue circles to compliment the smudges, along with a small bruise left behind by the baseball.

That alone should have warded off the man.

I snatched a cotton swab and got to work clearing away the mess.

Teeth brushed and makeup gone, I ran into my closet. "Now I need a burlap sack."

I didn't find one, of course. Thanks to my aunts' store, everything I had was either stylishly retro or for work. It may not have been a wardrobe to attract men, but it certainly wasn't a wardrobe to send them running either. If I was gonna be around Devin—a given since we lived next door to each other—I needed to go through the dregs of clothing downstairs and find something hideous to wear when I was at home.

While digging for a loose-fitting tee, my hand settled on a lavender-colored halter top I'd seized from a haul on a whim. I hesitated for a moment, Sienna's words echoing in my head.

Wear somethin' cute!

"Sienna clearly doesn't understand the seriousness of my situation," I muttered as I pulled the top from the closet rod and bit my lip. "Don't be stupid."

Short on time, I slammed the top back on the bar and grabbed my boots, jeans, and a tee from a hanger.

I should have looked at the shirt before putting it on. It was a vintage Lynyrd Skynyrd tee from their 1974 Sweet Home Alabama Tour, and it fit me like a glove. Devin wasn't wrong when he said Southern girls loved Skynyrd. I had all their albums. But I didn't want him to think I wore it for him.

I heard his door slam shut and panicked.

"Why couldn't he be the type of man who spent time on his appearance?"

Cause he's perfection already, you ninny.

With no time left, I ran into my closet, grabbed the first oversized shirt I came across, and headed for the door.

The minute I walked outside, I knew I'd made three fatal errors.

One, instead of taking time to change my shirt, I'd grabbed a long-sleeved one to cover it. A long-sleeved flannel shirt. It was springtime in Savannah. We only had a month of flannel weather year-round, so within five steps, I was sweating. But Devin was leaning against the gate waiting for me, so I couldn't turn back. My second error was forgetting to borrow the Jeep keys from my aunts. Of course, I didn't remember the blasted keys until Devin held the gate open and I saw his bike. My third mistake was apparent when I approached, and his mouth pulled into a sexy grin, causing my heart to skip a beat. I should have drawn him a map.

"I think it would be easier if I drew you a map," I rushed out. "I'll only get in the way."

I turned immediately to get pen and paper, but I only made it one step before he grabbed my arm and stopped me.

"No time. Get on the bike," he ordered.

"It'll just take a minute," I explained, tugging at his hand.

Devin looked down at my flannel-covered arm and his brows pinched together. "You wanna explain why you're wearin' flannel in eighty plus degrees?"

Of course, he'd ask.

"I was cold," I lied.

"Cold? Are you sick?"

"No. A little hungover, but I'll—"

In a move that could only be described as lightning fast, Devin pulled the flannel from my body before I could protest. He tossed the shirt into the courtyard while I stood gobsmacked, then grabbed my hand and yanked me toward his bike. I would have given him *what for* if I'd had my wits about me, but the moment his warm hand wrapped around mine, he cast his voodoo spell again.

An electric current buzzed up my arm, rounded my shoulder, and settled in my chest like a warm memory, so I followed him like children followed the Pied Piper. It wasn't until he turned and handed me a leather jacket, his eyes settling on my chest, before I broke from his spell.

"Great tee," he drawled, winking at me.

Dammitalltohell.

I should have worn the purple halter.

"Address?" I asked between clenched teeth.

"Eight Thousand Waters Street," he answered, his lips twitching at my discomfort.

He was definitely the Devil.

Ignoring him, I searched my memory as I pulled on the jacket. I remembered brightly painted apartments in the Highland Park neighborhood built on stilts. They were cheerful and inviting, and spoke of the coastal living in this part of the state.

"Eight Thousand Waters Street is an apartment complex. Take Fahm Street and head west, but the fastest route is Interstate 516."

"We'll take Fahm," he returned immediately, then grabbed a helmet hanging off his handlebars and secured it snugly to my head. When he was done, he climbed on his bike and started it, then reached out to me.

I looked at his outstretched hand then at the imposing man. Blazing blue eyes sparkled brightly in the morning sun, but there was a dark sense of danger about him, a sense of uncompromising masculinity that warned me that one false step would spell my doom. In spite of all that, I still found myself taking his hand and climbing onto the back, but keeping as much distance as possible between us. As if he knew what I was thinking, he reached down and wrapped his warm hands around my legs and pulled until I was snugged up to his back, then grabbed my arms and wrapped them around his waist before he released the kickstand.

My breath caught on contact, and my body hummed. There was no distance between us now. My breasts were pressed to his back, every inch of my body touching his. It was both exhilarating and terrifying.

However, terrifying won out in a moment of clarity, and I loosened my grip on his waist only to have Devin run his hands across mine, pulling them back firmly on his steel-like abs. He let go when I didn't pull away and gunned the engine, easing off the clutch. Moments later, we were cruising up the ramp toward Bay Street, the wind whipping around us as I hung on tight. But I couldn't deny that as frightened as I was at losing my heart to him, for the first time since I was a child, I felt alive.

✿ ✿ ✿

"Stay here. We might have a problem," Devin ordered as he helped Calla off his bike.

Expecting to be obeyed, he pulled out his 9mm from under his shirt and checked the safety before heading toward the staircase. On the third step up, he heard a creak behind him and turned to find Calla on his heels.

After traveling miles with her wrapped around his body like a second skin, her baby fresh scent invading his senses every time they stopped for a light, he had no patience. Especially after seeing Maria's apartment door ajar when he pulled under the flamingo-pink apartment building.

Maria's apartment fronted a greenbelt. It was secluded from the street with no neighbors nearby to hear her scream, adding tension to the already urgent need to find her.

"I thought I told you to stay with the bike," he bit out.

"You did," she replied nonplussed by his tone as she passed him heading up. "But you also said there might be a problem, and from my point of view, stayin' close to you is safer than standin' alone unprotected."

Devin reached out and snagged her hand, halting her. "Stubborn woman," he growled in annoyance then started up the stairs. At the top step, he raised his gun. "Stay right behind me."

She didn't argue, thank Christ.

With his right hand, he pushed open Maria's door and scanned the inside of her apartment. The living room had been tossed. Her cushions were shredded, her drawers dumped and their contents strewn across the floor.

Calla's head popped around his shoulder as he surveyed the mess and she gasped. Looking down at her, Devin raised his finger, pointing to the spot where she stood. "Don't move," he whispered. She nodded with wide eyes, then crossed her heart like a child making a solemn promise.

His mouth twitched.

Fuck, but she was frustratingly cute.

Turning his attention back to the apartment, Devin entered slowly, sweeping each room for intruders. He saw the same destruction in each one. Someone had been looking for something.

"It's clear," he told Calla as he made his way back to the door, holstering his gun as he went. "I need to call this in to the police."

"Someone was lookin' for somethin'," she muttered as she took in the room.

"Yeah. And whatever it was may have sent Maria into hidin' or worse."

"Maria?"

Devin pulled the missing woman's photo from his back pocket and showed it to Calla. "Maria Espinoza. Do you know her?"

Calla took the picture and gasped. "That's Maria from Happy Maids."

"You know her?"

Calla shook her head. "We've spoken a few times when I worked late, but I don't know her outside the office."

"She ever mention any trouble? A man who might be botherin'

her?"

Calla ignored Devin and looked around Maria's living room, lost to the destruction, so he stepped in front of her to block out the view. "Babe. Did she ever mention havin' problems?"

She closed her eyes and shook her head. "No," she finally responded. "She never said anything like that. She was friendly; always had a smile. She mentioned readin' a book we'd published and talked about workin' with her mother, but nothin' as personal as any trouble she might be havin'."

"When was the last time you saw her?"

Calla didn't answer. She was trying to look over his shoulder, so he moved her farther away from the door and turned her to look at him.

"Devin, her apartment," she whispered, vulnerability clouding her expression. "She's in real trouble, isn't she?"

Cupping both sides of her face, he waited until she looked at him. The soft purple brightened with moisture, so he replied gently, "I'll do my best to find her. I promise. Now, tell me the last time you saw her."

She nodded, then her eyes clouded with concentration and her brows pinched together as she searched her memory.

"Last week. Tuesday night."

"You're sure?"

She pulled her bottom lip between her teeth and nodded. "I saw her enter the buildin' from the side entrance. I was leavin', so I didn't talk to her."

"How do you know it was Tuesday?

"'Cause I went to the library last Tuesday. I left early that day to get there before they closed and I remember it was rainin'. That's one of the reasons I didn't call out to her and say hi. Maria didn't have an umbrella. She was gettin' drenched."

"Is that her normal day for cleanin'?"

She shook her head. "No, I didn't even think about that. It's Monday, Wednesday, and Friday. She told me we're one of the only offices she cleans. Mostly, her business is residential houses."

Devin pulled out his phone and googled the weather for the week prior. It had rained on Tuesday like Calla had said.

"Does that help?" she asked, looking at his phone.

"Yeah. Maria disappeared on Tuesday. According to Nate, she wanted to meet her mother after work. She never showed. The question is, why did she go to a job she wasn't scheduled for and not call her mother?"

"It's a big buildin'. Could she be hidin' out there?"

"Good question," he answered, impressed with her observation. "Only one way to find out. You got a key?"

"Yes. But I left my keys at home."

"Then let's roll," he stated, grabbing her hand, pulling her toward the stairs.

"But Maria's apartment is wide open," she called out as he led her down.

"I'll have Nate call it in after we're gone. If I stay, I'll get stuck answerin' questions, and I want to check out your buildin'."

When they reached his bike, Devin grabbed his helmet and put it back on Calla's head. Baby powder scented the air again, causing his teeth to clench. The overwhelming desire to kiss her battled for dominance over finding Maria, and he would have breached her walls like a conquering knight if they weren't standing in front of Maria's apartment with her life in tatters.

"You know you should be wearin' a helmet, too," she replied, her body tense as he drew her closer to him instinctually.

"It's busy coverin' a much more valuable head."

Calla's breath hitched at his meaning, so he took a step closer. She needed to get used to having him in her personal space, because he wasn't going anywhere.

"How's that?" he asked in a husky voice once the helmet was secured.

Calla blinked twice before her cheeks turned pink.

Taking a step back to put distance between them, she rushed out, "Fine. Fine," then turned quickly and tried to climb on his bike.

Grabbing her around the waist, he pulled her back into his chest, whispering, "Steady, sugar. I gotta climb on first." This time, however, instead of tensing at his touch, she melted into his body, allowing him to move her back without complaint.

Brick by fuckin' brick.

Just like the Duke, he would win over his modern-day Wallflower.

✿ ✿ ✿

I whipped out my cell phone on my way up to my apartment. I'd left Devin downstairs with his bike while I grabbed my keys. I was still shaken by the fact that sweet Maria was the missing woman Devin was looking for. What were the odds I knew the woman in a city the size of Savannah?

The ringing in my ear stopped abruptly as I opened my door.

"Did you survive the ride on the back of his bike?" Sienna chuckled as I searched for my purse.

"Forget about that. Maria is missin'!"

"Maria, who?" she asked with concern, Devin's voodoo forgotten in the wake of my announcement.

"Maria from Happy Maids."

"The sweet girl who cleans our buildin'?"

"The same one. Devin took me to her apartment, not that I knew it was hers when we left, and it had been tossed, her furniture slashed, and everything gone through like somethin' out of a movie."

"That sounds like someone was lookin' for somethin'."

"Exactly."

"When was the last time she was at work?" Sienna asked.

"The last time I saw her was the day she disappeared. She was comin' into the buildin' as I was leavin'."

"Does he think she was taken from our buildin'?" she gasped.

"No idea. He said she called her mother and wanted to talk to her about somethin', but never showed. Sienna, I may have been the last person to see her."

"What's Devin gonna do to find her?"

"We're headed over to Poe now to look around. We thought she might be hidin' out there, scared to call her mother or the police for fear she'd be found."

"I'll call Poppy, and we'll meet you there. Four sets of eyes are better than two. If she's there, we'll find her!"

"Good thinkin'," I responded. "See you in a few."

I found my keys in my purse and headed back downstairs. I cut through Frock You and heard my aunts talkin' in the stock room, so I popped my head inside.

"I'm headin' to Poe with Devin. A girl named Maria who works for the cleanin' service we use is missin', and I saw her on Tuesday at Poe. We're gonna look around."

Both were digging through a box, but paused when I started speaking.

"Are you talkin' about Maria, Carmella's daughter?"

"You know her?"

"Since she was knee high to a grasshopper. Her momma came here from Mexico City before she was born. We used to give them free clothes while they were gettin' established here," Bernice explained.

"Sister, we should go over and see if Carmella needs anything," Eunice threw out.

"Tell her we're on the case, and we'll find Maria," I shouted as I turned to find Devin.

My aunts followed me as I wound through the racks of clothes. When I got to the front door, I looked out the side window and stopped dead in my tracks. Devin was standing by his bike, looking down at his arm as Bridget Donavan, a highly endowed brunette with legs long enough to walk to Atlanta in a day, ran a finger across his forearm.

"She didn't waste time," Bernice stated sarcastically from behind me.

"How would she even know about Devin?" I asked as a knot tightened in my chest.

"Butterbean, you've had your head buried in your books so long you have no idea how this town works," Eunice snorted. "Devin had to file for a business license, sugar. The biggest gossip in town runs that particular city office. She called me before the ink was dry to verify he was rentin' from us. And Devin's cousin is married to Greg Pierce, a divorce attorney with a client list as long and wide as the Savannah River, and she runs in the same circles as Bridget. I imagine when Devin told her he was movin' here, she told all her eligible female friends, and they've been waitin' by the alley hopin' to walk past just as he came home."

I looked back at them in disbelief. Savannah was like Peyton Place.

"Her boobs are fake," I snipped, pushing open the door. Devin heard the bell ring signaling my exit and turned to look at me as I rounded the corner.

"I see you've met Bridget." The words may have come out accusingly as I raised a brow at him in question.

He cocked his head in response and raised one back.

"If it isn't Calla Lily Armstrong," Bridget replied, flipping her hair for maximum effect.

Bridget and I went to high school together. She was one year ahead of me, so we didn't run in the same circles, but I'd been to enough charity events at my grandparents' request that she knew who I was.

"Bridget Donavan. How are things hangin'?" I looked at her chest and raised my forehead in mock surprise then dropped my mouth open for that 'wow, you've gone from an A to a DD cup' look of astonishment. "Clearly not hangin' since your trip to Atlanta."

I heard Devin grunt, so I turned and glared at him. "Are you ready?" I asked between my teeth.

His response was to grin and throw a leg over his bike. I moved to the side, and he handed me his helmet. Bridget just stood there with her mouth pulled tightly as I shoved the helmet on and then reached out and took hold of Devin's hand. When I climbed on, I wrapped my arms around his waist and snuggled in closer on purpose. When I rested my chin on his shoulder, I could feel his body quaking with a chuckle.

Yes, I just made a ninny out of myself; laugh it up.

Ignoring him, I turned to Bridget and said, because bitch or not, good manners were always in fashion, "You have a nice day now, Bridget."

Devin burst out laughing.

Whatever.

Bridget Donavan pissed me off on a good day. I didn't want to see her get her claws into Devin. No one deserved that misery. At least that's what I told myself as we pulled away from the curb and I flicked a wave at her.

He drove twenty feet up the ramp then stopped and looked back at me.

"What?" I asked.

"Where're we goin'?"

"Oh. Um. Turn left on Bay Street and then hang a right at the second light. It's the large rock three-story building on the left about a mile up."

He looked in his rearview before taking off, then paused and glanced back at me, jerking his head, indicating something behind me. "Interestin' woman. Friend of yours?"

I turned around and found Bridget walking toward her car. It was parked across River Street in the city parking, so it had a clear shot of Frock You and his office. Eunice was right, she'd sat in her car and waited for Devin to arrive home and then she'd pounced.

"She's a barracuda. You'd be wise to steer clear of her."

"I'll bear that in mind," he drawled.

"You can date who you want, of course," I rushed out, not sure why I was clarifying my opinion, "but that one isn't worth your time."

Devin rolled his lips between his teeth, which made my stomach flip. "I know plenty of nice women I can introduce you to," I continued like a loon, staring at his mouth. "Just say the word, and I'll make a call."

Oh, God. I've lost my mind!

"Also good to know," he grinned. "Tell you what. I promise when I'm ready to get mixed up with a woman, *you'll* be the first to know."

My flipping stomach plunged, and I felt sick. "Can't wait," I grumbled, but he wasn't finished.

"I prefer blondes, by the way. Keep that in mind while you're lookin' for someone."

Yes, I'm officially an idiot.

With a deep chuckle I felt all the way down to my toes, Devin turned and gunned the engine, heading up the ramp.

I pointed out the turns as we came to them, and in less than five minutes we were pulling up outside Poe Publishing. I led Devin to the door I'd seen Maria enter and unlocked it. As we entered, I switched on the lights and looked around. It was the entrance that led to the employee break room and lockers on the first floor.

"I think they keep the cleanin' supplies in the supply room. There are carts in there for the cleaners to use," I explained as we made our way down the hall. "Maybe she left a note or somethin' on the cart?"

"Your mind works like a cop's," Devin muttered as we navigated the long hallway. Peeking up at him, my gaze stopped on his thick, textured hair. It looked soft, and I wondered what it would feel like to run my hands through it.

I was so busy checking out his hair, in fact, that I didn't notice the hall had terminated until Devin grabbed my arm to halt me.

"You with me?" Devin asked, his mouth pulling into a sexy half-grin.

"I, uh, I can't stop thinkin' about Maria and her apartment," I rushed out to cover my blunder.

His grin pulled further across his mouth.

Shit! He knows I'm lying.

Turning my back to avoid his knowing eyes, I looked around. The storage room was five feet behind me, so I rushed over. It was locked, so I tried the keys on my ring.

None of them worked.

"I got this," he mumbled, then moved me out of the way and kneeled to his haunches, pulling out a square, black, zippered lock-pick kit from his back pocket. Moments later, he had two long instruments shoved inside the lock. Thirty seconds after that, the lock clicked and he opened the door.

"That's a handy skill," I mumbled as he flipped on the light and walked in.

"Which one is hers?" he asked, staring at the three carts parked inside the large, cluttered room.

"Maria's in charge, so she usually has a clipboard hangin' off hers." A cart in the far back corner had a hook on the side, so I pointed toward it. "That one, I think."

Devin made his way over and began pulling the supplies from the cart, digging around the edges as he went. Once the cart was empty, he flipped it on its top and began searching the bottom.

"You think she came here to hide somethin'?"

"I don't know what I'm thinkin' other than someone flipped her apartment lookin' for somethin' they want back. My gut tells me she stumbled across somethin' while she was cleanin'. Somethin' that sent her into hidin'. I'll know more once I interview her clients."

"So you're hopin' she taped it to her cart for safekeepin'?"

"Brains and beauty," he drawled, winking at me.

I bit my lip to keep from grinning like a ninny, but the heat rising up my throat at his compliment would soon flush my face, so I stood and moved to another cart to hide my reaction and began searching.

When Devin finished with Maria's cart, he helped me search the other two.

Nothing.

He scanned the room when we finished, frustration etched on his face.

"What were you doin' here?" he asked the room.

"Should we check the buildin' to see if she's still here?"

Devin nodded then grabbed my hand and led me out of the room and down the hall. Each room we came to, we flipped on the lights, and looked for any sign that Maria had been there.

"Most of the staff's offices, along with mine, are on the second and third floors. Other than a kitchen, there's no place to hide that we wouldn't see her. But we do have a basement, where we store old manuscripts from years past. Everything is on computer now, so no one ventures down there anymore, but it would be the perfect place to hide," I said as we shut a door.

"Show me," Devin ordered, so I led him to the elevators at the end of the hall. Before I could push the *down* button, the lights on the elevator indicated the car was heading down.

"Someone's on the elevator."

Devin pushed me behind him, and we waited to see where the car would stop. When the doors opened on our floor, I peeked around his shoulder and sighed.

"I forgot you two were comin'."

Poppy and Sienna rushed out of the elevator followed, incidentally, by Eunice and Bernice.

"Did you find her?" Bernice asked.

"Why are you two here? I thought you were goin' over to see Maria's momma?"

"She wasn't home, so we came here to help," Bernice replied. "Did you find her yet?"

"Not yet," I answered.

"I take it you know Maria as well," Devin sighed.

Four voices talked over each other, leveling question after question at Devin.

He turned and glared at me.

I shrugged. "They wanted to help."

Devin dropped his head back on his shoulders and looked at the ceiling like he was waiting for patience. When he righted his head and muttered "Christ," then pushed the *down* button on the elevator, I looked at my aunts and bugged out my eyes.

The door opened immediately, and he stepped back, his arm sweeping wide for all of us to enter first.

"Ladies," he gritted out.

"Such a gentleman," Bernice said, looking back at me.

I rolled my eyes and tried to keep from sighing.

Once we were all in the elevator, Sienna leaned in close and mumbled low, "Has he cast his voodoo spell yet?"

If I had luck, it was only bad luck. Poppy somehow heard Sienna.

"Who casts voodoo spells?" Poppy inquired loudly.

My eyes shot to Devin in horror, and he looked down at me and raised a brow.

"Uh. Old man Murphy," I stupidly said.

"Mr. Murphy doesn't cast voodoo spells," Eunice stated instead of letting it lie.

Devin's other brow joined the first, and he crossed his arms.

"He threatened to cast one on me if I rode my bike in his garden again," I lied.

He rolled his lips between his teeth, his eyes gleaming with hilarity, then leaned over and hit the button for the basement.

"Somebody kill me now," I mouthed to Sienna.

"Calla Lily, why would you ride your bike through his garden? You know how particular he is about his flowers," Eunice admonished, not letting the subject go.

I groaned.

"Moment of insanity," I mumbled. "It seems to be happenin' a lot lately."

We reached the basement, and the doors slid open, saving me from further humiliation. We started to move to exit when a smell so putrid, so overwhelmingly rank, filled the elevator. Devin pulled me back and growled, "Don't move," then exited the elevator, disappearing into the gloom as he drew his gun.

Blood rushed from my face and ice replaced it, chilling my veins. I froze. Everyone froze. Death had a certain smell that was unmistakable.

Bernice whispered, "No."

Eunice gasped, "Not sweet Maria."

And I closed my eyes and prayed.

Poppy and Sienna reached out and grabbed my hands, and we held on tight, waiting for Devin to return.

"She was in the basement this whole time while we were upstairs workin'," Poppy said softly, her voice hitching on the words. "Her poor mother."

Devin appeared out of thin air a moment later; the line of his jaw was so sharp he could have chewed steel. He stepped inside the elevator and pushed the button for the lobby, then turned to the five of us. "We've got a John Doe with a letter opener in his chest."

The whole car erupted into cries of relief for Maria, then we began asking questions as to who the man was.

Devin raised his hand to quiet us when the door opened at the lobby. Surprisingly, it worked.

"I need for you ladies to head home," he looked at Poppy, Sienna, and my aunts. "There's no need to drag you into this. I just need Calla to confirm she let me into the buildin'." He turned to look at me, then continued. "As far as the police are concerned, I was accompanyin' you to the office to retrieve a manuscript. I don't want them knowin' I'm workin' Maria's case."

"You think she stabbed this man, don't you?" I asked.

His jaw tightened further.

"It was self-defense; it had to be," Eunice cried out.

"What did this man look like?" Bernice asked.

Devin turned his eyes to her. "Sharply dressed, manicured nails."

"Paunch in his gut?" she questioned.

"Hard to say."

I turned and looked at her.

"What are you thinkin'?"

"Billy Ray Stutter," was her answer. "If there was trouble in this town, he always had a hand in it, and he hasn't been seen since last week."

"You said he was up whorin' around in Atlanta."

"Or he's lyin' dead in a basement with a letter opener in his chest."

A vision of a dead Billy Ray made my nose scrunch, but we needed to know who the man was to help Maria.

I turned to Devin. "I'll look at the body and tell you if it's Billy Ray," I announced, hitting the button for the basement. "You need to know so you can help Maria."

"No," Devin growled, placing himself between the elevators doors so they wouldn't close. "I don't want you seein' that."

"I can handle it. Billy Ray wasn't a close friend."

"Calla, he's been dead five days . . . In a hot basement."

"I'll hold my breath."

He sighed with impatience.

"His own mother wouldn't recognize him," he finally answered.

"Oh . . . Well, then . . . I'll just . . ." I pointed to the lobby and he moved aside then I took off, followed by my aunts, Poppy, and Sienna.

I hugged my aunts and promised to call them as soon as we knew who the man was, while Devin was on the phone detailing what we'd found for his friend Nate.

Unable to keep my eyes off Devin, I watched him run his hand through his hair in frustration as he paced. Someone called out my name, but I was too busy watching how the light cast a blue shadow across his hair to listen.

"He definitely cast a voodoo spell on you," Sienna whispered in my ear.

I jumped, then shrugged. "Yeah. But I'm an Armstrong. My aunt says we're made of sterner stuff, so I should be able to hold myself back."

"You know how we agreed to tell the others if we were makin' a mistake where a man was concerned?" Poppy asked.

"Trust me, I know I am. You don't need to warn me off."

She shook her head. "You're makin' a mistake, but not the kind you think," she countered, looking back at Devin. "He's one of the good guys. You'll see that when we go speed datin' tomorrow night."

I looked back at Devin. "He is a good man," I agreed. "One who's got half the female population of Savannah gunnin' for him, accordin' to my aunts."

"So?" she said.

"So I'm takin' a big risk lettin' *any* man in. If I open up my heart to him and one of those long-legged socialites catches his eye, I'll be crushed."

"First off, your aunt was right," Sienna sighed. "You really don't see yourself the way the rest of us do. And secondly, if a man is so easily swayed by another woman, then you don't want him anyway. He wouldn't be worth the salt in your tears."

"I'm not sittin' around thinkin' I'm not good enough for him. I'm just cautious."

"Aren't you?" Poppy questioned.

My head jerked back at her comment and I looked at Sienna, who was nodding in agreement.

Am I?

I started to defend my decision, sure I was doing what was right for me, but Devin called out, "I'm callin' this in now," before I could respond.

They nodded at him, and then each gave me a hug before heading for the door. When Poppy started to exit, she paused and looked back at me. "Think about what I said," she called out then waved at Devin and left.

Devin appeared at my shoulder, watching as they disappeared around the corner. "Think about what?" he asked with his phone to his ear.

I turned and looked at him.

Blazing blue eyes looked back at me.

He'd been working himself under my skin all day by standing too close, brushing his hand on my back as we entered a room, and whispering in that gravelly voice of his until my toes curled. I was weakening, and I knew it.

He raised a brow in question, and his mouth quirked in a devilish grin as I stared at him. My heart leapt at the effect.

I'd decided a day ago to stop hiding from life, yet here I stood, holding back because I was scared. Bernice was sure that Devin was the type of man I needed, and Poppy was right; he *was* a good man. That much was obvious. He cared about a missing woman he'd never met; was determined to find her at all costs.

So why am I holding back?

Because he's perfect and I don't deserve him, echoed back at me.

"Calla?" he drawled, his smoky voice washing over me like a warm blanket.

I closed my eyes and let it fold around me.

God, my aunt was right. Poppy was right. I don't think I'm good enough.

Devin reached out and ran his hand down my arm, his touch warming my blood. He murmured, "Babe?" and my eyes snapped open, landing on his blue.

The little girl I'd been, the one who'd haunted my dreams for twenty-one years, screaming for her parents as her nanny held her tight, was silent for once. And in that moment of quiet, I threw caution to the wind and reached up, snagging Devin around the neck, bringing his mouth to mine. He was shocked at first, then arms like warm steel curled around my back, pinning me to his body. His head angled as my mouth opened, and he took control of the kiss. He tasted like sin, and I felt like a seductress.

Clinging to his shoulders, I moaned into his mouth as the hard muscle beneath my fingers tightened in response. Heat bloomed and spread like wildfire, melting my bones as my nipples hardened.

I was lost, oblivious to the world around me, the dead body in the basement forgotten until a far-off voice broke the spell with the words, "Hello? Is anyone there? Are you able to respond?"

I broke from his mouth suddenly and looked up. His eyes had turned midnight blue; the pupils were dilated with what I thought was lust.

"Phone," I rasped, out of breath.

Slowly, his eyes changed, the lust-filled haze morphing into anger, and he raised the phone to his ear without another glance at me and bit out, "I need to report a murder," between clenched teeth, and then turned his back on me and walked away.

That was not the reaction I'd been expecting.

Heat curled up my neck, and adrenaline pumped my heart at a faster rate, so I turned toward the window to cover my embarrassment, staring blankly at the blue sky.

White clouds shaped like gossamer cobwebs dotted the horizon. I barely noticed them.

How had I made such a colossal mistake?

I'd assumed his behavior was the result of a mutual attraction, but I'd been wrong.

I looked back at Devin and found his back still turned.

Yep, definitely not wrong.

And now I have to live next door to him after throwing myself at him like a dog in heat.

I wanted to bang my head on the window to knock some much-needed sense into my brain. This was what I got for listening to someone else. I should have stuck with my original plan to stay away from him, then I wouldn't be in this mess.

Sirens broke through the afternoon air, disrupting my pity party of one.

Poe Publishing wasn't far from a police station, and since Alexandra Poe was a figurehead in Savannah society, I had no doubt the whole damn station rushed to their cars when Devin gave them the body's location.

Before Devin could hang up, the first car slid to a stop in front of the building, followed by three more. At their screeching halt, Devin turned toward the door, his gaze fixed on the street. I didn't want to see the rejection written on his face, so I moved to the door and opened it, putting as much distance between Devin and myself as I possibly could. Though it would take a distance the size of

Georgia before I'd stop kicking myself for being an idiot.

As the police approached, I realized I'd have to answer their questions before I could put said distance between Devin and myself, so I figured it was time to get down to the business at hand. I'd answer their questions quickly, then make a hasty retreat when Devin wasn't looking, saving us both the embarrassment of him having to let me down easy.

Five

Worth lyin', stealin', or killin' for

LEANING AGAINST A WALL in Poe Publishing's lobby, Devin cracked his neck from side to side trying to alleviate the headache brewing thanks to Calla and the John Doe lying on the floor in the basement.

He'd yet to confirm the identity of the body, but from the reaction of the first officer on scene, he didn't need one. He'd heard the patrolman mumble, "Billy Ray," the same name Bernice had uttered in the elevator.

His case just became more complicated.

Add to the mix that Calla took off the minute the police were done questioning her, it would take a double dose of painkiller to calm his head.

To say he'd been caught off guard when Calla had kissed him would be an understatement. He'd been prepared to take his time in his quest for the beauty, so when she grabbed his neck and kissed him, he'd hesitated for a fraction of a second. Then her tongue touched his lips, and he'd let instinct take over.

Lust ran hot and fast through his veins as he'd tangled his tongue with hers, his body's reaction to Calla's warm mouth immediate. He'd wanted to lay her down where they stood until he was between her legs, but she'd ended the kiss abruptly, whispering, "Phone," before he'd lost all control.

Being interrupted by the 911 operator wasn't as effective as a cold shower, so he'd clenched his jaw and turned from Calla until his body was under control. It had taken Herculean restraint not to hang up the phone without reporting the murder and continue what she'd started.

Now she was gone without a word to him, and he was pissed. He didn't know what was running through that damn head of hers. Whether she was resigned to the fact that they'd been dancing around each other all day in a prelude to that kiss, or if she was still trying to make up her mind. Either way, if she thought she could give him a taste of sweet Georgia Peach and then disappear, he'd set her straight and terminate any ideas she had of running from him. With extreme prejudice.

He looked toward the street where his bike was parked and saw Nate standing behind yellow police tape. Pushing off the wall, Devin headed for the nearest officer.

"Are you done with me?" he asked Officer Granger, who looked fresh out of the academy.

"Detective Strawn will be up shortly. You'll have to ask him."

His headache pounded harder.

"Then I'm gonna step outside for a moment and have a smoke. I won't leave the premises."

Officer Granger eyed Devin for a moment then nodded. "Go ahead," he replied jerking his head toward the door. "Not every day you see a dead body."

Devin turned from the rookie and frowned.

He'd seen enough dead bodies for two lifetimes, but he'd left his former profession out of the interrogation. To everyone involved he was on an errand with his woman, an employee of Poe Publishing.

When Nate saw Devin heading in his direction, he moved to the side, away from the gathering crowd.

"Did you call in the break-in at Maria's?" Devin asked as he walked up.

"Yeah. They were on the scene before you found the body here."

"Good. You got a smoke on you?"

"Gave them up two years ago," Nate answered.

Devin noticed a man standing directly behind Nate with a cigarette dangling from his lips, so he said, "I'll give you a buck for a smoke."

"Since when do you smoke?" Nate asked.

"I don't. But I can taste death in my mouth. At this point, anything would be better."

Devin pulled out his wallet as the man moved forward.

"Keep your money," the stranger mumbled, handing him the cigarette. "Saw you leave the buildin'. You with the police?"

"No comment," Devin answered automatically and put the cigarette to his lips. The man handed him a lighter and Devin lit the cigarette, drawing the smoke deep into his lungs.

He grimaced. Now he tasted smoke and decomp.

"You sound like a cop." The man grinned.

"Old habits die hard," Devin murmured under his breath.

"You got a name for the deceased?" the man continued.

A warning bell went off, so he looked closer at the man.

In his forties with salt and pepper hair, the man was built, but with a beer belly that spoke of overindulgence. His eyes were sharp, alert. Like he didn't miss details and committed them to memory. It was a look he'd seen many times in his ten years on the force.

"Press?" Devin asked, but it was more accusatory than question.

The man bowed. "Charles Taft. Savannah Register."

Devin pulled out his wallet again and handed Taft a dollar.

"Like I said, no comment."

Taft grinned and took the dollar. "Suit yourself," he drawled, "I'll find out one way or another."

"Beat it," Nate barked, and Taft bowed again then turned and moved back.

"Fuckin' vultures have a nose for trouble," Devin growled.

"Tell me what you know," Nate asked.

Devin took another draw on the cigarette then dropped it on the ground and snuffed it out with the toe of his boot. He scanned the crowd again then murmured low, "Does the name Billy Ray mean anything to you?"

"Billy Ray Stutter?"

"Didn't catch a last name."

"If it's Stutter, then Maria's in over her head," Nate replied. "Stutter's an asshole with connections and deep pockets. Runs in the same circle as the mayor."

"What's his business?"

"Import/export. You name it, he'll buy it and sell it."

"I need to know if Maria cleaned for him," Devin said.

"I'll call Carmella."

Officer Granger took that moment to step outside, eyeing Devin with suspicion before raising his hand, indicating Devin should return. Devin jerked his head at the officer in response.

"Get me her full client list," Devin ordered then turned toward Granger and headed in his direction.

"Strawn wants a word with you," Granger said as Devin approached.

Nodding, Devin headed back inside the building, scanning the lobby for the detective in charge. He found him towering over the ME as he signed off on the body. Their eyes met, and the detective jerked his head for Devin to follow.

"Tell me again why you're here?" Strawn ordered.

Devin sized up the man.

At six foot three, Devin dwarfed most men. Not Strawn. He stood eye-to-eye and toe-to-toe with him. Built solid, but lean around the waist, he looked like he could handle anything the job threw his way.

Gray eyes narrowed on Devin when he didn't answer.

"I pulled your record," Strawn growled. "I know who you are and what you do. What I don't know is, how you connect to my dead body."

"You mean Stutter, don't you?"

Strawn's jaw ticked, confirming it was Billy Ray Stutter.

"I'll ask you again," Strawn growled, "what the fuck are you doin' at my crime scene?"

Devin shrugged. "Came with Calla while she picked up her work. Found the body like I told your officer."

Strawn chewed on that for a moment, then sized Devin up as he'd done Strawn. "We could use a man with your experience on the force."

"Been there, done that," Devin answered. "I prefer helpin' people without all the red tape."

"Are you admittin' you're helpin' someone now?"

Devin's mouth twitched then a half-grin emerged.

"Just givin' my woman a ride to her place of business."

"The same woman who took off after I interrogated her?"

"The same," Devin gritted out between his teeth.

When he was done here, he would hunt Calla down. Leaving made them look suspicious, and he didn't want to answer more questions than necessary. But mostly, he wanted to know what the hell was going through her head.

"Did you fight? Is that why she left you high and dry?"

Devin didn't answer. He stared blankly at Strawn.

Strawn sighed and changed tactics. "Can you confirm your whereabouts on Tuesday night?"

"Are you sayin' Stutter died on Tuesday?"

Strawn ignored Devin's question, and the beginning of an eye twitch emerged. "I just had to land a case with a former homicide detective as a witness." Strawn looked down and scanned his notes, then tapped the page with his finger. "According to Ms. Armstrong, she needed a manuscript from the basement, and she asked you, her *new neighbor*, to come with her, because, and I quote, 'it gives me the heebie-jeebies.'"

Devin tried to hold his face passive, but hearing what Calla had said caused him to grunt to cover a laugh. When that didn't work, he rolled his teeth between his lips to keep from smiling. Strawn caught his reaction and his own lips twitched. After a pregnant pause, both men chuckled, and the air that had been wired tight with accusation finally lifted.

"You're her neighbor, *not* her man," Strawn stated. "You wanna start at the beginnin?"

"I'm both," Devin replied. "She just doesn't know she's mine yet."

Strawn crossed his arms, his legs spread wide for effect.

"Would you say she's worth perjurin' yourself for?"

"You've seen her," Devin stated. "In a world where women are plastic, pretendin' to be somethin' they're not, and have personalities that change with the breeze, would you let anyone or anything come between you and a woman like Calla Lily Armstrong? . . . Christ, the heebie-jeebies?"

"So you're freely admittin' you'd say or do anything you had to for Ms. Armstrong."

"What I'll admit is that a woman like that would be worth lyin', stealin', or killin' for, but I didn't. I was still in Atlanta packin' up my apartment on Tuesday. Call my landlord if you have any doubts." When Strawn started to speak, Devin decided to halt any thoughts the detective had about trying to pin the murder on Calla. "And for the record, if you're thinkin' of pinnin' this on Calla, you're way off track. She's not capable of stabbin' a man with anything but her sharp tongue."

Strawn raised his hand and pinched the bridge of his nose. "All right, let's say for the record that's true. If you're convinced she couldn't be involved, do you have any information that *might* shed some light on this clusterfuck?"

"Yeah." Devin moved further away from the patrolmen gathered in the lobby, and Strawn followed. When they were more than an earshot away, Devin spoke. "Stutter laced the drinks of every man who participated in some golf club invitational."

Strawn raised his hand to interrupt. "For someone who just moved here, you know this how?"

"I have it on good authority. I overheard a conversation between Calla and her Aunt Eunice."

"Eunice Armstrong? Daughter of Preston Armstrong? Christ, I didn't make the connection when I interviewed her," Strawn muttered.

"If you say so," Devin said. "I don't know the man."

"Asshole. More money than God."

"Are there any other kind of rich people?"

Strawn shook his head. "And you're goin' after his only grandchild," he chuckled. "Heads up, you'll have trouble from him, that I can guarantee. His blood's so blue he looks like a Smurf, so I doubt he'll welcome you with open arms."

"Duly noted, but if Calla's the woman I think she is, her grandfather hasn't told her what to do since she was a kid."

Done with the topic of Preston Armstrong, Strawn said, "Tell me about Stutter and this alleged spikin' of drinks."

"Eunice told Calla that Stutter has a man at the club who spiked the drinks of the other players during the celebratory toast. That's why he's won the past few years. She also said that when his wife tossed his shit out the window, several of your prominent citizens were in attendance and fought over his clubs. If I were you, I'd ask myself how they knew his belongin's were bein' tossed at that very moment, and why they weren't concerned he'd show up and put a stop to it."

Strawn gritted his teeth. "You wanna be more specific on the who?"

"A judge, a senator, and the chief of police."

Strawn closed his eyes slowly, his jaw ticking as he absorbed the information, and mumbled, "Fuck," under his breath.

"That about sums it up," Devin agreed.

He had no idea if Maria killed Stutter in self-defense or by someone else, but he had no doubt Strawn would find out. He didn't strike Devin as a man who did what he was told, but as a man who did what was right. Finding Maria alive was Devin's job, and if Strawn shook the bushes for him, he'd get to the bottom of what she was hiding from quicker.

Shoving his notepad into the back pocket of his jeans, Strawn stuck out his hand to Devin. "Bo Strawn."

Devin immediately took the man's hand. "Devin Hawthorne. Am I free to go?"

Strawn jerked his head toward the side door. "I saw Ms. Armstrong hightail it on foot headin' north."

Devin clapped Strawn on the shoulder in thanks then headed for the door and his bike. When he exited, Nate was waiting for him, anger shadowing his features, his hands curled into fists.

"Talk to me," Devin said as he approached.

"Carmella heard about the body on the radio. Seein' as they clean here, she put two and two together and panicked, thinkin' it was Maria. She called me, and I spent the last ten minutes reassurin' her that you'd find her daughter."

"That's a big promise to make."

His face hardened. "You remember that stolen test?" Nate asked. "You didn't stop until you had that kid dead to rights. You're part bloodhound, my friend. I figure if Maria's still alive, you'll find her, and that's what I promised her mother."

Devin's head pounded harder with the added pressure, but he nodded.

"Did you find out if they cleaned for Stutter?"

"They don't. But when I told Carmella it might be Stutter who was dead, she said she'd seen him at one of her other customers' homes and they looked to be arguin'."

"Did she give you the name of the client?"

"Yeah. Fang Ken Yoo. The last place Maria worked."

"Fang Ken Yoo? Jesus, what a name."

Nate cracked a smile for the first time since he'd arrived. "Puts a whole new spin on "what the fuck were her parents thinkin' naming her that.""

"At least the dots are connectin'," Devin replied.

"What's your next move?"

"Coffee. I have a feelin' it's gonna be a long night."

"You gonna stake out Yoo?"

"As soon as you give me the keys to your truck."

Nate grinned and pulled the keys from his front pocket, tossing them to Devin.

"Been a while since I rode a bike," Nate said, eyeing Devin's Harley.

"You put so much as a scratch on her, we'll have problems," Devin warned, tossing his own keys to Nate.

"Wouldn't dream of it," Nate answered then swung a leg over the bike. After he donned the helmet left behind by Calla, he started the Harley and shouted, "Keep in touch," over the roar of the engine, speeding off down the street as Devin watched.

Devin turned and looked at Nate's black Ford F-150. At least he'd be comfortable while he kept tabs on Yoo for the night.

As he headed for the truck, he caught a glimpse of blonde hair the color of Calla's. As much as he wanted to hunt her down that very instant, he'd have to wait until tomorrow to take her pulse.

✿ ✿ ✿

My phone buzzed in my back pocket as I made my way home. I'd taken an alternate route back from Poe, hoping to avoid Devin for as long as possible so I could gather my nerves to face him, but it wasn't working. A knot had formed in my stomach after his reaction to my kiss, and it hadn't eased in the twenty minutes it had taken me to make my way back toward my apartment, further emphasizing my earlier belief that a man like Devin would be hard to get over.

If I was this upset after one unbelievably hot kiss, one he clearly didn't want, how would I have reacted if we'd entered into a relationship and he left?

"Fat chance of that happenin', so problem solved," I mumbled as I pulled out my phone.

The display said *Poppy calling*, so I swiped *Answer* and put the phone to my ear.

"Hello."

"Did you find out who the dead body was?"

I'd stopped at an intersection as I answered, but I paused and looked back, because I could hear a bike roaring down the street. Not ready to deal with Devin yet, I turned and ducked inside a souvenir shop. The rider passed by a moment later, but it wasn't Devin. Though he looked familiar.

"Cali?" Poppy called out.

"Sorry, I was crossin' the street," I answered as I watched the biker turn left onto Broughton Street.

Was that Devin's friend, Nate?

"Are you home already?"

I tried to pull up the man's face from the night before and remembered eyes like the night, so brown they looked black, but his face wasn't coming to me.

"Almost. I'm gettin' ready to cross Broughton, so I'll be there in about five minutes," I answered without thinking.

"Wait, are you walkin' home? Why aren't you with Devin?"

Shit!

Rider forgotten, I hesitated before answering. I wasn't about to tell her I'd taken her advice only to be shot down. She and Sienna would bug me for details, and I just wanted to forget about the whole embarrassing episode.

Now what?

LIE!!

"I, um. He was tied up with the police, so I walked home," I replied, stumbling over the lie as I walked back outside.

There was dead air for a moment.

"He let you walk home?"

"Um, yes," I answered, but even I didn't believe it. I couldn't lie worth a damn.

More dead air.

"All right, spill."

"About what?" I played dumb, but I knew she wouldn't buy it. Even I knew that Devin, interested in me or not, wouldn't have let me walk home after finding a dead body.

"What happened? Why'd you leave?" she asked on a sigh.

"Nothin'. I just needed to get out of there. Devin had to stay and talk to police, and I needed air. I'm worried about Maria, and I didn't want to see the body brought up from the basement, so I left. Simple as that."

"Okaaaaay." She dragged out the word, and I could tell she wasn't buying it.

"Where are you?" I asked to change the subject.

"We're at Jacobs' Ladder. Why don't you come join us?"

"Oh. Well, I'm headin' to," I looked around the street for a plausible destination. "Blends. For coffee and a muffin."

There was no way I was gonna meet up with them at Jacobs' Ladder. Devin would no doubt head there when he was finished with the police to debrief his friend. But I didn't want to head home either. The closer I got to my apartment, the faster my heart raced. I knew he'd show up there eventually and confront me for taking off.

Jesus. I'd essentially turned into a big fat scaredy-cat all because of a man. *Maybe I should rethink the whole notion of love?*

"After what we've been through, I would think tequila was the order of the day."

She wasn't wrong.

"I didn't get any caffeine this mornin', and I need to refuel," I hedged. "Besides, I still have a hangover."

I could tell she'd covered the phone and was talking to Sienna, so I waited, hoping they would come to me.

"We'll be there in ten," she finally said, so I did a U-turn and headed for Blends.

Thank you, God, for small miracles.

"See you soon," I responded and swiped my phone off.

As I entered Blends, I saw a circular for area apartments and grabbed one on a whim. I'd considered moving in the past to get out from underneath my family, but now, after making a ninny out of myself with Devin, would be the perfect time to stretch my wings. I knew I'd be miserable watching Devin take women into his apartment, hearing his gravelly voice chuckle as he entertained someone like Bridget Donavan.

I'm an idiot. I should have never listened to Poppy.

I berated myself as I flipped through the listings of cute, homey apartments.

Pausing on a listing for a one-bedroom at Eight Thousand Waters Street, my mind drifted to Maria. If she *had* killed the man in the basement, she must have feared for her life. The Maria I knew wouldn't hurt a fly.

Slamming the circular shut, I headed to the counter and ordered a café mocha. I wasn't lying when I said I needed caffeine. I was also starving, so I eyed the muffins and grabbed a lemon poppy seed. I'd drown my sorrow in coffee and bakery delights, then I'd focus on how we could help poor Maria.

I'd no more taken a sip of the rich hickory coffee with just the right amount of chocolate, when the girls walked in and made a beeline for my table. Their mouths were set in hard lines, their brows drawn low as they bore down on me.

They were ready for answers I didn't want to give.

Dammit. I really have to learn how to lie.

Sienna dropped her purse on the table, then her hands went to her hips as she glared down at me. "If this Wallflower thing is gonna work, we have to be completely honest with each other."

I looked at Poppy, and she'd crossed her arms in agreement, jerking her head slightly at Sienna in a *what she said* action.

Argh. Why had I thought it would be great to have friends?

"Sit," I finally said—resigned to my fate—and pulled out a chair for each of them.

Then I took a sip of coffee to stall.

Poppy began tapping her fingers on the table, her nails clipping the wood in a *rat-a-tat-tat*. "Any time would be good," she stated.

Blowing air from my lungs in a whoosh, sending strands of my hair off my forehead, I nodded and began.

"I kissed Devin, and he didn't like it."

Sienna snorted. "I doubt that."

"We'll be the judge of that," Poppy stated. "Start at the beginnin' and leave nothin' out."

I proceeded to explain in detail the events that transpired, leaving nothing out, not even the part about them being right about my not feeling good enough for a man like Devin, and then waited as each one chewed on the information.

"That doesn't make sense," Sienna mumbled. "I may not have dated recently, but that doesn't mean I'm blind to men who find me desirable. And I'm tellin' you, that Devin has that same look on his face when he looks at you."

"You must have misread him," was Poppy's only explanation.

"How do you misread angry eyes, locked jaw, and a back to your face?"

"Not easily," Sienna mumbled, "I'll give you that. Let me think about it."

My head fell back on my shoulders, and I raised my hands to run them through my hair. "I'm done thinkin' about it," I muttered. "His reaction shook me, which reinforced my belief he is not a man I should get involved with. Even if I did misread him, which I don't think I did, my reaction was exactly what I was afraid of," I said matter-of-factly. "No man should have that much power over any woman's heart."

Sienna reached out and placed a hand on my arm. "I understand, more than you know."

I knew she did. She'd spent years pining for a man who didn't return her feelings, and I sure as hell didn't want to end up the same way.

"Let's talk about what we can do to help Maria instead," I said, wanting more than anything to change the subject.

Sienna shot Poppy a look. "How exactly do you think we can help her?" she asked cautiously.

I'd been thinking about how to help Maria in between feeling miserable for myself and came to some conclusions.

"Devin thinks she found somethin' while cleanin' and whoever is after her is one of her clients."

I paused to look between them both, unsure of what I was about to say.

"And?" Poppy asked.

Grabbing my coffee, I took a sip to stall again. Maria needed help, that much was certain, and Devin was only one man. No matter how good he was at his job, being new to Savannah, not knowing the ins and outs of the close-knit community, would be a hindrance. If Billy Ray *was* the dead man, then I had a better chance of ferreting out the truth with my family connections than he did.

"I think I should go to work for her mother and look around," I finally mumbled.

After a loaded pause, I peeked up to gauge their reaction. Sienna had leaned back and crossed her arms, staring at me like I'd grown a second head. "You can't be serious," she finally bit out. "A man is dead, and you want to run off playin' Nancy Drew?"

I sighed. "No. But how else can we find out what happened to her? I can't sit idly by while her mother is worried sick. And if Billy Ray *is* involved, then others who run in the same circles as my grandparents might be as well. I know these people. I would know what to look for."

"I'll help," Poppy jumped in unexpectedly. "We can work together, keep an eye out for the other while one of us snoops. Sienna can cover for us at work, keep Alexandra and Jolene off the scent. She could tell them we're workin' from home since we've got the Unbridled Passion deadline loomin' next month. They'd believe that excuse."

"You're both nuts," Sienna hissed, looking around the coffee shop to see if she was overheard, "and forgettin' two things."

"What's that?" I asked.

She raised her hand and ticked off the points on her fingers. "One. *Devin.* He'll no doubt see you and blow your cover, if he doesn't kill you first. And two, you're Calla Armstrong, heir to Preston Armstrong's fortune. Maria probably cleaned for the who's who of Savannah. You may not live in their world, but they sure as hell know who you are."

"Devin won't care. I've already established that," I pointed out.

Sienna rolled her eyes. "I don't care what you say, you're wrong about Devin. He'll care, trust me. In fact, I guarantee after the way he acted about you viewin' the body, he'll lose his mind if he finds out you're puttin' yourself in harm's way."

"Oh, he'll mind," Poppy threw in, too, not willing to let go of the topic. "Even if it's just about his neighbor nosin' around where she doesn't belong."

"I'll cross that bridge *if* he finds out," I stated, though I'd decided in recent minutes that I had no intention of ever speaking to the man again if I could help it. "Besides, *he* can't nose around without bein' questioned and *we* can. No one will think twice about the cleanin' staff tidyin' a desk."

"Ok. Then how do you get around bein' recognized by half of Savannah?"

"Easy. I'll just wear a wig and glasses. I'll make myself look so different that Devin could walk right past me and never know."

"That could actually work," Poppy chuckled. "Should we begin tomorrow?"

Sienna gaped at us. "That's assumin' you can talk her mother into givin' you jobs without prior experience cleanin' or, I might add, without givin' her your *real* name so she can run a background check, little miss heir to the Armstrong throne. There is no way you can pull this off without bein' found out."

"Piece of cake," I said. "I'll just tell her we were sent to investigate by the PI workin' the case. By the time Devin or Maria's mother figure out what we're doin', we'll have searched for the evidence."

"Oh, that's good," Poppy beamed.

Sienna looked between Poppy and me and shook her head. "You both are T.S.T.L.; you know that, right?" she argued, referencing the acronym bibliophiles use about fictional characters that are so ridiculous in their behavior that they're 'too stupid to live.'

I looked at Poppy and smiled. "Good thing we read so much. We'll know exactly what not to do."

"Right. Like runnin' out of a house instead of investigatin' a creepy noise," Poppy chuckled.

"Or knowin' that the least likely person is usually the killer," I added.

Sienna smirked at us, rolling her eyes. "I still think you're nuts," she said rising from her chair, "but I'll help if you're really gonna do this."

"Easy peasy," I smiled. "We can be in and out in a day or two, and no one will be the wiser."

"Easy remains to be seen, but if you're plannin' on startin' tomorrow, you need to find Maria's mother and outfit yourselves with one of those cute uniforms they wear."

"Oh goodie," Poppy chuckled as she stood. "I look hot in gray scrubs. Maybe I'll catch the eye of a hot guy while I'm scrubbin' a toilet."

"Yeah," I joined in, rising, too. "Who needs speed datin' when you can find your future man while washin' his dirty clothes?"

Poppy's nose scrunched. "Lordy, we better find somethin' quickly. I'm not washin' dirty drawers unless there's orgasms involved."

"Eww. I'm not washin' dirty drawers period."

"Ladies, you gotta take one for the team," Sienna snickered, holding open the door for us to leave. "You know what they say, '*No pain, no gain.*'"

Six

MONDAY MORNING CAME WITHOUT a single lead after a long night spent in Nate's truck. Foo had stayed home all night—acting the innocent citizen Devin doubted she was—but looked out her blinds several times, scanning the street as if she could feel him watching.

Devin had kept watch all night to make sure she didn't sneak out the back door and slither into the night. She hadn't, and now he was headed home for a shower.

Frustrated about the progress he'd made, Devin climbed the outside stairs that led to his apartment and yanked open the door, coming face-to-face with Calla's apartment.

Time to mark one item off my to-do list for the day.

He didn't care if it was seven a.m.; it was time to settle things between them so he could concentrate on the job.

Moving to her door, he pounded hard enough to wake the dead. Nothing.

He pounded again and called out, "Calla," through gritted teeth. Still nothing.

Reaching into his back pocket, he pulled out his lock pick and went to work on her deadbolt. He didn't care if he was being intrusive. He'd had no sleep and fought a headache all night while trying to keep his mind on the job and off the kiss they'd shared. Her mouth won out every time his thoughts ventured there, warming his body with no chance of relief, so she owed him. He'd start with an explanation as to why she left him high and dry, then he'd take that mouth of hers until he'd had his fill and could function again.

He finally felt the cylinder turn, allowing the bolt assembly to retract inside the frame. As he opened the door, he called out Calla's name one more time to keep from startling her.

She still didn't respond.

Finding a light switch, Devin flipped it on and then grinned. Calla's apartment was laid out like his but reversed, with the living room and dining room off the entry, but he could feel Calla's presence on every surface.

Walls the color of her eyes were the backdrop for oversized down couches dressed in white covers that looked like you could sink into them and never get up. There were pillows in different hues of purple on every surface and soft-looking throws in the same light lavender as the walls. She had an old, weathered chest as a coffee table that looked to have been blue at one time, then painted white. The sky-blue color peeked out from beneath the white, giving the chest dimension and character. Her sofa tables were mismatched, but she'd painted them to match the walls then lightly sanded them until a layer of white shone through. There were also books scattered on every table, their covers as unique as the woman who lived there.

Devin moved to her bedroom door and opened it slowly. The light spilling in from the living room gave him a clear shot inside. In the center of her bedroom was a metal canopy bed with white billowing panels of sheer fabric designed to make her feel like a fairy princess and any man who entered her domain a conquering hero.

It was also empty. She'd already left for work.

Devin raised his hand to his nose and pinched the bridge. He was bone tired and didn't have time to hunt Calla down until tonight. He had a full day ahead of him dealing with Carmella's clients, and at some point, he had to catch a few hours of sleep before he headed out again to keep an eye on Foo.

Exhausted and frustrated, he left Calla's apartment and headed to his own.

When he opened his door, the apartment felt off, so he scanned his living room. The boxes he'd yet to unpack were where he'd left them, but the feeling someone had been inside didn't leave. Moving to his desk, Devin studied the contents and tried to picture how he'd left it. Everything seemed to be untouched until his eyes landed on a notepad. He'd used it to write down Maria's address then tossed it toward the desk before leaving, but he'd missed the desk. It had fallen to the floor, and he hadn't picked it up. Now it was on a stack of papers at the corner.

On a hunch, he flipped open his laptop and waited for it to wake up. Once it had booted up, he checked his *Quick Access* to see which files were opened last. He'd purchased the computer before moving to Savannah, and he hadn't had time to transfer many of his files, but he had started one on Maria Espinoza. It was the last file accessed, which he knew was correct, so he moved to his browser history. The last website he'd visited was Amazon, searching for the Duke of St. Ives, but his history showed the Eight Thousand Waters Apartments.

"Jesus." He hadn't googled the apartment complex, because Calla was going with him.

Dropping his eyes to the next link on the list, his jaw tightened. He clicked the website and waited for it to load. Within seconds, he was staring back at a picture of himself, one of him shielding his face as he entered his former station in Atlanta. The caption read '*Supercop Tracks Down Serial Killer.*' It was a byline a reporter by the name of Kendall Brown had given him after he'd rebuked her invitation to warm her bed. In her mind, she thought she could win him over by painting him as some sort of Superman. She'd even gone as far as talking to his elementary school teachers to find anything she needed to romanticize him in the public eye as a modern-day white knight.

It didn't work. Instead, it pissed him off.

When he didn't respond as she expected, she took to stalking him so he'd talk to her. But the final straw was when she broke into his apartment and climbed into his bed naked. He had her arrested for breaking and entering and hadn't seen her since her arraignment, where he'd agreed to drop the charges if she sought counseling. She'd agreed, and the last he'd heard she'd left Atlanta.

The headache he'd been fighting all night came back with full force.

Pounding on his front door drew his attention, so he closed his computer and moved toward the door on silent feet, pulling out his gun as he went. Peering through the peephole, he grumbled, "Just what I need," as he holstered his gun and ripped open the door.

Bo Strawn was on the other side.

The detective didn't look happy.

Proving Devin's assessment of his mood, Strawn shoved a newspaper in his gut and entered his apartment without invitation, growling, "We need to talk."

"Make yourself at home," Devin answered sarcastically then unfolded the newspaper, scanned it, bit out, "Christ," and then slammed the door.

❀ ❀ ❀

"I took his monster cock into my mouth and . . ."

"Ugh, Wuthering Heights it's not," I grumbled as I reached half-asleep for my second cup of coffee for the day.

After taking food over to Maria's mother and explaining our plan to work for her on Tuesday, the same work day Maria disappeared, I'd had a sleepless night—sleepless because I'd spent the night listening for Devin to come home, which he didn't, I might add—and given up and come to work early.

I'd tossed and turned wondering when he would come home and confront me, and then, the later it got, I began wondering where he was and just who the hell he was with until I'd driven myself crazy. When I took to looking out the window, hoping to see his Harley pull up, I'd called myself all kinds of a ninny and gotten dressed.

Now I was sitting at my desk still wondering what he was doing and who he was doing it with while attempting to edit *The Way to a Man's Heart is Through His Dick.*

I heard my name called out and turned to see Sienna coming my way at a clipped pace, clutching a newspaper to her chest. When I opened my mouth to say hi, she grabbed my arm and pulled me out of my chair, dragging me toward the break room.

"What's goin' on?"

"The dead man *was* Billy Ray Stutter," she said as she closed the door, ensuring we had privacy, then handed me the newspaper.

"I heard on the radio already," I told her.

"There's more," she returned.

Opening the newspaper, I scanned the headline and froze.

In bold print above a picture of Devin were the words "There's a New Sheriff in Town."

"Oh my God," I whispered as I began reading the account of how Devin and an unidentified female had found Billy Ray after following leads in the disappearance of Maria Espinoza.

"This is bad," I mumbled. "How the hell did this guy know about Maria?"

"This Charles Taft guy says Devin is some kind of Supercop. The article is more about Devin than Billy Ray's murder. He even talks about how he's single and ripe for the pickin'."

"What?"

She pointed to the paragraph, and my stomach dropped. Women

would be pounding down his door now. I kept reading about Devin's accomplishments, but something more important occurred to me, and my stomach dropped again.

"Oh. My. God. Whoever's after Maria is gonna know that Devin is looking for them! After reading this," I shook the paper, "I bet they've cleaned every surface of their house and gotten rid of any evidence."

"You're right," she gasped. "Is it still worth snooping tomorrow?"

"I don't think we have a choice if we want to help find Maria, but I doubt we'll find anything now."

"Maybe you should let it go? I've had a bad feelin' about this insane plan of yours from the start."

Leaning against the wall, I closed my eyes and tried to think.

"No, I think we should still try. If the person knows Devin is lookin' for them, they're bound to be nervous. And with the cops involved now, that means added pressure. They may have gotten rid of evidence, but they'll be jumpy. We could still clean and look for odd behavior while we're there."

"This is true, but you gotta remember, they'll also be on the lookout for anyone snoopin' around. You could be puttin' yourself and Poppy in danger."

She had a point.

Pushing off the wall, I began pacing. "Dammitalltohell," I bit out. "Who is this Taft guy, and how did he find out about Maria?"

"He's a reporter," was her helpful response.

"I know that," I snapped. "But how?"

"They're all like dogs with a bone. He probably has informants at the police station."

"Yes, but how did he know about Maria? We didn't say anything to the police."

There was a knock at the door, followed by Poppy saying, "Let me in." Sienna opened the door for her, and she slid inside as I paced.

"Cali," she said, her voice a hushed whisper, "there's a Detective Strawn here to see you, and he looks really pissed."

I spun around and stared at the door, expecting the detective to burst through at any moment.

"Shit. I'm going to jail for lyin' to the man, I just know it."

"Do you want me to stall him while you sneak out the back stairs?" Poppy asked.

I looked at Sienna then back at Poppy and actually considered fleeing for a half a second.

"No," I sighed, shaking my head. "I'll go face the music."

"Don't worry about it," Sienna said as she opened the door, "You're Preston Armstrong's granddaughter. The man would have to be an idiot to lock you—"

We'd no more exited the break room when Sienna stopped dead in her tracks, causing Poppy and me to collide with her back. I looked over her shoulder to see what had stopped her and found Detective Strawn standing right in front of us, his attention fully on Sienna.

"He heard you, didn't he?" I whispered in her ear.

She confirmed my suspicion by nodding slowly.

"Great. Just great," I bit out, pushing past Sienna. "This is what I get for steppin' outside my comfort zone. *You* told me to get on the back of his bike when all I wanted to do was draw a map." I pointed at Sienna in accusation, ignoring the detective. "Wear somethin' cute, you said. Not run the other way! I should have called Poppy, *she* would have told me to run. Now I'm goin' to jail for listenin' to you!"

"Ms. Armstrong," Detective Strawn said, but I ignored him.

"You were bein' stupid," Sienna argued back. "Devin's a good man."

"If he's such a good man, then why am I goin' to jail? A good man wouldn't have dragged me into this!"

"Ms. Armstrong," the detective tried again, but I threw up my hand to silence him.

"And not only am I goin' to jail, I also have to move, thanks to Poppy and her, *'He's a good man. You're makin' a mistake.'*"

"I think she's losin' it," Poppy mumbled to Sienna, and they both had the nerve to smile.

"I'm not losin' it," I bit out, then turned to the detective and put my hands together so he could slap on the handcuffs, turning my head for a parting shot before I was hauled away. "I want a Wallflower divorce!"

Both women gasped at that announcement then started talking over each other.

"Marriage is for life," Sienna cried out.

"Wallflowers don't turn their backs on each other," Poppy joined in.

"We've only been Wallflowers a whole two days," I pointed out. "I'll get an annulment, and it'll be like it never happened."

I turned to Detective Strawn to see why he hadn't slapped the cuffs on yet and found he'd moved and was leaning against a wall with his arms crossed.

"Are we doin' this or what?"

He grinned. Actually grinned like he thought something was funny.

"Definitely worth lyin', stealin' or killin' for," he oddly said, his gaze scanning the three of us. "And Wallflowers to boot."

"Ex-Wallflowers," I reminded him. "Now, haul me downtown so I can call my lawyer."

"You're not under arrest," Detective Strawn announced.

I blinked once. Twice. Then narrowed my eyes.

"You better not be afraid to arrest me 'cause of my granddaddy. I will not be treated differently just 'cause he has money."

"Nope."

"Then I don't understand?"

Strawn looked at Poppy and Sienna then jerked his head toward the break room. "Since I found your accomplices right along with you, I might as well make this speech once. Follow me," he said, then turned and started walking.

"Oh, God. He found out we were there yesterday and he's makin' a group arrest," Poppy whispered as we followed. But Strawn heard her with the bat hearing all cops have and stopped in his tracks, his head falling back on his shoulders.

"You have the right to remain silent," Strawn grumbled at the ceiling, "I suggest you use it before I change my mind."

I elbowed Poppy in the side, then followed the man.

Strawn was tall like Devin, well built with medium brown hair and gray eyes that spoke of intelligence. Intelligence that said he missed nothing. I knew it would be pointless to lie to the man, which was a good thing, because the minute the door closed behind the four of us, he whipped around and bit out, "I'm gonna say this one time and you'd better listen. Leave the investigatin' to me. Whatever harebrained scheme you ladies have to dig around in an official investigation will land you in jail."

"Um," was my intelligent response as I looked at Poppy and Sienna.

"How did you know?" Sienna questioned.

"I met with Carmella Espinoza this morning."

"She ratted us out?" Poppy gasped.

Strawn narrowed his eyes. "She brought me up-to-date on Hawthorne's investigation and mentioned he had female partners who were gonna go undercover for him." Strawn moved closer to me and leaned down, getting right in my face. "She said the ladies in question were two blondes and a brunette named after flowers, but couldn't remember the names. She said she thought one of them was named Poppy." He shot a look at Poppy, who grimaced. She also remembered that the leader of the pack had the most unusual color of eyes. Said they were like periwinkles on a spring day."

"*Your* eyes are pretty spectacular," Sienna interjected. "And unforgettable."

"All of you are unforgettable," Strawn said, scanning Sienna with what looked like interest, "which is bad for undercover work. You need to blend in to go undetected, not stand out. Not to mention, none of you have a fuckin' clue what you're doin'. You'd end up dead right along with Stutter."

"So if *you're* investigatin' Maria's disappearance now, does that mean you threw Devin off the case?" I asked.

"I'm not at liberty to discuss the investigation. But I'll tell you that I've already had it out with Hawthorne, and if he were any other man, he'd be in jail. But he's not. He broke the law, and he knows it but didn't impede my case since he's lookin' for the killer as well. We're short-staffed and in need of a man with his qualifications, so I let it slide. All *you* need to know at this point is you're done. Don't get near my case again, or I'll haul you all down to the station and lock you up."

We nodded immediately.

"We only wanted to help, because Devin's on his own and needed it. Now that you're involved, there's no reason," I explained.

A sparkle of laughter lit his eyes. "If you tell Hawthorne that when he finds out what you were up to, call me. I'll do my best to keep him from wringin' your neck."

"He isn't gonna find out," I replied tersely. "I have no intention of speakin' to the man again."

A grin broke across his face before he reached out and grabbed hold of the doorknob, opening the door. "Just so you know, I'll be callin' Hawthorne as soon as I leave to update him on what I found out this mornin'. That should give you about a five-minute head start."

I swallowed hard at that news.

I wasn't sure why I needed a head start. Well, I kinda did, but it didn't make any sense, because we didn't snoop like we'd planned, so he shouldn't be mad.

I asked anyway, 'cause curiosity killed the cat and all. "Why do I need a head start?"

He grinned even wider. "'Cause you say words like heebie-jeebies," was his cryptic response, and then he disappeared through the door.

"That makes no sense," I told the girls. "Is it possible Detective Strawn is just tryin' to scare me 'cause I lied to him?"

"Yep," Poppy answered. "That bein' said . . . I'd hide if I were you."

"Hide?"

"For a day at least," Sienna threw in.

"For goodness sake," I huffed. "Devin's not gonna do anything."

Both women scoffed and then threw an arm around me, herding me toward the door. When we walked out, Detective Strawn was standing near the elevator with his cell phone at his ear, and my heart leapt.

Is he talking to Devin?

When the doors opened, he looked at the three of us and grinned before entering the elevator. We watched silently as he slid his phone into his back pocket, a look of male satisfaction on his face as he flicked a salute at us before the doors closed.

"He looked smug," I whispered as trepidation caused my heart to pump faster.

"Like we said," Sienna chuckled. "Hide."

"I'm not hidin'. No man is gonna—"

My cell phone started ringing on my desk, so I walked over and picked it up.

"Don't answer it," Poppy said. "It's probably Devin."

"I'm not hidin' from the man."

They both snorted.

"I'm not. I'm just not speakin' to him."

"Then answer it," Sienna returned, pushing the phone toward me.

I looked at the display and didn't recognize the number.

It was a Savannah area code, so I took a chance it wasn't Devin. I doubted he'd changed his number yet, and I knew I hadn't given him mine.

Swiping *Answer*, I took a deep breath and said, "Hello?"

"This is Carmella Espinoza. Is this Calla Armstrong?"

I let out my breath and took another. Saved by Mrs. Espinoza.

"Yes, this is Cali. How did you get my number?"

"Detective Strawn told me your name, so I called your aunts and got your number."

"What can I do for you, Mrs. Espinoza?"

"Detective Strawn said he was pulling you off the case, but I need a favor from you if you're willing."

"Mrs. Espinoza, I promised the detective I wouldn't get involved. He'll lock me up if I do."

"It doesn't involve Maria's disappearance," she rushed out.

"What does it involve?"

Poppy and Sienna crowded in closer, trying to hear what Mrs. Espinoza was saying.

"I've been so worried about my Maria that I forgot to clean a business yesterday. They called me this mornin', but I've already sent out my girls and my schedule is full."

"Are you askin' if the girls and I will clean for you?"

"Yes, that's it exactly. I can't afford to lose this client, Ms. Calla. My company is all I have until my Maria comes home."

I looked at the girls to see if they'd heard, and they nodded.

"Give me the address, and we'll be there within the hour."

Poppy's uniform was still in her car from the night before, so we'd gone to my apartment so I could change, checking ahead of time, of course, to make sure Devin wasn't home. I'd called Bernice, and she told me she'd seen him leave an hour before with another man, so I'd dashed up and donned my disguise to keep from being recognized.

"You look hot as a brunette," Poppy snorted when I climbed into the car.

I pulled down the visor and looked in the mirror. I'd chosen a wig from my aunts' stash in Frock You that was cut sassy and short. It had plenty of bangs to hide my face, but wasn't so bulky it looked like a wig, and I'd paired it with huge, black, Buddy Holly glasses. I looked unrecognizable, which was good since we didn't know who we were cleaning for until we arrived. With everything else going on, the last thing I needed was a lecture from my grandfather on how an Armstrong should conduct themselves.

"I don't think anyone will recognize me," I answered, adjusting the wig in the mirror. "You know this bruise gives me an edge of danger." I chuckled looking at the yellow shading on my face.

"We can call you Bruiser," she laughed then put the car in drive and pulled away from the curb. "So," she asked cautiously, "you haven't mentioned whether or not you saw Devin last night. I know you told Strawn you're avoidin' him an' all, but is there a particular reason, other than him knowin' about our plan to snoop, that is?"

"I'm avoidin' him, 'cause I want to forget about the colossal mistake I made yesterday."

"But you haven't seen him, so you don't know you made a mistake."

I gave her a look. She was still hanging on to the silly notion that Devin was interested in me.

"As far as I can tell, he didn't come home until this mornin', so no, I haven't seen him."

"Never came home?" she questioned.

"Nope. So you see, I was right. If it had mattered to him, he would have come home and confronted me," I answered breezily as if it didn't matter to me in the least.

Her brows pursed in confusion.

"I don't understand," she mumbled, but I didn't think she was talking to me.

"There's nothin' to understand. I told you yesterday he wasn't interested in me, and last night proved my point. He probably didn't come home to avoid me and any conversation that needed to be had. In fact, I bet he spent the evenin' at his friend's bar and then went home with some woman just so he didn't have to run into me this mornin'."

I kept my face neutral on purpose. I was laidback and relaxed like everything coming out of my mouth wasn't gutting me to say. Another reason I should have stayed in my comfort zone: if you don't put yourself out there, you can't be humiliated and forced to move to save face.

"So, you're really okay with the whole rejection thing?" she asked, her brows high on her forehead.

My hand came up and I flipped my wrist, pffting air from my lungs in a whoosh. "I'm totally okay with it. I must have misunderstood his flirtin' for somethin' more than it was. He probably acts like that with all women, so I can hardly hold it against the man for not bein' attracted to me," I lied. Lied so convincingly for once that I almost believed myself.

"Well, that's good to hear. Especially since I googled the address while you were changin' and . . ." she looked at me and grinned.

"And?" I asked cautiously, but I knew by her face I wasn't going to like her answer.

"And . . . it's Greg Pierce, Devin's cousin's husband."

"What!"

"Didn't Bernice say his cousin was married to Greg Pierce, the divorce attorney?"

I groaned. "I swear if I had any luck at all, it's bad."

"But you've never met the husband, and since Devin isn't in the equation, then it shouldn't matter, right?"

I narrowed my eyes at her. She was enjoying seeing me squirm.

"Right," I answered through my teeth. "But you're forgettin' my grandparents. If they find out I cleaned a house for someone, they know they'll take it out on my aunts for raisin' me wrong, and I don't want them bullied by either one."

"You worry too much. You haven't met the husband, and I doubt she'll be there."

She had a point. And there was no reason his cousin should recognize me either way.

"True," I finally acknowledged. "I don't recall seein' her in social circles, so I doubt she knows me on sight."

"Then there's nothin' to worry about."

"Right," I answered, but I had a sinking feeling this was gonna explode in my face.

We were quiet for a moment, lost in thought, then Poppy blurted out, "Do you think Maria killed Billy Ray Stutter?"

I considered that for a moment.

"If she did, I'm convinced he must have been threatenin' her life. Though, I can't see Maria havin' the strength to kill someone as big as Billy Ray."

"Maybe she didn't. Maybe there was someone else there, and *they* killed Billy Ray."

"That's a good theory."

Carmella had given us the list of jobs Maria had worked the day she disappeared, and Billy Ray wasn't one of them. So how *did* Billy

Ray figure into this mess?

"Have you talked to Sienna?" I asked as I mulled over the puzzle.

"Yeah. She said Jolene is out of the office today, so no worries there. And Alexandra is tied up in meetings all day, so she won't notice we're gone."

"So far, so good," I mumbled.

My phone began to ring, and Poppy and I both looked at my purse like it was a snake. I didn't know what I expected Devin to say if he did reach me, but Detective Strawn's answer was so cryptic he had me on edge.

She bugged out her eyes at me and I rolled mine to continue with my charade of not giving two hoots about Devin Hawthorne. She snorted in return, telling me she didn't buy my calm façade in the least.

Pulling my phone from my purse, I saw my grandfather's number on the display and groaned.

Just what I needed.

I sat a little straighter as I swiped *Answer*, conditioning from years of my grandmother exalting the reasons ladies do not slouch. "Hello?"

"Calla!" he shouted in the phone. "Explain to me why you're on the front page of the paper."

Shit. I'd forgotten about the newspaper article.

"Granddaddy—"I began, then it hit me my name wasn't mentioned in the article. "How'd you know it was me?"

He paused briefly, then bit out, "The chief of police is a friend of mine and keeps me appraised when my granddaughter is involved, now explain to me what you were doin' in the company of a private investigator."

His snobbery was an annoyance most of the time, but hearing the disdain in his voice concerning Devin pissed me off.

"What's wrong with bein' a private investigator?" I bit back.

"They're bottom feeders. They make their livin' off of destroyin' people's lives."

"That's not true," I defended. "The whole reason I was with him is because he's lookin for a missin' woman."

"I can read," he returned. "He's lookin' for a woman who cleans for a livin' and probably stabbed Stutter when he wouldn't leave his wife for her."

I gasped. "You know, Granddaddy, your blue blood came from simple cotton farmers, so you have no room to judge anyone for their profession," I answered then swiped *Off* on my phone.

The original Armstrongs were cotton farmers, but sometime after the Civil War, my family turned from farming to shipping after Yankee soldiers burned most of our crops. My great-great-great-great-grandfather had foresight, knew that the world was getting bigger and Savannah would need goods shipped in and out of it if it was going to rebuild after the war. So Armstrong Shipping was established in 1867, and it's been a powerhouse in the industry ever since.

"I take it you're not close to your grandparents?"

"They don't exactly do close," I explained. "They're more like 'stand up straight and we'll see you next Christmas' kind of grandparents."

My son would still be alive if it weren't for you.

"And your aunts?"

"Sorry?" I asked, pulling back from the painful memory.

"Are your aunts close to them?"

"No. They were disowned before my parents died for bein' rebels."

"That's harsh," Poppy gasped.

"That's Preston and Margaret. Toe the line, or they'll act like you don't exist."

"So you toe the line then?" she questioned.

"I don't see them enough to get close to the line. Though I'm sure I'm close after hangin' up on him. Hell, if they knew what I was doin' today, they'd have a stroke and strike me from their life. But I don't intentionally ruffle their feathers like my aunts do, out of respect for my father."

And guilt.

I turned and looked out the passenger side window as the old bitterness set in.

Poppy must have cottoned onto the fact that I didn't like talking about my grandparents, because we traveled in companionable silence the rest of the way to Pierce's building.

The old home sat across from Chippewa Square, a picturesque park that is famously known for the park bench scene in the movie Forrest Gump. Named after the Battle of Chippewa in the War of 1812, the peaceful square, with its abundance of trees and flowers, drew tourists daily, causing congestion on the street.

I stared up at the two-story brownstone and sighed. "Let's get this over with quickly."

"Um. What exactly are we supposed to do?" Poppy asked.

I turned and looked at her. "Clean," I responded.

"Yes, I'm aware of that," Poppy answered. "But isn't there a list or something we have to follow?"

"How hard can it be?" I asked. "We'll just wing it. Clean anything that looks dirty and empty all the trash cans."

Poppy nodded then exited the car. I followed, pulling my wig further down on my head.

Here goes nothing.

I might not know Devin's cousin, but I'd been in enough society pages with my grandparents that it was possible Pierce might recognize me. And the last thing I needed was Devin finding out what I was doing after the lecture we got from Strawn. He'd never believe we were actually helping, not snooping.

Avoidance 101: Avoid confrontation at all costs lest you be noticed by one and all.

I had a Ph.D. in avoiding life, so I should have no problems keeping my distance from the man.

"Carmella said to go around to the back door," Poppy said, so I followed her around back.

We scanned the back of the house until we saw an oversized glass door. We walked to it and tugged. Locked.

"Guess we should knock," I mumbled.

Poppy rapped on the door three times then we waited.

Footsteps could be heard inside heading our direction. I prayed it wasn't someone I knew.

The door swung open, and I looked up into the face of Devin's cousin.

This day keeps getting better by the minute.

"Come in," she whispered. "We have a bit of a situation, so if you could start upstairs and give us some privacy, it would be appreciated."

Either my wig passed the test—she hadn't paid that much attention to me when I'd fallen off the ladder—or she was distracted by the wailing emanating from deep in the bowels of the home.

Poppy and I both nodded then scooted past her.

"Carmella called to say you were new employees, so I'll show you to the storage closet."

I kept my mouth shut and nodded again. The less I said, the less I could incriminate myself unwittingly.

As we followed Devin's cousin, a cry so mournful blasted us from the left and we stopped in our tracks. Inside an office with divided light doors that we could see through, was Billy Ray Stutter's wife, Danielle Stutter. The always coiffed woman was a mess.

Her makeup ran down her face in rivers of black, coating the white shirt of a good-looking man with brown hair and kind eyes I recognized from Saturday night at Jacobs' Ladder. Greg Pierce. She wailed again, and I jumped from the impact of it. Bernice and Eunice always called her a shrew, but the woman standing in front of me was visibly distraught over her husband's death.

"You have to find out who murdered my husband," she cried out.

"Danielle," Pierce said, patting her on the back, "I'm not the police. You need to leave it to them to find out who killed Billy Ray."

"No," she argued, shaking her head in aggravation. "I need someone who will dedicate all his time to finding out who killed my Billy Ray."

Pierce moved to a sideboard and poured a glass of water. "Even if I had the time, I'm not a criminal investigator. I handle civil disputes," Pierce pressed, handing her the water.

"Then find me someone who won't sleep until my husband's killer is caught. Get me that man who was in the paper, the one who found my Billy Ray. The newspaper says he's some kind of Supercop."

Devin's cousin had stopped at the outburst, as well, then realized we were gawking. "Shit, come with me," she ordered, and we followed. "Guess I'm gonna have to call in a favor," she mumbled to herself as we proceeded down the hall. "Her husband was murdered," she continued, turning back to look at us, explaining as if we hadn't heard the conversation. "My husband is a friend of his, so naturally, she came to us for advice. I'm Megan Pierce, by the way, you can call me Megan." She stopped next to a closet and opened the door. "Everything you need is in here. Just holler if you have any questions."

She turned on her heel and headed back down the hallway toward her husband's office, pulling out her cell as she disappeared around the corner.

"Let's get this over with as soon as possible," I whispered, grabbing cleaning solution and rags from the shelves. "I feel guilty. I feel it in my bones Maria didn't kill Billy Ray, but hearing that woman cry . . . "

Poppy glanced over her shoulder to make sure Megan wasn't close by. "According to Author Karen Rosemond, a person is capable of anything if their life's in danger."

"Jesus, Poppy. Fictional characters don't count," I said.

"Cali, it's common knowledge she interviews the police extensively for her books," Poppy defended.

I narrowed my eyes.

"I'm just sayin', anything is possible."

"No way. Not that sweet girl."

Sighing, she nodded. "You're right. Let's get this done and get back to work."

We struggled with the supplies until we got to the top of the stairs. The second-floor bedrooms had been converted into a filing room and a single conference room with views of Chippewa Square. There was a bathroom between the two rooms and a long runner covering the hardwood floor.

"I'll take the bathroom, you start in the conference room," I told Poppy.

She grabbed the vacuum, and I grabbed the cleaning supplies then walked into the bathroom. It was larger than I expected. A walk-in closet and double sink vanity stood on one side and a large glass shower was situated on the other. I looked inside the shower to see if it had been used and found it still looked clean. In an attempt to finish quickly, I sprayed the tile with Windex to give it a just-cleaned shine and wiped it down.

The toilet was next.

I looked at the ceiling, wondering how I'd gotten myself into this. Cleaning my own toilet when I knew I was the only one who used it was one thing, but a toilet that only God knew how many people had used was akin to torture.

cp smith

Rummaging through the supplies, I realized I didn't have rubber gloves, so I opened the bathroom door to ask Poppy if she had any. As soon as I opened the door, I shut it again. Then I cracked it, and my eyes widened at the sound of Devin's voice. "I was in the neighborhood when you called."

"You look like crap, Devin, and you look like you slept in your clothes."

"Yeah," he answered, his voice filled with exhaustion. "I had a hell of a night stakin' out a suspect and one hell of a mornin'. I haven't been to sleep yet."

"I'm guessin' your bad mornin' has to do with the article in the paper. What case kept you up?"

"I can't discuss my cases, Meg."

"Were you workin' the Billy Ray case?" she whispered.

"What part of 'I can't discuss my cases' doesn't compute with you?"

"Billy Ray's wife is here," she whispered again. "That's why I called you. She wants to hire you to find his killer."

"She needs to leave it to the police," he answered.

"But you found his body. Doesn't that mean you're already involved?"

I leaned out of the bathroom enough so I could see down into the lobby. He looked exhausted, rumpled, and sexy as hell. His hair was messy, like he'd been running his fingers through it all night in frustration.

He crossed his arms and looked blankly at his cousin. "Meg," he warned.

With a huff, Megan reached up and ran her hand through his hair in motherly disgust. "You need a woman to take care of you, because you clearly aren't takin' care of yourself."

Devin grinned.

"And a haircut," she groused. "Have you eaten?"

126

"Not since yesterday. I'll pick somethin' up on my way back to my apartment."

"You'll do no such thing. I have food in the kitchen," she said then linked an arm with Devin. As they headed toward the back of the house, Megan stopped, then leaned in and sniffed his clothes. "Why do you smell like . . . a dead body?"

He looked down at her and raised a brow. "Shit," she mumbled, then pointed at the stairs. "Shower. Now."

"Meg," he chuckled, but she pointed again and stomped her foot. "Right. NOW!"

I could tell by the look on his face he was going to acquiesce. Hell, I'd agree if I'd been sitting in clothes that smelled like a dead body for more than a minute.

When he looked back at the stairs, I stepped back and closed the door then started gathering my supplies.

Poppy opened the door as I was almost done and whisper-shouted, "Is that Devin downstairs?"

I nodded frantically, then we heard footsteps on the stairs.

"Oh, God. Now what?"

"The bathroom's right through that door, towels are in the linen closet."

Poppy and I looked at each other then looked at the closet. She ripped it open, grabbed a handful of towels, and shoved them at me. "Put them on the counter."

I did what she said, then she grabbed my hand and pulled me into the closet, closing the door.

There was a knock on the bathroom door a second later, then it opened. I covered my mouth to keep from laughing.

This was like something out of a *Three Stooges* movie.

Poppy and I barely fit in the closet, so I held onto the doorknob and leaned back to keep from falling out.

"I'll get you some of Greg's clothes to wear home, just leave those smelly things in here, and I'll wash them for you . . . or burn them."

The door closed behind her, and then the shower turned on.

"When he gets in the shower, open the door a smidge and see if we can escape," Poppy whispered.

"This is ridiculous," I whispered back. "I should just walk out there and confront him. We're not doin' anything but helpin' out Carmella."

"Works for me," she answered, nudging me in the back, but I couldn't bring myself to move. Twenty-four hours ago, I'd kissed that man and I didn't want to see the rejection on his face again. Add to that we tried to interfere in his investigation, and I figured he'd be pretty pissed. No, I wasn't ready for the confrontation yet.

"Are we leaving or what?" she whispered in my ear.

I sighed. "Or what."

"You were lyin' when you said you didn't care he rejected you."

I didn't answer immediately, then nodded. "I'm an idiot. I shouldn't have kissed him, and now I can't bring myself to face him."

"I understand," she replied. "But just so you know, I still think you're wrong about Devin."

I started to answer, but I heard the shower door slide closed, and then a low moan filled the room.

"He's in the shower."

"Look and see if he has his back to the door."

Very slowly, I cracked the door a hair and peeked out. Then my breath caught.

Devin's eyes were closed in relaxation as he supported his weight with one hand on the shower wall. His expression was one of relief as water cascaded over his body in rivers. His profile was beautiful. Breathtaking. Like Michelangelo's David, he looked like he'd been carved from smooth stone.

Scanning his hard lines and muscles, I stopped on his fantastic ass. Michelangelo himself couldn't have sculpted one that firm, round, or bitable. If he had, it would have been called Michelangelo's Devin.

But Devin's backside was in a stratosphere all on its own; it was its own masterpiece.

It was Devinangelo, naked butt from the gods.

"Well?" Poppy whispered.

"We can't leave yet," I answered as my mouth ran dry, unable to peel my eyes off Devin. I was hypnotized watching the water curl down, around, and over his ass. That is, until he turned and gave me a full frontal shot.

Oh . . . my.

I gasped and pulled the door closed too hard, slamming into Poppy. She steadied me when I fell back, whispering, "What? Did he see you?"

I shook my head in quick jerking motions and tried to breathe. The image of Devin fully naked was cauterized into my memory.

"Can we escape?" she asked, and I shook my head again.

"The shower door is clear glass," I finally answered.

She didn't respond for a moment, then she snorted. "You got an eyeful, didn't you?"

"And back."

"You're an ass woman?"

I licked my lips. "I was until he turned . . ."

We both threw our hands over our mouths to keep from laughing, but our laughter died when the closet door was ripped open, and I fell face first into a very naked, very wet, and *very* pissed off man.

I lost my glasses as I tumbled forward and slid down his body. Then Poppy reached out to grab hold, but missed and took the wig right off my head.

I didn't dare look up. I'd be eye level with his— well, you know.

"This day just keeps gettin' better and better," Devin growled.

Flipping over, I scrambled to my feet and stood up, grabbing a towel in the process and tossing it over my shoulder.

"You've got two seconds to explain what the fuck you're doin' here," Devin hissed as I turned to face him. Oh, he was pissed all right. He looked like the Devil himself with his arms crossed over his chest while his jaw worked overtime. He also, I might add, hadn't covered himself yet, which made it really hard to concentrate.

I bent down with my eyes closed and picked up the towel, throwing it at him again.

"Don't use that tone with me, Devil man," I bit back.

He ignored my warning and leaned in further until his crystalline eyes were all I saw. They weren't cool like ice this time; they were molten fire directed at me. "Talk," he bit out between clenched teeth, "Or so help me God."

Yikes!

Okay, maybe I should tread lightly here. This *was* his family's business and I was just his neighbor who'd crossed two lines in less than twenty-four hours.

Shit. Shit. Shit!

"Carmella called and needed our help, so we agreed. It was nothin' nefarious."

His jaw ticked.

Then he looked at the wig on the floor. "Wearin' a wig to disguise your identity?"

My hand rose to my head. "Shit."

"I'll ask again," he growled low, "what are you doin' here?"

Avoidance 102: when confronted, turn the tables on the accuser to throw them off.

"Are you calling me a liar?" I bit out.

I wasn't lying, of course, but considering the phone call he'd gotten from Strawn I could see why he would think I was.

He looked to the ceiling for patience, his jaw working the whole time. After a moment of reflection, which I figured included how to keep from wringing my neck, he answered. "I came home after a long fuckin' night on a stakeout to find out you and your friends are nosin' around in a murder investigation, and you expect me to believe you're not here doin' exactly what you've been ordered not to do?"

I crossed my arms and narrowed my eyes. "If I say I'm helping Carmella, then I'm helping Carmella."

He moved toward me then, crowding me deeper into the bathroom, his face a perfect example of a man done playing games.

"This is the last time I'm gonna ask you what the fuck you're doin' here," he stated flatly, in a tone that brokered no argument.

"Or what?" I asked out of curiosity. "What are you gonna do, Devin? Call the police and tell them I cleaned a toilet wearin' a wig?"

"I'll just step outside and give you two some privacy," Poppy said, inching for the bathroom door.

Devin turned on her as she opened it. "You've got two seconds to tell me what the fuck *you're* doin' here, as well."

"Um . . . cleanin'?" she squeaked out, her eyes rounder than a hoot owl.

"I told you why we were here," I butted in, glaring for all I was worth. "Carmella called us this mornin' and told us Pierce's office hadn't been cleaned, what with Maria missin', so we agreed to clean it for her."

"That doesn't explain the wig," he returned.

I crossed my arms and bit my tongue. I didn't want to explain my grandparents. There weren't enough hours in a day to explain my grandparents properly, and one should never attempt it without an alcoholic beverage at hand.

He looked between the two of us when I didn't answer, his eyes flashing with anger again.

"Ladies?" A call from downstairs broke the tension, and our

attention swung to the open door.

Saved by Megan!

Since I'd vowed to take my life by the horns a few days ago, it had been turned upside down. But I was learning on the fly when to stand my ground and when to back down.

This, however, was another running situation. Strawn had been right when he said Devin would be pissed and I should hide. Time to take his advice.

I saw Megan's distraction as an opportunity to make a break for it, so I pushed past Devin and grabbed Poppy by the hand, heading for the stairs and freedom.

"Later, Devil," I shouted over my shoulder.

I chanced a look back to see if he was following us, and almost stumbled at what I saw. He was grinning from ear to ear as he *finally* wrapped a towel around his hips.

"I think he's allergic to clothing," I mumbled as we cleared the bottom step and ran smack dab into Megan.

"Is there a problem . . . wait, aren't you the woman from the window?" she accused, then looked up the stairs at Devin.

"Devil will no doubt explain it all after we're gone," I said by way of explanation.

"Devil?" she asked.

"Devin," I answered. "Same thing."

Seven

This isn't my Dress

ARRIVING BACK AT POE an hour after our encounter with Devin, Sienna shut and locked the bathroom door as Poppy and I changed our clothes. She turned to us and leaned against the door, smugness written clearly across her face.

"I told ya you should have hidden. I'd say his reaction proves he's interested in you," she gloated.

I looked up and glared. "He was pissed because it looked like we were investigatin' his cousin. Nothin' more."

Poppy snorted. "She's S.O.S on this topic, so don't even try."

I directed my glare at Poppy. "S.O.S?"

"Stuck on stupid," she answered.

"Am not," I argued.

"Sugar, if you were any blinder to Devin, you'd need a cane," Sienna laughed.

"You should have seen him, Sienna. If it weren't for his cousin draggin' him off to meet Billy Ray's widow, he'd have cornered Cali again, I just know it. He kept glarin' at her, yet ignored me. It was the classic 'do I put her over my knee or kiss her 'til she obeys me' look you read about in books. I'm certain he would have hauled her into a closet and kissed some sense into her if we hadn't hightailed it out of there before he could finish with Megan."

I flipped my head over and pulled my long hair into a ponytail, ignoring their chuckles.

"He was pissed on Megan's behalf," I defended. "It didn't have anything to do with me. He kept askin' me what I was doin' there. I get that. After Strawn's phone call, I imagine findin' us at his cousin's place of business made it look like we were investigatin' her. He was bein' territorial about his family, is all."

Sienna looked at Poppy, and she shrugged. "He did keep sayin' 'what are you doin' *here*,' not 'what are you doin' I forbid you from gettin' involved with my case 'cause you'll get hurt.'"

"Hmm," Sienna said. "Maybe we aren't experienced enough to read this guy," she finally admitted.

"Exactly," I agreed. "None of us know men well enough to know what they're thinkin'."

"Okay, I'll agree to that, but I know when a man is attracted to a woman," Sienna returned. "I had to watch it for too many years while lusting after Chase, and the way he looked at his wife when they first met is exactly what I see in Devin's eyes when he looks at you."

"He looked like he wanted to kill her?"

She snorted.

"No. He had lazy eyes that smoldered when he followed her with them. He looked like he wanted to eat her pretty much twenty-four hours a day."

"That must have been hard to watch," Poppy murmured.

She shrugged it off, but I could tell by the way her eyes blanked that it cut deeper than she let on.

"Well, it doesn't matter how he looks at me," I said, trying to take Sienna's mind off her past. "As I said yesterday, even if I misread him, it doesn't matter. I took a chance, and when he turned his back to me, it hurt. I don't want to experience that again. If I started somethin' with him and he left, it would probably devastate me."

"You know you can't avoid heartache no matter who you go out with," Sienna mumbled. "Life isn't a bed of roses; there are plenty of thorns." I started to open my mouth, but she held up her hand and stopped me. "I know you know this, Cali, but everyone in this room has lost somethin' important to them. None of us want to experience that pain again, and you don't see us holdin' back."

My head jerked back as if I'd been struck, and I looked between them both. God, she was right. We'd all lost someone important, yet they were more willing than I was to let go of the past.

"Your aunt was right, you know," she continued, "You can't choose who your heart wants. It doesn't work like that. All you can do is follow it and hope that when you find what you're lookin' for, it wants you too."

I opened my mouth again and then shut it.

There were no guarantees in life; I knew this. You lived each day the best you could while sailing on a sea of what ifs and should bes. Sometimes you made the right choice and sometimes you didn't. It was a crapshoot, a roll of the dice how it all turned out. And if you weren't living it to its fullest, then you were cheating yourself out of a full life . . . And I'd already lost twenty-one years thinking I could protect myself instead of really living.

"In the end, only three things matter: how much you loved, how gently you lived, and how gracefully you let go of the things not meant for you," I said under my breath.

"Pardon?" Sienna asked.

"It's supposedly a Buddhist sayin', but there's truth there. I'm thinkin' the last bit is what I need to work on," I answered. "I try to treat people with kindness, and I'm not a bitch takin' advantage of people, but gracefully lettin' go of things not meant for me clearly needs work."

"You've lost me," Poppy said. "Are you sayin' you agree with us and you'll give Devin a shot if he makes a move?"

I took a deep breath and slowly let it out.

Am I?

I nodded.

"I won't push him away IF he makes a move," I said, raising my hand to stop Poppy and Sienna's outburst. "But I think you're wrong."

"Finally," Sienna hooted.

I shrugged. "I can be a tad bit stubborn."

"Tad?" Poppy snorted.

"Whatever." I rolled my eyes. "Now that that's settled, let's get back to work."

Sienna stopped me as I opened the door. "What about tonight? Are you still goin' speed datin'?"

I shrugged. "I don't see why not. I'd be a ninny to put all my eggs in one basket, as Neecy says."

Sienna smiled, but there was a twinkle in her eyes I didn't like. "What?"

"Nothin'," she denied, then winked at Poppy.

At ten after six, Devin walked into Jacobs' Ladder. He scanned the bar until he found who he was looking for. Moving toward the back of the room, he jerked his head at Nate to follow him as he passed. Nate followed, neither speaking until they'd reached the table in the farthest reaches of the bar and sat down.

"Nate, meet Bo Strawn," Devin said.

Nate reached out and shook Strawn's hand.

"Devin tells me your department is finally lookin' into Maria's disappearance." It was a statement laced with accusation.

"Nate," Devin warned as they sat down.

Nate leaned back and crossed his arms.

"We'll do our best to find out what happened the night Ms.

Espinoza disappeared," Strawn replied with cold eyes.

"Because she's your number one suspect?"

Strawn leaned back and mirrored Nate's posture.

"We don't think she murdered Stutter," Strawn drawled, shocking Nate. "Evidence suggests there was someone else in the basement beside Stutter and Ms. Espinoza."

"What evidence?" Nate asked.

"There were two stab wounds. One was shallow, at an angle that suggests someone the same height as Maria struck out. The wound was debilitating, but it wasn't lethal if he'd sought medical attention. The stab wound that killed him was driven deep into his chest, suggesting the perpetrator was a man. Stutter was on his back when someone delivered the deathblow. By someone left-handed." He paused and looked at both men. "Maria is right-handed."

"So she's innocent," Nate stated.

"That's what the evidence suggests."

"Did you pull the security footage on the buildin'?" Devin asked.

Strawn's jaw tightened. "The power was cut to the buildin' five minutes after Maria entered. Most employees had left by the time she arrived."

"All but Calla," Devin bit out, anger settling in his gut. If she'd stayed later at work, she could be missing as well.

Strawn turned to Devin and shook his head. "There was another. They called in the power outage before leavin'."

"Did they see Maria?"

"Yeah." Strawn pulled out his notebook. "A Ms. Jolene Cartwright said Maria came up to her floor looking for Calla."

"What?" Devin snapped.

"Ms. Cartwright indicated that Maria seemed fine. Said she was leavin' when Maria walked into the office looking for Calla. Cartwright was in a hurry, and assumed Maria was there to clean, so she headed downstairs while Maria stayed behind. She indicated the lights went out as she was heading through the lobby, so she called the power company from her cell phone and left."

"You're sayin' whatever Maria is messed up in has to do with Calla?" Nate asked, shocked.

"No," Devin bit out. "Calla edits books for a livin'. She spends all her time off readin' romance novels as near as I can tell. If this has anything to do with her, it's by association." He turned his attention back to Strawn. "The grandfather?"

"That's what comes to mind."

"So Maria saw or heard somethin' about Calla's family and decided to go to her with the information?" Nate asked.

"How does Armstrong make his money?" Devin questioned.

"He owns the largest shippin' business in the state."

"And Stutter made his money through import/export," Devin stated, his mind already working the illegal scenarios that would partner Stutter to Armstrong. And considering what he found out that afternoon, none of the possibilities were good.

"And Yoo? How does she fit in? Carmella said Stutter was seen at her house and they were arguin'," Nate asked.

"I spent the afternoon diggin' into her finances," Devin said. "I found a dummy corporation in the Virgin Islands that links back to Stutter."

"So they were in business together," Nate returned.

"Looks like."

"Payments?" Strawn asked.

"Middle East."

"Fuck," Strawn muttered.

"Clusterfuck," Devin agreed. "If this leads back to Armstrong, then one of your most prominent citizens is in bed with our enemies."

Strawn waited a beat then pointed out something Devin had already considered.

"He's *also* your woman's grandfather. Are you prepared to help bring him down if he's guilty?"

His jaw tightened. This wasn't the scenario that had played out in his head. He'd imagined having to win the old man over, not bring him down.

"I'll do whatever I have to, then deal with the fallout if it comes to that. If he's guilty, I'll make sure justice is served."

Strawn grinned. "Jesus, you've got cojones. You sure you don't want back on the force? We could use a man like you."

"You don't want me on the force," Devin returned.

"I don't?"

"Nope. As you said this mornin', your hands are tied by the same red tape I left behind. You need me on the outside doin' the dirty work, askin' the questions you can't."

"You have a point," Strawn agreed. "And speakin' of that dirty work,"—Strawn continued, opening a file—"I need you to run a check on Armstrong's employees. There are too many eyes at the station, and it'll ping the wrong people's curiosity."

"You got a list?"

Strawn pulled out a sheet of paper from the file and handed it to Devin.

"Is Armstrong still at the helm?"

"He retired two years ago. The man runnin' things now is Bobby Jones. His family is close friends with the Armstrongs." Strawn hesitated a moment, then continued. "You should know that rumors have been flyin' for years that Preston Armstrong wants Calla to marry Jones."

Devin thought back to the day he first saw Calla with the man in the window. "Blond man. Spit-shined with an arrogant face?"

"That's Jones," Nate responded.

"Pissant," Devin growled. "Armstrong should want better for his granddaughter."

"He won't think it's you," Strawn pointed out.

"He can think what he wants."

Devin wasn't going to let Armstrong or anyone else get in his way. Not after spending the last ten years looking for a woman like Calla. One who wasn't superficial, one who wanted the same things he did, like hearth and home. A woman who stirred his blood to the point that all others vanished from his sight. He knew he could find that with her if she'd quit running from him long enough to set her straight.

"Speakin' of Calla," Nate chuckled. "Megan stopped by. I heard you caught Calla in a disguise cleanin' for Carmella."

Strawn's eyes shot to Devin's and his brows pulled across his forehead. "After I threatened to lock them up?"

"That's what I thought," Devin answered. "Damn near lost hold of my temper when I caught them. They got out of there before I could wring their necks, so I called Carmella. She confirmed they were there at her request."

"I'd have locked them up first, then called," Strawn replied. "Just to teach them a lesson."

"I may still," Devin stated. "Now that I know this connects back to Calla, I'm keepin' her close."

"I doubt Armstrong would hurt his only grandchild," Strawn said.

Devin shook his head. "You and I both know when money and power are involved, people will do whatever they have to do to keep it," Devin replied then stood and put out his hand to Strawn. "I'll be in touch, but right now I need to hunt her down and put her under lock and key."

"I'll help," Nate threw out. "You want your bike back?"

"Keep it. She's still in escape mode and won't see me comin' in your truck."

Strawn stood, grinning. "With all you're havin' to deal with just to keep her in line, do you still think she's worth the trouble?"

Devin didn't hesitate to answer. "You won't get it until you meet the right woman, but the answer is yes. Every fuckin', irritatin' second."

Nate clapped Devin on the shoulder, his deep chuckle rolling through his chest. "Told you Savannah wouldn't be borin'."

"You weren't lyin'." Needing to find Calla immediately so he could rest easy, he turned to leave, then paused and looked back at Nate. "If you find her, call me. Don't confront her. I'm tired of this hide-and-seek game we've been playin', and she'll go to ground if she knows I'm lookin' for her."

"Fight or flight response kicked in, I see."

"Flight, yes. The woman's quicker than a jackrabbit with a wolf on its tail. Though, she has spunk like a raccoon when cornered."

"And now that the big bad wolf is pursuing her, she's panicked?"

"Nope. She hasn't got a clue she belongs to me."

"Then why's she hidin'?"

"'Cause I told her to," Strawn chuckled.

✿ ✿ ✿

I held up a skimpy black dress and my eyes grew wider. There would be no bending over unless I wanted to say ten Hail Marys. The back plunge was so low my ass would fall out if I so much as breathed. "The Baptists don't make you say confession, right?"

Sienna walked over and turned the dress around.

"You can't be serious?" I gasped. "If you make me wear this, I won't need to flirt. The dress will do the flirtin' for me."

Sienna shoved me toward the bathroom, giggling. "I'm just kiddin'; the plunge goes in the back."

"Why do I get the impression you enjoy seein' me suffer?"

"No idea," she answered, but I wasn't buying it. She and Poppy had been whispering all afternoon. Grinning innocently at me whenever I caught them.

They were definitely up to something. The question was, what?

Ten minutes later I'd stripped off my clothes and pulled the black, long-sleeved, cotton knit dress with a Sabrina neckline and plunging back, over my head. It was styled to draw a man in for a closer look, but soft like a T-shirt, so it was comfortable to wear. I turned around and looked at my back. *Just as I thought.* Panties wouldn't work, so I pulled them off and stared at my reflection. God was definitely going to strike me dead for not wearing panties in a church. At least the length wasn't sinful; it hit just above my knees, and it had built-in cups to keep my breasts from jiggling as I walked.

I twisted and turned in several directions, then took a deep breath and walked into the bedroom for the final verdict.

"Hot," Poppy said as she curled her hair.

"Devin would not approve, so it's perfect," Sienna giggled.

"Devin hasn't earned the right to complain yet," I mumbled.

"Yet," she parroted back, her eyes gleaming with mirth.

"Now, for the hair," Poppy said. "Sit."

I eyed the curling iron and sighed. "Just don't make me look like a hooker."

"Wouldn't dream of it," Poppy chuckled, but I caught the look she gave Sienna.

One excruciatingly long hour later, Poppy had curled and teased my hair into a wall of hair that would have made Farrah Fawcett proud.

"I can't go into a church looking like this. I said *no* big hair!"

"You need to trust us," Poppy mumbled. "We have it on good authority this is how we should dress for man hunting."

"Really? Was it from a current issue of Hookers R Us?"

Chuckling, Sienna handed me strappy black sandals with a killer heel. I shook my head. "I'll break an ankle in these."

"Possible, but we're told they'll make your legs look a mile long."

They had an excuse for everything.

I grabbed the sandals in a huff and headed for the bed. "This is punishment for a past life," I grumbled.

"Cali, you have to use all your weapons; make a good first impression. Everyone knows that," Poppy said. "And since we don't know what Devin's truly thinkin', then we don't want to waste an opportunity to find your happily ever after."

"Oh, I'll make an impression. *Especially* when I fall through the door and flash everyone my ass."

Sienna's eyes lit up and held a far-off look.

"You're calculatin' how quickly you can switch your cell to camera function, aren't you?"

"Two point five seconds," she answered.

I grinned and muttered, "Bitch," then stood. "Here goes nothin'." I took a step, then another. I was still standing, so I tried a faster pace.

"You're a natural," Poppy beamed.

"I think she's ready," Sienna agreed.

I sashayed back to the bed and grabbed the clutch Sienna had lent me, surprised I hadn't twisted an ankle.

"Are we doin' this or what?" I asked the girls.

It was now or never. If I didn't leave soon, I wouldn't walk out the door.

Sienna shouted, "Hold that thought," and ran out of the room, teetering on her three-inch heels like a five-year-old wearing her mother's shoes, pulling on the hem of her dress in hopes it would grow a foot.

She and Poppy were both dressed as sinfully as me. Poppy in a red dress with a plunging neckline that was just south of shameful, and Sienna had on pale yellow sundress that matched her hair, but barely covered her ass. I didn't know what the Baptist would make of the three of us, but I had a feeling God was still rooting for us to find a match.

Poppy and I followed Sienna into her living room and found her in the kitchen with three shot glasses and a bottle of booze.

"I figured if the old coots at the golf club can start a tournament with a shot, we can start the night off with a toast."

I grabbed a glass filled with amber liquid and raised it. "I'll go first . . . For courage to break down my walls and let love in."

Poppy raised hers, smiling. "For wisdom to not judge a book by its cover."

"Definitely somethin' you need to work on," I giggled.

We both looked at Sienna, and she raised her glass, lifting it to the ceiling. "For lettin' go of the past and seein' what life brings our way."

We started to put the shots to our lips, but I raised my glass higher. We weren't the only Wallflowers in need of help. "To Wallflowers everywhere: may you find your Happily Ever After in whatever form you choose. Be it with a man, woman, or dancing to the beat of your own music."

We grinned at each other and threw back our shots.

Then we choked on the hellfire burning our throats.

Apparently, we were *delicate* Wallflowers.

After we had regained our breath, Poppy and Sienna grabbed their purses, and I followed them out to Sienna's car. I climbed into the back—more like crawled in out of fear I'd rip the dress—and settled in. When Sienna pulled out of her parking lot, she turned right instead of left as I was expecting.

"Um, ladies. Did you forget which way the Baptist church is?"

"Nope," Poppy said, turning back to look at me. "We agreed you'd be the first in this Wallflower experiment, and since you've agreed to give Devin a chance, Sienna and I decided there was no need to go. We're headed to Jacobs' Ladder in search of Devin."

It occurred to me in that moment if I jumped out of the car while it was in motion, I might ruin Sienna's dress, so my immediate reaction was squashed. But that didn't stop me from begging them to stop.

"No. Not like this. Please, just take me home," I kinda whined.

Sienna snorted. "No way."

"I told you, we have it on good authority this is how all women dress when huntin' men," Poppy defended.

"By whom? A street walker?"

"Hardly," she scoffed. "Gayla Brown."

It keeps getting better and better.

"Gayla?" I exploded. "She goes through men like water goes over Niagara Falls. Fast and furious. She's no role model for Wallflowers paddling in uncharted waters."

We were on a collision course for relationship disaster if we took advice from the office slut.

"Stop the car," I demanded.

Sienna glanced at Poppy, uncertain, but shook her head no.

Screw it. I will buy Sienna a new dress if I have to.

I reached out my hand to the door handle, but the locks clicked into place.

"Unlock the door," I bit out.

"Not a chance. You look hot, Cali. If there's any flame burnin' in that blood of Devin's, that outfit will shoot it straight to an inferno."

"But it's not *me*." Poppy regarded me with concern, so I explained. "Look, I know I agreed to see where it went with Devin if he made a move, but this isn't me, not by a long shot. I want him to like me for who I am, not Gayla's big-haired, slutty version. I'm a book nerd. One who prefers jeans and boots to dresses, not this sex kitten you've turned me into."

Poppy looked at Sienna, and I hoped I'd scored a point.

I wasn't sure why I was freaked out, but I was. The hair, the makeup, *the dress.* It was too much in the light of day—or night—in

145

this instance. Dressed like this for speed dating, where I didn't know anyone, was like playing dress-up. But this was Devin. I didn't want him to want me for any other reason than plain ole me. Not sexy, dressed for a ball—more like a night of sin—Callarella.

"Pull into the McDonalds ahead," Poppy told Sienna. "We'll just be a minute."

Thank you, God.

If I had to, I'd refuse to get back into the car and call a cab.

Sienna hit the locks after she parked, and I bailed out of the car. Poppy climbed out behind me with her purse and grabbed my hand. I followed her, stumbling once on my stilettoes on our way to the ladies' room as catcalls rang out. When the door closed behind me, I pointed at it and cried out, "See? So not me."

"I know," she mumbled, and moved to the sink. "Come here, and I'll fix your hair and makeup. When I'm done with you, you'll look like you again, only in an attractive dress. Will that work?"

I hesitated a moment then moved to the sink. "Get rid of 'hooker Cali', and we'll talk."

Ten minutes later, she'd smoothed my hair into a stylish ponytail, wrapped low at the base of my neck, and removed all the eye makeup. I now had a clean face with ruby red lips and sleek hair. This was a look that I would wear out and not think twice about. This was the Cali I knew, but with flair.

"Better?" she asked.

I looked from side to side and smiled. "You do a good 'Cali, but with flair,'" I said. "Thank you!"

"You're welcome," she chuckled.

"No, really. Thank you," I muttered. "For listenin', for takin' me seriously, for makin' me look . . . hot on my own terms."

"You're welcome," she smiled. "Now, let's go find Devin and see if we can rev his engine."

I looked in the mirror again and decided if this didn't catch his attention, then nothing would. Tonight I'd find out if the Devil with fire in his eyes was the man I'd been hoping for, or if he was just a poser.

❁ ❁ ❁

Wine number three was getting warm, and there was still no sign of Devin. We'd sat at the bar with our backs to the restaurant so we could see when he came in. It was ladies' night, so the bar was full, which meant we'd had plenty of attention dressed the way we were. It was approaching ten, and I'd had a long day; it was time to throw in the towel and go home.

"He must be on another stakeout," Poppy said.

"Maybe," I agreed.

"Don't go there," Sienna said. "He's dedicated to findin' Maria."

I turned on my stool and looked at her. "I didn't go anywhere."

"You were thinkin' he was out with someone else."

"No, I wasn't. I was thinkin' he might still be interviewin' Carmella's clients."

"Oh," she answered, looking chagrined.

"I'm not insecure." They both raised their brows. "Okay, I can be in certain situations, but not until I have a reason. Now that I've had time to think about it, I realize he isn't the type of man to ignore a missin' woman for a good time with a loose woman. If he hasn't stopped by to say hi to his friend, then I figured he's workin'."

"Speakin' of his friend," Poppy said. "I haven't seen him tonight either."

I looked around the bar and realized she was right. Nate Jacobs was a tall, good-looking man. He'd be hard to miss if he was working.

"That settles it," I said, standing from the barstool. "If Nate isn't here, then there's no reason for Devin to stop by."

Poppy and Sienna both nodded in agreement and stood as well.

"It was a good test run for these dresses at least. Though, you may need to disinfect your back after all the hands that touched it," Poppy said.

"Yes, I think the attention we received proves my point: Gayla's a man-eater who reels men in like a spider with her looks."

Groaning, Sienna looked around the bar then leaned in so I could hear her.

"We have a confession."

"Okay."

"We hate the way we look as well. We only listened to Gayla, because she seemed to know what she was talkin' about. We didn't want to let you down, 'cause you were lookin' to us for advice on datin', but we're almost as green as you."

The hilarity of the three of us pretending to be something we weren't made me laugh. Linking my arms with both women, I started dragging them to the door. "New rule," I hollered over the noise. "From this day forward, let's just be us. None of us need a man who doesn't want us just the way we are. Jeans and all."

"Deal," Poppy smiled. "No more sex kitten outfits."

"Thank God. I'm with you. If I had it my way, I'd be in jeans and boots twenty-four seven," Sienna announced as we cleared the door and headed for my apartment.

When we made it to the corner by my aunts' building, a beast of a Harley pulled up across the street, waiting for a car to turn right into the alley. I held my breath, sure it was Devin, then saw the rider had longer hair.

"I think that's Nate," Poppy whispered.

The three of us stared through the gloom at the rider until he pulled forward and we could see it was definitely Nate. I raised my hand and waved just as he turned his head and saw us. His face went from relaxed to taut in the blink of an eye. He scanned our group, his eyes landing on Poppy and holding longer than the rest of us.

Then he looked behind him for a moment before gunning the engine and taking off toward Jacobs' Ladder.

"I'm sure that's Devin's bike," I told the girls.

"Maybe he's driving Nate's vehicle while he's on these stake-outs," Poppy offered, turning back to follow him with her eyes.

We crossed the street and then turned down the alley to head back to Sienna's car.

"Do you want us to walk you to your door?" Poppy asked.

"No, I'm good."

We hugged, and then I watched the girls as they climbed into the car and pulled out. I moved to the back gate and opened it, then walked through the courtyard to the stairs.

Normally, I would have checked on Bernice and Eunice before heading to bed, but my feet were killing me in these ridiculous heels, and all I could think about was taking my shoes off and then soaking in a scalding hot bath.

When I pulled open the door to the second floor, I startled when I found Bobby Jones leaning against the wall next to my door. I sighed loudly in frustration, hoping he would hear me. Two visits in three days felt more like stalking than friends.

Bobby pushed off the wall when he saw me, and his mouth dropped open as he scanned my body from head to toe.

Yes, I'm dressed in a sexy dress. No, you won't be getting your hands in my panties tonight—or any other night.

"What are you doin' here, Bobby?"

He didn't answer. He kept staring.

"Bobby. Answer me. What are you doin' here this late?" I bit out as I unlocked my door and opened it.

He looked up finally, his mouth pulling into a devilish grin that wasn't nearly as handsome as Devin's. "Jesus, Calla Lily. You look . . . different."

"Is that an attempt at a compliment?" I asked crossing my arms.

He nodded slowly and licked his lips.

Not in this lifetime, pal.

"Get that look off your face, Bobby. You're not gettin' in my panties tonight or any other—"

The door ripped open behind me, and I spun around. Devin stepped through looking dark and formidable. He glared at Bobby, then turned to me and froze. Scanning my body slowly, his gaze heated as it inspected every inch of my skin. When he was done, he sucked in air then let it out slowly, breathing deep and controlled as his eyes settled on mine.

"You know this guy, sugar?" Bobby asked.

I didn't answer. I was caught in a vortex of heat that ran down my neck and settled between my legs as Devin's gaze ignited. I thought I'd seen lust when I'd kissed him the day before, but I'd been wrong. This look was lust personified. It was primal, possessive, and all-encompassing. The world simply ceased to exist when a man looked at you that way.

"Devin," I whispered, licking my lips, because my mouth had run dry.

"Calla, who is this?" Bobby asked again, but I ignored him.

Devin moved then, heading straight for me. He kept coming until he'd backed me into the wall. When my back hit the sheetrock, I dropped my purse and put my hands to his chest, grabbing hold of his shirt as my heart thundered. I swallowed hard for control and looked up. Blatant desire reflected back at me.

I'd never seen a man act like this. I'd read about it in books, but passed the behavior off as figments of the author's wonderful imagination.

God, I'd been wrong. About so many things.

Raising his hands, Devin cupped my face gently and leaned his head down. I closed my eyes against the emotions, rioting for control as he rested his forehead on mine and hissed, "Fuck, baby."

"Who the fuck are you?" Bobby seethed, stepping in closer to my side.

Opening my eyes sluggishly, I found Devin's staring back at me. The color was so blue I knew only God could have designed them.

"I'm her man," Devin mumbled, turning his attention to my mouth. I watched with interest as his eyes lost focus and turned lazy like Sienna had described. She was right. He looked like he wanted to gobble me up whole.

"Her man? Since when?" Bobby asked, incredulous.

"Since she placed her hand on my chest and called me Devil," he answered, and the air left my lungs on a breathy, "Oh my God."

"For God's sake, Calla. Is this the *PI* from the paper?" Bobby hissed. He said PI like it was a terminal disease.

"I take it you like the dress?" I asked Devin, ignoring Bobby.

He nodded slowly as he ran his thumb across my bottom lip, his gaze following it as it went.

"I demand to know who this man is," Bobby ordered.

"I've told you who I am," Devin growled, "and you've got two seconds to leave, or I'll show you to the door."

Bobby was used to giving orders, not taking them, so he stepped in closer and arrogantly said, "If you had a clue who you're dealin' with, you'd take your hands off Preston Armstrong's granddaughter and leave immediately. If you don't, then I can promise you this won't end well for you."

Devin turned his head at the threat and looked down at Bobby. "I know *exactly* who I'm dealin' with, and now you've got one second to remove yourself from the premises, or I'll be happy to do it for you."

Bobby didn't clue in to how much danger he was in until Devin flinched in his direction. He stepped back hurriedly as Devin sneered at him. A moment later, I heard the door being ripped open and took my eyes off Devin long enough to watch Bobby storm out.

Devin turned his attention back to me, crowding me further into the wall. "I'm gonna kiss you now," Devin whispered, his gravelly voice thick with lust.

"I have to know somethin' first."

His lazy eyes came back to mine. "Anything," he answered, pulling me closer to his body.

"Do you really want a relationship?"

He blinked at the question.

From his reaction, I expected him to pull away. Expected to find out what was happening between us was hormones brought on by a sexy dress. Instead, his eyes warmed to a cobalt blue, and he lowered his head to mine, drawling out, "Oh, yeah," in a deep husky voice.

To my mortification, tears began to sting my eyes. I wanted to believe him. Wanted what he was offering to the very depths of my being, but old insecurities die hard, and I shook my head in disbelief.

When the first tear started its slow descent down my cheek, Devin's hands came up to cup my face. He tilted my head back until our eyes locked, brushing away a single tear with his thumb, and then leaned in closer until our mouths were inches apart. I wasn't sure if I wanted him to kiss me. After spending half the night looking for the man, now that I had exactly what I wanted within my reach, I was hesitating.

He either sensed it or read the uncertainty written across my face, because he mumbled, "No turning back," as he continued to inch closer, as if to see how long it would take for our lips to touch.

With tenderness I wasn't expecting, he kissed the corner of my mouth, not touching my lips, mumbling, "Brick by fuckin' brick," as he moved to the opposite side and repeated the action.

"What?" I asked, confused.

"I'll break down that wall you've erected brick by brick until you don't feel the need to run scared from me."

He was definitely a mind reader.

"I—I'm a little terrified you know that about me."

He grinned slow and easy.

"All *you* need to know"—he whispered, his voice deep and husky—"is that the second my lips touch yours, it's over. You're mine."

My eyes hooded, and my knees grew weak hearing that declaration. Who would have thought having a caveman beat his chest, declaring you're his woman, would be hot?

I licked my lips, then opened my mouth to argue, to say we needed to slow down, but Devin halted my response with his mouth. He touched his tongue to my bottom lip, and my ability to form a coherent thought vanished. I opened for him and tasted coffee laced with mint as he tangled his tongue with mine. Heat exploded through my veins, my body tingling with sexual awareness, and I lost control. Wrapping my fingers in his hair, I tugged on the longish strands, and he moaned his approval, kissing me harder, deeper, and wetter, stealing my breath.

I thought when I rode on the back of his bike I'd felt alive, felt free for the first time in years. I was wrong. Having this man kiss me as if he needed it in order to live was far more exhilarating.

I could fall so easily, lose myself to him . . .

And with that thought, I panicked.

Ripping my mouth from his, panting as I tried to catch my breath, I declared, "We need to talk."

✿ ✿ ✿

Resting his forehead against Calla's, Devin tried to catch his breath. The force of his reaction to Bobby Jones being that close to her had caught him off guard. His attraction to her had been strong, almost distracting to the point of madness since he'd laid eyes on her, but seeing another man staring at her with blatant lust had tipped him over the edge. So he'd staked his claim the minute he could think clearly, so Jones had no doubt whom she belonged to.

Burying his face in her neck, Devin breathed deep, taking in her powder-fresh scent as he ran his tongue up her neck, mumbling, "We'll talk," before he nipped her ear.

She shuddered beneath his hands, and he smiled.

"We don't know each other that well," she started off in a shaky voice. "We should—"

Devin took her mouth again, drinking in the taste of her. He wasn't ready to leave her lips long enough to form a single word. He'd suffered through a long night with only the memory of her kiss to keep him company, then spent the rest of the day fighting the urge to storm into Poe so he could get a few things straight. Namely, put her on notice that he wanted her. Secondly, assuaging his anger that she'd considered putting herself in danger by investigating Maria's disappearance.

If she wanted to talk, they'd talk. But not before he was good and ready.

Lifting her at the waist, Devin pinned Calla to the wall so he had better access to her sweet mouth. He deepened their kiss as he ran a hand down her side and then to her back. When he reached her heart-shaped ass, he palmed it, running his hand over a firm cheek. And then he froze. Breaking from her mouth, Devin narrowed his eyes at her.

"You wanna talk, we'll talk," he rumbled low in warning. "Next time you dress for sex, I'd better be the man you're lookin' for."

Her eyes grew wide in surprise. "I'm not dressed for sex."

Pissed off by her answer, he pressed her further into the wall then ran his hand up her leg, hooking it on his hip, causing the fabric to ride up until he could cup her bare ass. Her breath hitched on contact, and her eyes grew lazy.

"I rest my case," he bit out, squeezing gently to make his point, then stroking her warm skin.

"The back was cut too low for panties," she said by way of an explanation. "I wasn't looking. I mean, I was looking, but not for . . . Devin, I think we should slow down."

Reaching for her other leg, Devin wrapped them both around his waist and turned for her open door.

"Tell me why we should slow down?" he asked into her neck as he nipped his way to her shoulder.

"You don't know anything about me. I may be the last woman on earth you should get involved with."

He kicked the door shut as she answered and headed for her bedroom. He wanted her on that fuckin' bed, had a feeling no man had been invited in there, and he wanted to claim that privilege as his own.

"You have a tender heart, but you're strong-willed. You're stubborn when you think you're right and your opinion isn't easily swayed. You have walls up to keep people out, and you accomplish that by avoidin' life at all costs. You spend most of your time readin', use words like heebie-jeebies to express your mood, and your favorite color is purple."

She inhaled loudly as he crossed the threshold of her bedroom and flipped on the light. He had her attention, so he went in for the kill. "You're lookin' for someone who will put you first, just like you'll put him first. Someone who will protect you, keep the world at bay. But mostly someone who heats your blood to the point you can't breathe for wanting him."

She licked her lips and swallowed hard when he stopped at the foot of her bed. "But I don't know *you*," she husked out, raising a shaking hand to his face. Her body trembled as she stroked his jaw, and his fuckin' knees went weak.

"All you need to know about me"—he answered, nipping her finger as she drew a line across his mouth—"is that I'm playin' for keeps . . . and I never lose."

A grin pulled across her mouth. "You're arrogant, Devil man."

Devin put a knee to the bed and dropped down, landing on top of Calla. "I wanted you the moment I laid eyes on you in the window, and now I'm lyin' on your bed. That's not arrogance, babe, that's goin' after what you want and not lettin' anything get in your way. Not even you."

Her eyes widened as if she'd just realized where they were, and she tried to roll out from underneath him.

"This is a bad idea," she said, struggling.

"Bad for whom?"

She didn't answer; she ignored his question and kept trying to extract her limbs from his.

"Stop tryin' to run from me and tell me why this is a bad idea," he bit out, pinning her arms above her head.

Turning her head, Calla avoided eye contact and stared at her bedroom wall, worrying at her lip.

Sighing in frustration, Devin let go of her arms and reached down, turning her face toward him. "Answer me. Why are you so hell-bent on denyin' what we both want?"

"This isn't my dress," she rushed out, oddly. "I'm a book nerd who prefers boots to heels."

"And?" he asked in confusion, trying to hold on to what was left of his patience.

He knew she'd be a hard sell, but figured getting past her defenses was more than half the battle. Now she had thrown up a new wall that didn't make sense.

"And I'm inexperienced. I have no idea how to have a relationship."

"And?"

"And?" she parroted back. "You need more?"

Rising up on one arm so he didn't crush her, Devin growled, "I haven't heard a viable reason yet."

Her face turned pink, and for a moment he thought she was blushing. He was wrong. Raising her arms, she put them to his chest and shoved, so he fell to his side, taking her with him. She crawled around until she'd straddled his stomach, her dress inching up to barely cover her ass, then she sat up, glared at him, and began ticking off her reasons one by one.

"You're too handsome, too intimidatin', and I'm clueless when it comes to men. I need a man who's safe, easy to figure out, and you're anything but safe, what with your gravelly voice that melts panties off both sexes with a single utterance . . . Not to mention, my family's a big fat pain in the twiddle diddles," she groused. Devin started to ask what he thought was the obvious question in the room, but she continued. "And I can already tell you're a man who takes orders from no one, so their constant interference will wear you down 'til you realize I'm not worth the hassle. So, as you can plainly see, it's a bad idea. I'm just savin' both of us the time and trouble of investin' in somethin' that's gonna end."

There was a lot there that needed to be addressed, mainly what the hell twiddle diddles were. He chose to focus on one.

Rolling until he had Calla pinned again, Devin shoved his face into her neck, muttering in that gravelly voice she loved and hated equally, asking, "So my voice melts your panties off?"

She gasped, her breath coming in deep gulps, and then threw a hand to her face and groaned, "I said that out loud, didn't I?"

Running his hand down her bare leg, he curled it over his hip and ground into her heat. "Is that why you aren't wearin' panties?"

She whimpered at his contact, her hips rising to keep the connection. "I told you. The dress was cut too low to wear them."

Devin took hold of the shoulder of her dress and pulled it until her skin was exposed. "I'm sensing from your ramblings this dress needs to go," he murmured against her skin, his tongue snaking out to taste the ivory pallor as he exposed one breast. Her breath caught when he circled her nipple, and she moaned, arching into his mouth when he sucked the pebbled bud deep inside.

Grinding into her core, he jerked down the other side of her dress until she was bare to him from the waist up, and ran his tongue down the valley between her breasts, then further to her belly button. He looked up and locked eyes with her as he grabbed both sides of her dress and yanked it off past the fuck-me heels she still wore. She was the sexiest woman he'd seen in his life, and he had to clench his jaw to keep from ravaging her.

He needed to proceed with caution. It wasn't what she said but what was left unsaid that bothered him. She was trying to convince him of her faults. Said she wasn't worth the hassle, and that was a red flag that told him he needed to be careful. She belonged to him now, so he'd figure out what was broken and then he'd fix it.

When her hands came up to cover her breasts, he shook his head. "I told you the moment our lips touched you were mine. Don't hide from me."

She hesitated, working at her lip again, indecision painting her face, so he drawled low, "Show me what's mine."

Calla took a deep breath and let it out slowly. Then, with shaking hands, she uncovered her breasts, consenting she was his, and he took in his fill.

Generous breasts the color of cream made his hands itch to touch them, followed by hips that were meant to hold a man deep inside. He wanted to bury his face between her silky thighs until she cried out with pleasure, but he stayed his actions.

Running a hand down her stomach, he held her eyes as her breathing increased.

"You want this as much as I do, so listen closely. I don't give a shit about your inexperience, whatever hang-ups you have about your past, or what your family will throw my way. I'm intimidatin', because you're scared about how you feel when you're with me," he explained. "As for needin' a man who's safe, I can't help you there. I live my life like a man. I work like a man. And I'll protect you like a man. Safe will give you nothin' but a borin' life filled with regret."

She shook her head. "But you'll regret this in a month or two. I'm borin' like you said."

"Bullshit," he growled. "Since I've known you, you've climbed on the back of my bike when it was the last place you wanted to be, then charged up a flight of stairs with little thought for your own safety to help find a missin' woman. You put a man-eater in her place with a single remark then offered to view a dead body so I could keep lookin' for Maria. You shocked me into silence by kissin' me when I thought I needed to take it slower with you. And then, after you took off because you couldn't handle what you were feelin' about me, you still organized a harebrained scheme thinkin' I needed help. You're fuckin' fearless, not borin'."

Her eyes widened at his statement, then widened further when he pulled the shirt from his body and fell onto hers. "This is happenin' between us. You know it, and I know it," he mumbled against her lips, and then kissed her hot and hungry, his hand finding her breast.

He rolled her nipple between his thumb and finger then broke from her mouth to watch her face grow hungry with need and pleasure. "I'm gonna enjoy watchin' you come for me," he whispered before taking the nipple in his mouth.

She arched, burying her hands in his hair, holding him in place, then groaned, "Yes."

The cat-like sounds she made as he feasted on her body urged him on. Urged him to take her, to claim her, but he paced himself. He wanted her writhing with need, sweat dripping from her body, so she'd know exactly whom she belonged to when he surged in, sealing their fate.

His cell began to ring as he moved to the neglected nipple. He

159

ignored it, and nipped the pebbled bud, grunting with approval when she moaned deep in her throat as his fingers thrust inside her slick, hot heat.

Fever racked his body, and his control began to slip as she whimpered in pleasure, her hips slamming down on his hand as she reached for bliss.

He wanted to bury himself deep inside her, but he was hungry for a taste of what belonged to him.

He began working his way down her body, giving attention to each soft curve. As he reached the apex of her thighs, her hips rose, inviting him to take what was his. He didn't hesitate. With a groan, he buried his face between her legs, claiming her for his own.

She gasped when his tongue found her bundle of nerves and he went to work, using his fingers as well as his tongue to tip her over the edge.

Then his phone rang again.

He paused, gritting his teeth for control. A single call at midnight could be a wrong number, twice in a few minutes meant he had to answer.

"Fuck," he muttered against her smooth thigh, dropping a kiss before looking up at her glassy eyes.

"Don't move," he ordered before reaching into his back pocket.

Pulling out his phone, he looked at the screen.

Bo Strawn was calling him.

Devin bowed his head and took a deep breath to calm his rioting hormones, then looked back at Calla. "I have to take this, baby. It could be important."

Her expression sharpened, the glassy, heated look clearing as it registered what he said. She nodded, then jumped up, wordless, and headed for her bathroom, teetering on her fuck-me heels. He watched her hips sway, knowing full-well she was hiding from him. She may have given in for the moment, but he could tell there was something deep-seated in her psyche that held her back from him. Held back her passion. He wanted one hundred percent of her, not just the parts she allowed people to see. Only then would she truly be his.

"This better be good," he growled into the phone when he answered.

"We've got a floater. Liberty Terminals off Harbor Street." Strawn paused, and the air around Devin grew heavy. He knew what was coming. "Pick up Nate and meet me at the morgue."

Eight

Granddaddy's a Dick

A KNOCK ON THE bathroom door pulled my attention away from my reflection in the mirror.

"Baby, I have to leave."

Baby.

I closed my eyes and drank in the sound of it. Every time he called me baby, warmth shrouded me like a cocoon, and I felt safe.

I looked back at my reflection. My cheeks were flushed, my eyes bright from sexual arousal. Turning my head from side to side, I smiled at the results. It was a look I'd never seen on my face.

"Calla?" Devin rumbled in his gravelly voice. It reached through the door to wrap around my body, heating it instantly, just like his touch.

I liked how this felt.

No. I *loved* how this felt, and I wanted more.

Turning, I tightened the tie on my robe and ripped the door open. Devin was leaning one arm against the jamb, his face painted with concern.

I wanted to dip my head and hide, feeling shy at how close we'd come to making love. Instead, I walked into his body and wrapped my arms around his waist, dropping my head back so I could touch my lips to his.

He wrapped a hand in my hair and tugged gently, his gaze moving over my face, searching, trying to read my thoughts. So I licked my lips in invitation. Heat flared across his expression, and he mumbled, "Jesus," before capturing my mouth for a brief, but very hot kiss.

"I have to leave," he gruffed out. "Swear to God I wouldn't if it wasn't important."

"I know." I wanted to ask him if his reason for leaving was about Maria, considering she was his only case, but I could tell he didn't want to talk about the call.

"I want you to sleep at your aunts' tonight."

My brows drew together. "What? Why?"

"We'll talk about it later. Just do this for me. I don't want you alone 'til I know what's goin' on," he explained.

I searched his face. His jaw was taut and his eyes burned with anger. Something was going on that I didn't understand, but I trusted him, so I yielded immediately. "I'll grab a bag for work and head right up."

He'd expected me to argue, that much was clear when his body relaxed and he leaned down and touched his lips to mine, his way of saying thank you for not questioning him.

Wrapping his arm around my shoulder, he walked me to my front door. "Locks engaged until you leave. Don't answer the door for anyone, and call your aunts and let them know you're on your way up, so they'll keep an eye out for you."

What has him spooked?

"I know you won't tell me what's going on, but you're scaring me a little."

"I'd rather you be scared than dead," he returned frankly.

I knew then, knew to my very core. "They found Maria, didn't they?" I choked out, trembling as my blood ran cold with fear.

He didn't answer. He pulled me into his arms and held me tight until the shaking calmed to a minor tremor.

"I'll call you when I'm done," he mumbled in my hair, squeezing me once for support before turning to leave.

He opened the door then paused and dropped his head back. When he turned back to look at me, his face was grim. "I'll do whatever it takes to find justice for Maria. They won't get away with this," he bit out.

My bottom lip began to quiver, but I pushed through my sorrow for Carmella and answered. "I know you will."

"No matter who it is," he growled. "Remember that."

I puzzled over his answer then nodded. "I understand."

He started to leave again, but turned abruptly and took a step back, grabbing my neck, pulling me back to his mouth. The kiss was rough, almost desperate in its intensity, then he ripped his lips from mine and stormed off without looking back, pushing through the exit like a bull.

The tears I'd been holding back finally began to fall as I locked the door and rushed to my bedroom. I changed out of my robe and packed quickly, then called Bernice's number. It rang until voicemail picked up, so I hung up and dialed Eunice. She answered on the second ring, her voice sharp and alert.

"Butterbean?"

"Devin just left. He wants me with you two until he can get back."

"Devin? What's goin' on?"

The word stuck in my throat. "Maria," I whispered.

Eunice cried out, "No," and I let out a muffled sob.

"I'm coming up."

"We'll meet you halfway," she said and hung up.

I grabbed my bag and headed for the door.

To get to my aunts' apartment, I had to go outside to reach the third floor. Their building was an old cotton warehouse and the back access to the building required climbing steep cobblestone steps to reach each floor.

Bernice and Eunice were both waiting at the top with the door open as I came up, keeping an eye on me like always, and just like with Devin, I walked right into their arms. These women were my mother, my father, my saving grace. If they couldn't fix a problem, it wasn't fixable, and Maria's death was unfixable, so we held on tight to each other.

When we broke apart, I caught sight of Odis Lee. He looked grim-faced as well. He'd been in our lives for so long I didn't think twice about seeing him any time of the day or night, so when he opened his arms for a fatherly hug, I took it.

"You're safe now," he muttered.

"I know. I wasn't scared; I'm just upset about Maria."

"What was the detective doin' at your place this time of night?" he asked point-blankly

Umm. How do I answer this?

"Umm. Well."

Nope. I wasn't about to share.

I looked at Bernice for an excuse, but her eyes twinkled with mirth and she blurted out, "Same thing you're doin' at my house this time of night, you old coot."

"Bernice," I bit out, "TMI!"

Odis sighed and let me go as I glared at Bernice.

"Calla, girl, you don't know anything about this man. He probably looked you up and saw how much money you're comin' into. You have to be careful, so you're not taken advantage of."

I stiffened, caught off-guard by his remark.

"Odis," Eunice hissed. "What the hell is wrong with you? Now's not the time. We should be thinkin' about poor Maria, not buttin' our noses in where it doesn't belong."

"When's a good time to warn her off, Neecy? After she's been made a fool? Calla's like a daughter to me, as well. I don't want her gettin' her hopes up with a man that will likely leave her high and dry. Not after I heard half of Savannah has their claws out for him."

It was like he'd read my inner-most thoughts, knew exactly which insecurity to pick at for maximum effect, and the happiness I'd experienced wrapped in Devin's arms just a few short minutes ago dissolved in a puff of smoke.

"I'm goin' to bed," I mumbled then pushed past them, heading for my old room and the escape it would afford me. But I couldn't let his remarks stand. It pissed me off that Odis would throw accusations willy-nilly without cause, so when I reached their front door, I turned to Odis Lee. "You don't know his character, Odis. It's wrong for you to judge him. Devin cares about findin' justice. Cares that Maria's missin'. He's been losin' sleep tryin' to find her when the police have done nothin' to help. That's not the type of man who'd search me out for my money, just to leave me high and dry for a pretty face."

The truthfulness in that statement hit me as I defended Devin. He wasn't the type of man to use a woman. He was the best kind of man. Principled. Dedicated. Honest. Also the kind that would be hard to get over when he left.

"Perhaps," he answered. "But I'd be remiss in my duties as your friend not to warn you."

I glanced at Bernice, who was staring at me with concern, then looked at Eunice and found her glaring at him. I had a feeling he'd be spending the night at his own place.

Wanting more than anything to be alone with my thoughts, so I could dissect every detail of the evening, I mumbled, "Night all," and went inside.

Bernice followed me into their apartment and slammed the door behind her, leaving Odis and Eunice in the hall.

"Don't you give a moment's thought to what he said," Bernice called out as I opened my former bedroom door.

"I won't," I lied. Odis loved me, I knew this, but it hurt deep in that hollow place we all carry within us that he assumed I couldn't hold a man like Devin's attention away from the city's Bold and Beautiful.

"Devin isn't the type of man to entangle himself with the harpies in this town."

I paused at the door and asked, "How do you know?" without looking at her.

"Only weak men want weak women. Devin's a man's man. He'll want a real woman, a strong one with backbone, not some shallow marshmallow who can't think for herself."

"And you think I'm a woman like that?" I questioned, glancing over my shoulder.

She took a step closer and met me eye to eye, her expression riddled with pride. "No matter what they threw at you, you never caved, butterbean. You didn't kowtow even as a child. You stood up to my daddy and refused to bend to his will. I'd say that's real enough."

I stood a little straighter at the compliment, the hollowness inside me filling just a tad.

"Thanks, Bernie."

"No thanks needed when you're speakin' the truth."

I smiled and started toward my bed. "Calla?" Bernice called out again, so I stepped back out the door and looked at her. "You deserve this."

My brows pulled together in confusion. "Deserve what?"

"I know you think you don't deserve to be happy, but you're wrong. Preston Armstrong will do or say whatever he has to, to get his way. Even with you."

"You've lost me, Bernie." But she'd scored a direct hit to my heart.

"We screwed up with you, sweet girl. We didn't force you to talk about it when it happened. We foolishly thought you'd come to us, but you never did. You were so damn strong, always were, that we thought you'd seen it for what is was."

"Bernie, you're gonna have to speak English or, at the very least, like you're talkin' to someone who doesn't have a clue what you're goin' on about."

Bernice looked almost scared to speak, then she straightened her shoulders and explained. "Calla, no sane adult is gonna blame a six-year-old for the death of their son. And my father is anything but crazy. He was tryin' to manipulate you. He'd probably been savin' that emotional blackmail for years knowin' that you blamed yourself."

I blanched. I'd never told a single soul about that day. I'd wanted to forget it like yesterday's laundry. Tried for years to stop his accusation from replaying in a loop like a song on repeat.

"How? How did you know?"

"Betsy, the housekeeper at the time. She called me before you left, told me about the whole sordid mess. We didn't know what to do short of murdering our own father, so we played it by ear. We knew you'd shut down if we pushed you to talk, so we waited for you to come to us. But you acted fine when you got home, like his manipulation had rolled off your shoulders, so we misguidedly thought you saw through his bullcrap."

"But he wouldn't—I mean, I'm his granddaughter, he wouldn't . . ."

"Wouldn't what? Manipulate his only grandchild to further his purpose? Wouldn't disregard an innocent child's feelings he should have been protectin' to get his way? Wouldn't write off his daughters because they wanted to live life on their own terms and not some mapped-out course conceived before they were born?"

I was taken aback. Bernice was saying my grandfather, a man who should have been looking out for my best interests, had systematically destroyed my confidence, my emotional state, and my childhood in an effort to control my life.

"We'd foolishly hoped that with your daddy gone, he'd change his ways and soften with the loss. But it was apparent every time you came home after a visit that he hadn't. But you were so strong and never conformed, no matter how much he tried to shake your confidence, that we thought you were fine in spite of him. But, Calla, in all these years, not once did it ever occur to me that you actually believed it. That you believed you didn't deserve happiness as some sort of penance for your family's death."

With that one sentence, she ripped me open like a single slice of a blade. My chest felt tight, like the air in my lungs had been knocked out of me, and no matter how much I tried to fill them, it would never be enough. "How?" I finally muttered, swallowing past the lump in my throat. "How did you know?"

"The other night you said *when he leaves* not *if.* As if it's a forgone conclusion. People only think that way when their mind tells them they aren't good enough, that they don't deserve somethin' because of past actions."

She waited for me to confirm her suspicions, but I couldn't utter a word. She'd laid my deepest, darkest secret to bear witness to the light of day, and I didn't know how to process it.

"That's why you thought you should settle for a man who is safe, isn't it? You don't think a man like Devin will stay for the long-haul because he'll eventually see that you're not worth the effort."

"I—" I finally muttered, not sure of my response, but she cut me off.

"You. Are. Worth it," she bit out fiercely.

That took the wind right out of my sails and left me adrift. My ability to hold it together was slipping fast, so I threw my hands in the air and shouted, "FINE! I'm worth it," hoping she would let the subject drop. I needed space quickly or I'd lose control, and I've never, not once since my family died, cried in front of my aunts.

Bernice smiled at my outburst. "Good. Now keep tellin' yourself that until *you* believe it."

"Bossy old woman," I mumbled, then kissed her on the cheek and turned to escape to my room.

"I'm not old. Fifty-six is the new thirty-six," she shouted through the door, but I ignored her and leaned against the door, sliding to the floor as tears welled.

Did my grandparents truly manipulated me all these years to control me?

I thought back to all the times I'd been with them and couldn't recall a single instance when I'd felt loved. There was no warmth in that house, no concern for the child left behind by tragedy, only coolness that emphasized my loneliness.

"How could you?" I hiccuped as the tears I'd been holding back flowed freely. "I trusted you."

Devastated and heartsick, I crawled into bed with my clothes on and turned off my lamp. I tossed and turned, replaying conversations with my grandparents over in my head while wondering where Devin was. Somewhere in the wee hours of the morning, after I'd evaluated the last twenty-seven years of my life, I drifted off to sleep with my aunt's declaration whispering softly through my mind.

You're worth it.

Devin's hands clenched into fists as he watched Nate comfort Carmella Espinoza. Nate had viewed the body to confirm Strawn's suspicions, then went to Carmella's house and broke the news to her personally. She didn't believe him, insisted on seeing Maria with her own two eyes, so he'd driven her to the morgue.

Maria had been in the water almost a week, so any trace evidence that may have pointed them in the direction of the killer was lost in the murky waters of the Savannah River.

She'd been strangled to death, then dumped. If not for a downed tree that snagged her lifeless body, she could have washed out to sea, and they'd have never known what happened to her.

"Bobby Jones was waitin' for Calla when she got home last night," Devin told Strawn.

Turning to look at Devin, Strawn raised a brow but didn't respond.

"He threatened me."

"Verbally or physically?"

Devin stared blankly at Strawn. "The only way men like him know how," Devin growled.

"He'll ruin you?"

"More like Preston Armstrong will."

"I take it he figured out Calla's yours?"

For the first time since he received Strawn's call about Maria, he grinned. It was sinister. "Oh, yeah."

"Have you found anything that links Jones to Stutter?"

"Not yet. I spent last night huntin' for Calla. Give me a couple of hours, and I'll have enough information to hang him out to dry if it's there."

"Do I want to know where you'll come by this information?"

"Not unless you want the Feds breathin' down your back."

"Connections?"

"Yeah. Went to college with him. He's a few years older. From Savannah originally; lives in Baltimore now."

Movement caught Devin's eye and he turned to watch Nate lead Carmella out of the building. "If this leads back to Armstrong, your case has to be solid before you make a move," Devin mumbled, keeping his eyes on Carmella.

"Agreed," Strawn answered. "We'll need big guns if we're gonna accuse Armstrong or anyone connected to him."

"If we find enough to tie this to Armstrong, the Feds might tag along for the ride."

Strawn mulled that over for a moment. "You said Stutter had an offshore account and the payments were made from the Middle East?" he asked. "You think Homeland Security might be interested?"

Devin's attention turned to Strawn. "If they were, they'd tie up any loose ends, probably put a bow on it for good measure."

"I'll make a phone call," Strawn said, raising a hand to his neck to work out the kinks. "Find me somethin' that links Jones to Stutter or Foo, then call me and we'll meet at Jacobs' bar to keep a lid on this."

"On it," Devin replied and headed for the door.

They parted ways in the parking lot, each with a fire burning in their belly to catch Maria's killer.

Devin waved off Strawn as he pulled out then put on his helmet and looked at his watch. It was 7:45 a.m. He knew Calla would be heading to work, so he'd wait to call her. Throwing his leg over his Harley, he started it and put on his helmet. As he adjusted his mirrors, the reflection of a man sitting in a car across the street caught his attention. It was Taft, the reporter who'd written the article about him.

"Fuckin' vultures," he bit out as he opened the throttle, ripping out onto the street without yielding at the stop sign, hoping his quick exit would lose the reporter on his tail. He made a sharp right onto 66th Street then gunned the Harley to catch a green light before it changed. Twenty feet from his goal, a truck pulled out in front of him. He should have had enough time to stop safely, but his brakes didn't react like they should. He squeezed the hand brake harder, causing his front wheel to lock up. His choices were limited as he barreled down on the vehicle, so he made the quick decision to dump his bike and launched himself toward the back of the tuck, aiming for the bed.

Pain seared down his back when he hit the bed liner. The driver panicked with the impact, crashing into the car in front of him, propelling Devin backward to the tailgate. The gate popped open when he slammed into it and deposited him back onto the street with a jarring thud, knocking the breath out of him. Cars came to a screeching halt, the sound of metal hitting metal reverberating around him as the vehicles stopped mere feet from his head.

Trying to catch his breath, Devin lay still for a moment, inventorying his injuries. He was damn lucky he wasn't dead.

Turning his head slowly, he looked at his Harley.

It appeared to be totaled, pinned underneath a minivan.

"Fuck."

"You okay?" a man shouted.

"Define okay," Devin grunted, sitting up slowly. He pulled off his helmet and examined the back. It was cracked.

The clicking sound of a camera rapid-firing drew Devin's attention. To his right, Taft stood at the curb with a camera to his eye, shooting the scene in front of him.

Devin pushed through the pain and got to his feet, moving toward the reporter, stone-faced. Taft pulled the camera from his face and smiled, bowing once before hightailing it to his silver Camry.

The world spun suddenly as Devin gave pursuit. He put a knee to the ground to steady himself.

"An ambulance is on the way," a bystander shouted. "You shouldn't be movin'."

Reaching into his back pocket, Devin pulled out his cell. The screen was cracked, but it turned on. Swiping Strawn's number, he fell to his back and closed his eyes against the headache exploding through his temples.

Opening my eyes, I listened to the chirping sound of my cell phone ringing. Foggy from lack of sleep, I grabbed the phone and answered it without looking at the caller ID.

My heart raced as I put it to my ear, sure it was Devin calling to update me on Maria. I prayed silently before answering that I'd been mistaken the night before. That Maria *was* alive and well.

"Devin?" I croaked out, my throat dry as a desert.

"I have a car downstairs waitin' for you," my grandfather stated, his tone angry and deadly serious. "I expect to see you within the hour," he ordered and then hung up without waiting for my reply.

I fell back onto my pillow and groaned.

Then I got angry.

Ten years I'd carried around the guilt of his accusation. Ten years I'd I fought with the pain that nothing I did would ever atone for the part I played in my family's death, even when I knew deep down I shouldn't blame myself for the actions of a child. But that little girl had ruled my emotions like a puppet master, directing my actions with practiced ease, and no matter how many times I told myself it was an unfortunate accident, the stubborn child whispered inside my head that I was wrong.

Today, she was silent, the strings she'd pulled severed permanently because Bernice's words had curled around me like a suit of armor, deafening the voice.

For the first time since my family died, the pain I'd been holding on to, governing my life so I was only breathing, not actually living, was gone.

You're worth it!

Throwing the covers back, I marched to my bedroom door and flung it open.

My aunts' apartment was huge compared to mine. Decorated in muted tones of green and beige, their style was relaxed. A brown leather sofa and loveseat were the focal points in the living room, arranged so you could see the TV hanging over the old brick fireplace. The kitchen opened to the living room, and a large center island separated the two spaces.

Eunice was sitting at the bar when I walked in. As I approached, she lifted a mug of coffee to her lips then paused and smiled sadly at me.

"You know something?" I asked, rushing to her. "Did you hear about Maria?"

"No," she sighed, returning her mug to the counter then raising her hands to her face to give it a good rub in frustration. "About Odis Lee," she said after pulling her hand from her face. "Butterbean, I'm sorry about what he said last night. I want you to know if I'd had any inklin', I would have ended the relationship with him years ago."

"Sorry?" I asked, confused.

She turned in her seat and took my hands. "Odis, you see, has been keepin' an eye on things."

"On what things?"

"On you." Her voice faded away, her focus drifting over my shoulder at some unknown point as pain etched her face.

I felt my anger spike as what she said filtered through my brain and locked in tight. "Granddaddy," I bit out.

She nodded, then rubbed her chin against her shoulder—an action I was accustomed to when she was upset—looking older than she had the day before.

"Yes," she murmured. "Odis showed up last night after I'd already said good night to him for no other reason than to see me, he said. I found it odd, but invited him in. He was actin' funny, pacin' the floor, then asked how you were doin'. I told him I hadn't spoken with you this evenin', and he blurted out we should go downstairs and check on you. It was close to midnight, so I blew him off, sayin' you were probably asleep. He said he *swore* he saw you enter the buildin' just before him and that we should check on you. He wasn't makin' any sense at all, and I was about to ask him if he was on a new medication that caused hyperactivity, but then you called before I could.

When you came upstairs and he said what he said, I was angry and confronted him about it. In the course of the argument, it all clicked into place. He got agitated and defensive at first then spit out he was just doin' his job. When I pressed him for an explanation, he backtracked suddenly as if he had said somethin' he shouldn't have. Somethin' about the way he said *job*, coupled with his earlier behavior, hit home and I knew."

"Knew what?"

Eunice's bottom lip began to quiver, so I reached up to cup her cheek for strength. I knew what was coming had to be bad for her to lose her composure in front of anyone.

"That fifteen years ago when Odis started flirtin' with me, weavin' his way into my life, into my heart, he'd been sent by my father to keep an eye on what happened under this roof. To keep an eye on his only grandchild."

I shook my head in disbelief, shocked, yet again, that my grandfather could be so heartless. "No way. I can't believe that Odis would give up fifteen years just because Granddaddy wanted to know what I was up to at all times. I've seen the way he looks at you, Neecy. He loves you."

"He does," she confirmed. "You can't fake love. I would have known. He confessed, because he was tired of bein' blackmailed by Daddy. Said he wanted a relationship built on honesty instead of lies. Said it killed him to say what he did to you last night . . . I still can't believe my own father would go this far," she whispered.

A tear finally fell from her eyes and seeing it, I wanted to find my grandfather and make him pay for every single moment of pain Eunice was enduring.

When she swatted the tear away, I pretended not to see it. We Armstrong women hated showing weakness, and hated it more if someone saw it.

"How was Granddaddy blackmailing him?" I asked to distract her, running my hand gently up and down her arm for comfort.

"Oh, it started out as a loan," she explained, clearing her throat. "Odis had a gamblin' problem and owed big money to a loan shark. He approached Daddy about borrowin' money to pay them off. Daddy agreed on the condition that along with the repayments, Odis owed him a favor of his choosin'. He said it was two years before he called in the favor."

"What was the favor?"

"To distract me from the man I was datin' at the time."

"I don't recall anyone before Odis."

"Do you remember Elton Burrows?"

I thought for a moment and tried to pull up the man's face. He was tall, good-looking, and a Northerner who'd just moved to Savannah.

"The Yankee? I thought he was just a friend."

"That's him, and no, not just a friend." Eunice looked chagrined, so I rolled my eyes.

"Such a floozy," I teased to lighten the mood.

"Butterbean, don't say floozy. It's not ladylike," she chastised.

A sparkle had returned to her eyes, so I giggled in relief.

"So how does the Yankee figure into this?" I asked.

"Well," she began, running a hand through her hair, "it turns out my daddy was concerned I might fall for the Northerner, and since I was still young enough to bear children at the time, he couldn't stand the idea of the Armstrong name bein' polluted with Yankee blood. So, enter Odis Lee, a handsome Southerner who charmed me with his good looks, manners, and his sizable assets."

"TMI," I shouted. "I don't need to know this, Neecy."

She grinned. "I was referrin' to his bank account, but now that you mention it . . . "

"LALALALA," I sing-songed, covering my ears.

Eunice genuinely laughed at my reaction, and it sounded like music to my ears.

"So, why did Odis continue after he got rid of Burrows?" I questioned, wanting to hear the whole sordid tale to the bitter end.

Eunice stood and walked around the center island and grabbed a mug out of the cabinet, so I settled on the stool next to hers.

"Daddy threatened to sell his loan back to the original holder if he didn't keep courtin' me," she continued while pouring me a cup of coffee. "So he had no choice, you see. But this time, Daddy gave strict instructions to keep a close eye on you instead of me. After a few months, Odis said he fell in love with me, even wanted to marry me, but Daddy forbid it. Said he'd tell me he paid Odis to date me. Of course, he knew he'd lose me for good if I knew what he'd done, said he was damned if he did and damned if he didn't. He decided he'd rather have what time he had with me than none at all, and keepin' an eye on you seemed harmless until last night. Like I said, he didn't like interferin', puttin' negative thoughts into your head about Devin."

"Granddaddy told him to say that to me?"

"Daddy told him to do whatever he had to, to put a wedge between the two of you. Odis had overheard Bernie and me talkin' about your fears, so he used them, hopin' to put doubt in your mind."

I nodded. "He scored a hit," I admitted.

"I know he did, butterbean. That's why I confronted him."

"So where did you leave it with Odis? Are you done?"

Eunice tilted her head to one side and thought for a moment, her mouth twisting as she considered her answer. "To be honest," she said looking back at me, "I wasn't sure until this mornin'. You see,

I'm not so desperate for a man in my life that I would hang on to him to keep from bein' alone. But the more I thought about it, the more I knew I'd miss the old coot. It's simple really; I love him, and he loves me, and if I end things with him, the only one who wins is Daddy. Don't you think it's about time the man didn't get his way?"

A slow grin pulled across my mouth. "How long are you gonna make Odis suffer before you tell him he's forgiven?"

Bernice walked into the kitchen as I asked my question and looked between the two of us. "Sugar, have you learned nothin' while livin' under our roof?" she asked.

"Sorry?"

"One does not forgive a man for his transgressions. You make him earn it."

I looked back at Eunice. "So you're gonna keep him in the dark?'

"Of course, I'm not," Eunice chuckled. "I just won't tell him for a few months. That way he'll have to work for it." She winked.

"Like with dinner and gifts?"

"Oh, well, those are always appreciated." She smiled.

Bernice snorted and moved to the refrigerator, opening the door to look inside.

"She's talkin' about sex," Bernice called out. "She's gonna make him work off his betrayal with orgasms."

"Sister, don't be crass," Eunice hissed.

"She's not twelve, for goodness sake."

"She doesn't need to know the intimate details," Eunice returned.

"Guys," I interjected.

"Sister, she had a man in her apartment last night for the exact same reason Odis stays the night. I think she can handle the fact that you and Odis Lee get on like rabbits in heat."

I curled my tongue between my teeth and blew hard; the piercing sound of my whistle put an end to their fight. When they turned and looked at me, I smiled.

"Bernie, leave her alone. Neecy, it's fine. I'm a big girl."

"I was just tryin' to explain," Bernice groused, needing the last word like always, "that girls just wanna have fun like men do. Ask Cyndi Lauper."

"Speakin' of having fun," I replied, turning to Eunice. "It's obvious now that Odis knew Devin was with me, but how did he know?"

Eunice looked at Bernice and grimaced, and it hit me like a lightning bolt. "Bobby," I hissed.

She nodded slowly. "He called Daddy, and Daddy called Odis Lee. He appears to have more than one spy."

That was the last straw. Bobby may have been a pain in my ass, but I still thought of him as a friend. But no more. I was through with the both of them.

"He can spy all he wants," I bit out, grabbing my coffee from the counter. "In fact, he can spy on my ass all the way to work, 'cause that's as close to him as I'm gettin' from here on out."

Both women smiled.

"Sister, I do believe we raised a smartass," Eunice chuckled.

I rolled my eyes.

"Y'all are borderline crazy, you know that, right?"

"*Borderline*. Madonna. 1984. The first of her many top ten hits," Bernice beamed.

"Please don't start," I begged, heading for my room to dress for work.

"*Don't Tell Me* what to do, sugar," Bernice quipped back, using another Madonna song title to answer.

I waved them off. "*Unapologetic Bitch*," I shouted back, returning the favor with my own Madonna title. This was a game we used to play when I was little. Any time I asked a question, they would answer with a song title. We hadn't played it in years, but the memory of happier times made me smile.

I dressed quickly for work then kissed my aunts good-bye, promising to call when I heard from Devin about Maria. When I stepped outside the back gate to retrieve my bicycle, I saw a stretch limo waiting in the side alley. I recognized the burly driver immediately and glared.

"You can tell Granddaddy I won't be honorin' him with a visit today. Not after the bullcrap he's pulled."

Jessie, my grandfather's driver, stared blank-faced at me then opened the back door of the limo and waited. I shook my head and headed for my bike, ignoring the unspoken order. It would be a cold day in Hell before I spoke to him again.

I'd managed to enter one of the digits into the combination lock when two brawny arms wrapped around my waist and picked me up. I began kicking at his legs, shouting, "Put me down, you big brute," as he walked back to the limo and deposited me roughly into the back seat. He slammed the door and locked it before I could right myself and stop him. When I reached for the lock to let myself out, I realized there weren't any. I was locked in.

Dammitalltohell. I was trapped like a fox in a hole.

"Guess I'm goin' for a ride," I grumbled.

Fine. He wanted to talk, we'd talk. But I doubted he'd enjoy it.

The limo rocked forward, heading up the ramp that would take us up to Bay Street. When he turned right instead of left, I sighed. Right meant we were headed to Hilton Head instead of Armstrong Corporate Offices. I'd have to call work and tell them I wasn't coming in today, because I had no doubt my grandfather would keep me prisoner until he got his way.

Unless . . .

Pulling out my phone, I hit *Call Poppy.* It went directly to voicemail, so I spit out, "Mayday. Mayday. I need a Wallflower rescue at the Armstrong estate on Hilton Head Island. Pronto!" Then I worried that the message was too bossy, so I added, because really, it was just good manners to do so, "Or at your earliest convenience would be greatly appreciated. Thank you!"

Nine

Just Be

"I'M FINE," DEVIN GRUMBLED at the EMT, pushing the blood pressure cuff away from his arm.

"Are you refusing further medical attention?" the EMT asked.

Devin ignored the tech. His focus was on Strawn as he examined his Harley.

His brakes had been fine riding to the morgue. No hesitation engaging, no grinding. Complete failure without advance warning was rare.

He watched Strawn's face as he traced the rear brake line. When Strawn paused, his face growing darker with anger, Devin muttered, "Taft."

Strawn stood and headed in his direction, his jaw taut, his eyes sweeping the crowd as he approached.

"Sir, I recommend you get further evaluation at the hospital," the EMT tried again.

"I said I'm fine. Just give me the damn form to sign, and I'll get out of your hair."

The tech nodded and handed him an AMA. "Sign here, please. If your condition worsens or you change your mind, seek medical attention immediately or call 911."

Devin grabbed the metal clipboard and signed his name without answering the man, handing it back before standing from the back of the ambulance.

"Line was cut," Strawn confirmed.

"Add Charles Taft to our short list. If he cut my lines, I want his head on a platter."

"You said he was at Poe when we found Stutter?"

"Yep. And waiting for me to leave the morgue this mornin'."

"If he's a journalist with the Register, he could have heard about Maria on a scanner. It may be a coincidence."

"I don't believe in coincidences and neither do you," Devin answered, twisting his neck from side to side. He'd need an aspirin the size of Georgia and a hot shower before he'd feel close to human again.

Strawn nodded. "I'll add him to the list."

"Did you call a wrecker for my bike?"

"Yeah. You gonna try and fix it or scrap it?"

Devin looked at his hog and cursed. "Scrap it. Can you take me to get a loaner?"

"I'll take you to the airport. You won't find a rental agency in town."

A patrolman walked up, carrying his citation book, and ripped off a ticket, handing it to Devin. He took it and cursed under his breath again.

"Welcome to Savannah," Strawn chuckled.

"I'd rethink my decision to move here," Devin grumbled as they headed for Strawn's truck, tossing his broken helmet in a dumpster as they passed, "if it weren't for Calla."

"You get her sorted?" Strawn asked as they climbed inside the cab.

"She's as sorted as she can be with baggage the size of a steamer trunk."

"You tell her we're investigatin' her grandfather?" he asked as he pulled out and headed west.

"Not yet."

Strawn looked at Devin and grinned. "Got sidetracked, did you?"

Whenever he was near Calla, his brain function shut down and his baser needs kicked in. So, yeah, he got sidetracked in a big way.

"You've seen her," was the only answer he could give.

"That I have," Strawn chuckled.

Talking about Calla reminded him he'd yet to give her the news about Maria.

"Are we close to Poe?"

"About ten minutes north."

"You care if we swing past on our way to the airport?"

Strawn made a quick U-turn at the next block, his mouth twitching as he asked, "It's her eyes, isn't it?"

He didn't have to think about why he was attracted to Calla. It wasn't a single thing, but the whole package, so he answered without hesitation. "No. It's her *heart*, her *courage*, her ability to be so fuckin' innocent in a world full of shit that bein' around her is like steppin' inside a goddamned shower, makin' you feel *clean* for the first time in your life."

Strawn turned his focus from the road and looked at Devin. He held his eyes for a moment then turned his attention back to the asphalt and mumbled, "Jesus. All that and looks to boot?"

"Like I said the other day," Devin returned, "Worth lyin', stealin', or killin' for."

When they reached the brick building that housed Poe Publishing, Strawn parked in front and put his hazards on.

"I'll stay with the truck," Strawn said.

"I'll make it quick. She hasn't heard about Maria yet, and I don't want her hearin' about it on the news."

"Hold up," Strawn called out as Devin crawled out of the cab slowly, his muscles screaming at him to stop moving and lie down. "You move like you've been plowed over by a semi, and your shirt's ripped down the back. Take this."

Devin tagged the leather jacket Strawn tossed, mumbling, "Thanks," before inching into it through gritted teeth.

He checked his reflection in the window and knew he wouldn't fool anyone. The butterfly bandage above his eyebrow told the tale.

He checked the directory and found what floor she worked on then took the stairs to the third floor, trying to work out the kinks in his muscles. When he exited the stairwell, he found Poppy and Sienna leaning against a desk near a picture window and headed in their direction. Poppy saw him first and pushed off the desk, a quizzical look painting her features.

"What are you doin' here?" Poppy asked. "Holy moly, what happened to your face?"

"I'm here for Calla. Where is she?"

"We were just wonderin' the same thing. She hasn't shown up for work yet."

"Why are you here for Cali?" Sienna asked suspiciously.

"I take it you Wallflowers don't spend half your life textin' each other?"

"Meanin'?" Poppy questioned.

"Meanin', after two days of hidin' from me, I finally caught up with the woman and got a few things straight."

Sienna grinned and looked at Poppy.

"Such as?" Poppy asked.

Devin's mouth pulled into a slow, sexy grin. "Such as, no more harebrained schemes to help with my investigation, or I'll tan her hide. But mostly, since she belongs to me now and I don't share, no more harebrained schemes lookin' for men."

Both women burst out laughing then high-fived each other.

"I knew that dress would do the trick," Sienna laughed.

"Told you she was S.O.S where Devin was concerned."

Devin looked at his watch while the women congratulated

themselves and saw it was now after nine.

"What time does she normally show?"

"Normally? An hour ago, I'd say. But office hours are nine to five," Poppy replied. "I was just about to call her to see why she's late."

A tickle of unease surfaced, and Devin ordered, "Do it now."

Bugging her eyes at Sienna, Poppy pulled her phone from her pocket and mumbled, "Shit, I forgot to turn it on this mornin'."

When the phone opened, a beep sounded, indicating she had a missed call. "Yep, missed a call from Cali about ten-minutes ago. Hold on, I'll listen to her message."

Devin watched Poppy's face as she listened to the message. Her brows pulled together for a moment then she snorted, mumbling, "Why does she need a Wallflowers rescue from her own grandfather?"

His unease escalated twofold.

"Replay the message," Devin barked. "Put it on speaker."

Startled, Poppy looked at Sienna then fiddled with her phone and laid it down. Calla's frustrated voice called out *Mayday,* asking to be rescued from her grandfather's estate. She didn't sound frightened, so Devin relaxed by degrees as she continued. When her ever-present manners kicked in and she thanked them for their assistance, he couldn't help but grin. After the voicemail ended, an automated voice informed them there was one more message waiting, so Poppy hit *next* and Calla's voice rang out again.

Since I have forty-five minutes to kill, thanks to being kidnapped by my grandfather's brawny henchman, I thought I would inform you that Devin found me last night and things got—

Poppy muted the phone, looking chagrined, but Devin stopped listening after *kidnapped by my grandfather's brawny henchman*. He pulled out his phone, swiped *Call Strawn*, and headed for the stairs.

"Devin?" Poppy shouted. "Are you going after her?"

At the stairwell door, he turned his head and responded in the affirmative. "Yeah. If she calls again, tell her I'm on my way." And then he was gone, taking two stairs at a time, ignoring the pain that jarred his body as he connected with the concrete steps.

First his brakes and now Calla being forced against her will? Not a coincidence.

He looked at his watch again. She had a fifteen-minute head start. If Strawn let him drive, he'd make up the fifteen and then some.

✿ ✿ ✿

"I can find my own way," I hissed at Jessie. He'd pulled me from the limo with little regard for bodily injury, knocking my head against the doorframe in his quest to deliver me to my grandfather. Ripping my arm from his grip, I marched past him and climbed the steps to my grandparents' weekend home.

The two-story plantation was isolated on the beach, the nearest neighbor a good half-mile away. For all its grandeur, this mansion, a place that should have given me comfort, was nothing but a brick and mortar structure housing contemptible occupants to me now. What had once been a symbol of our family's heritage was now a reminder that those closest to you were sometimes the devil in disguise.

Ripping open the entry door, ignoring Douglas, the house steward who was making his way to the front door, I moved on swift feet to the back of the house and my grandfather's study.

My grandmother stood at the bay window when I approached, her hand at her neck playing with a perfect set of pearls. Margaret Armstrong was a petite woman with silver hair and impeccable taste in clothing. But she was distant, a scotch on the rocks never far from her hands.

She turned as I entered the room and said nothing. Her

expression spoke of weariness and complacency. There was no warmth at seeing me, only distance and acceptance that nothing she did or said would stop my grandfather in his quest to rule all.

"Is he in his study?" I shouted, my sights set on the closed door.

"Calla Lily, ladies don't shout," she admonished, picking a piece of lint from her sleeve.

"And gentlemen don't buy stud services for their daughters to keep them from fallin' in love," I bit back.

"Ah, I see Odis Lee finally let the cat out of the bag," she replied dryly. "Sugar, that was a simple business arrangement. Nothin' untoward." She waved off my complaint like so much water under the bridge.

"Are you pod people?" I asked, because that was the only explanation I could come up with. How do you give birth to someone and feel nothing? How do you raise a child and not want what's best for them until the day you die?

"Pardon?"

"Pod people. Aliens from another planet that have no feelings, no empathy, that care only about the prime directive."

She didn't respond. Instead, she raised her hand and snapped her finger, then waited for Douglas to enter the room.

"Douglas, fetch Calla an Arnold Palmer and go easy on the tea."

She must be joking.

"That's it? *That's* your solution to any ugliness that enters this house? To drink away the problem 'til it ceases to exist?"

For once, I saw a reaction from my grandmother. It was slight, but she jerked minutely.

"Please excuse me, butterbean," she drawled with a regal air. "I've just recalled a previous engagement I must attend to. Do make yourself comfortable in my absence." And just like that, she pivoted on her heel and strolled out without looking back, her head held high, ever the matriarch of the Armstrong family.

I followed her with my eyes and wondered why I'd tried so hard to win her approval. I should have seen it sooner, seen that she was a hollow shell of a woman who did only what she was instructed to do by my grandfather. I pitied her in that moment, but I didn't forgive her.

"That fire in your belly is why you should have been runnin' Armstrong Shippin' instead of wastin' that brain of yours editin' raunchy books."

I whipped around and came face-to-face with Preston Armstrong, my grandfather and driving force behind Armstrong Shipping. He was tall, silver-haired, with an aristocratic nose that spoke of Norman heritage, and a chin that looked like it was formed out of steel.

He was also pompous and smug.

He scanned me from head to toe, taking in my black slacks and pink silk blouse. I'd acquired both pieces from my aunts' shop. They were high quality, timeless in the way Audrey Hepburn's little black dress would never go out of style.

"Good to see those daughters of mine don't have you traipsin' about in polyester and denim."

"Cut the bull, Granddaddy, and get to the point. You hauled me out here for a reason, so we might as well get this over with so I can get back to my life."

His jaw tightened at my outburst. Not once in my twenty-seven years had I ever raised my voice like that to him. I'd listened, answered when spoken to, and refused when I didn't agree with their request, but never had I spoken in such an unladylike way in my life. It felt good. No. It felt great.

"Direct and to the point. I dare say you inherited that trait from me," he replied.

"Sorry? Which trait were you referin' to? Is it the one that manipulates young girls into believin' you blame them for your son's death, or is it the trait where you disown your own daughters for wantin' to choose their own path?"

He shrugged. Proof Bernice was right.

Jesus. All the years I've wasted over a lie.

"I do what I have to, to ensure the Armstrong name continues on with pride. This family's heritage, its roots, they're bigger than anyone standin' in this room. Armstrong Shippin's importance to the State of Georgia, to the city of Savannah, will be written about for generations."

My lip curled in disgust. "Yes, and you'll just be another footnote at the bottom that says *CEO from 1965 to 2014.*"

Slow clapping sounded from behind me, and I turned to find Bobby Jones leaning against the marble fireplace. "She one-upped you, Preston. There aren't many who can put you in your place."

"What are you doin' here?" I asked snippily.

He grinned slowly then moved toward me.

"Now, sugar, is that any way to greet an old friend?"

Bobby stopped in front of me and took hold of my hand, raising it to his mouth. I snatched my hand back before he had a chance to touch his lips to the back.

"Enough," my grandfather bit out. "Let's get down to the business at hand."

I turned back to my grandfather. "Please, by all means, enlighten me as to why I was brought here against my will."

My grandfather strolled to a wingback chair and sat, steepling his fingers across his chest.

"Well? What's so damn important you had your henchman kidnap me from my own back door?"

"I've had reports that this private detective and you are closer than earlier reports indicated."

There it was. Proof that he had spies everywhere.

I turned and glared at Bobby.

"I didn't spend my entire life safeguardin' this family's name to have you consort with white trash, Calla. Since Bobby seems to be unable to close the deal, then you leave me no choice."

"Devin is not white trash, Granddaddy."

"He's beneath this family. You're heir to an empire, for Christ's sake. Act like it."

"I'm heir to a life I don't want," I argued.

"It's not a choice," he bit out, standing from the chair. "You have a responsibility to this family, to its legacy, and by God, I'll make sure you keep it."

"I have a responsibility to no one but those I care about and who care about me. You've never given me a reason to care, to be proud of this family."

He shook his head slowly, the disdain on his face apparent. He didn't care about me; I was just his only option to carry on the family name.

"You're just like those daughters of mine," he sneered. "They turned their backs on this family, but I still had my son then, the one bright spot in my life, so it was of no consequence. But I don't now, thanks to you, so, unfortunately, you owe me, and you owe this family."

I didn't take the bait. He could blame me all he wanted, but I was done listening.

"So tell me, Granddaddy. What's your plan this time to control my life?"

He looked to my right and Bobby moved to my side, taking hold of my hand. I tried to pull it free, but he held tight.

"You will marry Bobby Jones," my grandfather said, cool as you like, and I laughed, cutting him off.

"You're crazy, there is no—"

"Silence," he bellowed with so much hate that it caught me off guard and I took a step back. "You *will* marry Bobby and take your rightful place at the helm of Armstrong Shippin', or so help me God I'll destroy the private investigator. When I'm done with him, he'll have to leave the State of Georgia to find work."

I wrenched my hand from Bobby's and took a step closer to the man who could have been like a father to me if he'd just tried. "Never," I shouted.

The soft color of hatred masking my grandfather's features was the last thing I saw before an open palm slapped me across the face.

✿ ✿ ✿

A massive rock wall, linked together with an iron gate worthy of the White House, designed to keep unwelcomed guests from entering the Armstrong estate, spanned the entirety of the palatial grounds.

They'd made the forty-five minute trip in thirty thanks to flashing turret lights and the occasional blast from Strawn's siren.

"We've crossed over into South Carolina, so I'm out of my jurisdiction. We have to play this smart."

"You play it smart," Devin said, reaching for the door handle. "I'm going over the wall."

Strawn sighed. "You're a fuckin' cowboy, you know that? You can't help Calla if you get arrested for trespassin'."

"You got a better idea?"

Strawn looked at the call button on the intercom. "We could ask nicely."

Devin scoffed. "No way in hell will that old man let me in. You push that button, I'll lose the element of surprise."

Strawn threw the truck in park and grumbled, "Fuck." Grabbing his door handle, he looked at Devin. "I lose my badge over this, I'm comin' to work with you."

"Quit tryin' to stop me from rescuin' Calla." Devin grinned.

Both men opened their doors and got one foot on the ground

when the iron gate hummed to life, swinging open for a limo to pass through.

"Flag it down," Devin barked. "Calla could be inside."

Pulling out his badge, Strawn raised it and stepped into the road, blocking their exit. A rear window rolled down, revealing an older woman holding a cut-crystal glass filled with amber liquid. She scanned both men then took a drink. "I take it you're here about my granddaughter?"

"Yes, Ma'am," Strawn answered.

"Which one of you gentlemen is the private investigator?"

"I am," Devin answered, stepping closer to the vehicle.

Her light blue eyes took him in from head to toe. "Are you a good man?"

"I try like hell to be."

She considered his answer for a moment then asked, "Do you *care* about my granddaughter, or is it her money that brings you here?"

Devin's jaw locked, his features shutting down at the insult.

"Fair enough. I'll take that as you care," she replied when he refused to answer. "You better get up there before my husband calls the preacher and marries her off."

Devin looked at Strawn then back at the woman.

"Say again?" Devin growled.

"Married," she enunciated. "To Bobby Jones. Though, Lord only knows why he'd pick such a weak man for Calla. She needs a man who can handle the hurricanes that are sure to surround her life." She narrowed her eyes at Devin. "Can you handle gale force winds?"

Devin's mouth pulled into a sinister grin. "Like a fuckin' lighthouse."

Calla's grandmother actually smiled. "Don't say fuck, it's not gentlemanly," she returned then opened her bag and wrote something on a scrap of paper. "Here's the code to get inside. Wait until we're gone, then enter."

Devin reached out and took the code. "Thank you."

She scanned him again, her dull eyes lighting with an inner spark for the first time. "Calla always did have good taste."

He smiled, nodded, then stepped back as she rolled her window up, saying, "Y'all have a nice day," as it closed.

"Did that just happen?" Strawn asked.

"Guess we'll find out," Devin returned, heading for the truck.

The code worked like she said it would, so they made the quarter-mile drive to the font of the estate.

"Play it cool," Strawn mumbled as he punched the doorbell.

"Not where Calla's concerned," he countered.

Whispering, "Jesus, fuckin' cowboy," as the door opened, he flipped his badge with authority he didn't have at that moment, as a man appeared in front of them.

He looked between them, clearly confused how they'd gained entrance to the estate.

"How may I help you?"

"We need to see Preston Armstrong," Strawn stated.

"He's not in residence. Do you have an appointment?"

"I don't give a shit if he's home or not. I'm here for Calla Armstrong," Devin explained.

"Miss Calla doesn't reside at Armstrong House."

Devin scowled at the old man. "I'm not playin' this game. I know she's here."

"Unless you have an appointment, I can't help you," the butler returned.

Devin was about to muscle his way past the older gentlemen when an angry voice bellowed, "Silence," causing the butler to turn in surprise. The space he created when he turned was all Devin needed, and he pushed past the man.

He made it two steps inside the marble foyer when a giant of a man stepped in front of him and crossed his arms. Devin stopped short, his muscles tensing for confrontation.

"Let me past," Devin clipped.

The goliath shook his head.

"This is not playin' it cool," Strawn advised from behind him.

He heard Calla shout, "Never," so he moved to sidestep the man. Lunging to stop Devin's advance, the man miscalculated, and Devin was ready. He put a shoulder to his gut, flipping the giant over his shoulder and onto his back, his head slamming against the floor with a resounding thud.

"Goddamnit, Hawthorne," Strawn bit out, but he ignored him and turned in the direction of the shouting. Halfway down the hall he heard the unmistakable sound of a face being slapped and Calla's startled voice crying out in pain.

Strawn shouted, "Go," following Devin as he barreled down the hallway, hell-bent for leather.

They both skidded to a halt when the hallway ended, then turned left and found Bobby Jones helping Calla up from the floor as she clutched her face.

Devin saw red instantly and made to move, ready to tear Jones limb from limb, but Strawn grabbed his arm and mumbled, "I can't protect you if you lay a finger on either man."

He shrugged off his hand and moved to Calla as she stared at her grandfather, pain, betrayal, and disbelief painting her features. He knew then who had struck the blow. He wanted to put his fist in the old man's jaw for the pain he caused her, both mentally and physically.

Preston Armstrong saw him first and brought himself up to his full height, bellowing, "Jessie," as Devin took hold of Calla's arm and pulled her to him. She gasped, caught off-guard by his presence, then tears flooded her eyes as he reached out and gently tilted her face to the side, taking in the red welt beginning to form. He could see each individual mark of a finger marring her ivory skin.

When she cast her eyes away from his and tried to step back, he whispered, "Baby?" She was withdrawing again; he could feel the wall going up. "We're leavin'," he bit out. He needed to get her alone so he could attempt to repair the damage her grandfather had caused.

"What'd I say last night, Hawthorne?" Bobby asked, stepping in front of Devin as he curled her into his body. "You brought this down on her yourself," he finished, jerking his head at Calla.

Devin released Calla and pushed her behind him. He stood toe-to-toe with Jones, taking deep, controlled breaths to cool the fury swirling through his body. His expression was flat. His blue eyes iced over with rage.

"The only reason I won't put my fist down your throat and pull out your heart is to protect Calla. Remember that. You come near her again,"—he turned and looked at her grandfather—"or lay a hand on her," he bit off, "I won't be so forgiving."

When he turned back to Calla, he put out his hand. "Let's go."

She reached out to take it, looked up at his face, and paused.

"What happened to your face?"

Christ, he'd forgotten about the bandage over his eye.

"Nothin'."

"Not nothin'," her grandfather called out, looking at Calla. "Seems he had an accident this mornin', isn't that right, Mr. Hawthorne? Seems his brakes failed. Curious how that could happen without warnin'."

Calla's eyes shot to her grandfather, then rounded with surprise—with fear.

"Baby, let's go," Devin barked, reaching out to take her arm, but she stepped back from him, shaking her head.

Jesus. The woman could build a wall quicker than Donald Trump.

"Calla," he warned.

"I can't," she whispered.

He ignored her. "Take my hand, babe. I'm not leavin' here

without you."

"I can't. I—I have to protect y—that is, I want to protect my family's legacy."

At her announcement, Preston Armstrong bellowed, "Jessie, I want this man removed from my home."

Ignoring him, Devin moved in closer to her. "I'm not leavin' you in this den of jackals. Now take my hand."

She shook her head then reached up and traced the bandage above his eye, tears falling down her cheeks in tiny rivers.

"I'd have given anything to know what it feels like to be loved by you."

Christ, she was saying good-bye to him, so he was done fucking around with the lot of them.

"You're gonna find out," he whispered back.

"No, this has to end before somethin' happens to—"

Bending at the waist, Devin put his shoulder to her gut then pitched her up and over his shoulder.

Calla cried out, "No!" but he was already moving.

Strawn blocked Jones with his badge, giving Devin clear passage out of the room. He kept walking down the hall as Armstrong continued to shout, "Jessie," stepping over the prone body of the man as he headed out the front door. He didn't put Calla down until he'd reached the truck. Ripping open the door, he grabbed her arm and shoved her gently inside, and then climbed in, securing her to his side so she couldn't escape.

"You can't stop him," she mumbled.

"I can stop him."

"He's gonna destroy you."

"He can try."

"You'll end up hating me."

He reached out and turned her face to look at him. Her eyes were red, weary in a way he hadn't seen before, and he cursed Armstrong, vowing to do whatever it took to bring him down. "Never," he whispered, brushing a kiss across her lips. "Not in a million years would I blame you for your fucked-up family."

She bit her lip then placed her head on his shoulder, curling her arms around his waist. "We'll see," she whispered.

She was quiet for a moment as he drew her deeper into his arms, then tensed and whispered, "Maria?"

He squeezed her tighter, but said nothing.

"Poor Carmella."

"We'll find them."

"Are you any closer?"

"Yeah."

"Anyone I know?"

"Later," he mumbled. "I'll explain tomorrow."

After her reaction to his accident, it was clear she suspected her grandfather was involved somehow. He wanted her away from that man's clutches and on firmer ground before he confided in her.

Strawn climbed into the cab and tossed a bag at Calla. "Guy named Douglas said this belonged to you," he explained then started the engine and turned to Devin, grumbling, "Fuckin' cowboy," before putting the truck into drive.

The sky above them turned gray as they headed in silence back to Savannah, the effect of a hurricane brewing off the coast of Florida. When they crossed the bridge into Georgia, Calla sat up and dug through her purse, pulling out a mirror. "Think they'll notice my face at work?"

"You're not goin' into work. Not after the mornin' you've had. Strawn's takin' me to rent a vehicle, then you and I are gonna take the rest of the day to just be."

"Just be?"

"Just be."

She smiled and curled her body back around his, whispering, "I don't know how to just be."

Devin placed his lips to the top of her head and smiled. "Then I'll teach you."

✿ ✿ ✿

"I don't think this is a good idea," I muttered to Devin, watching Strawn pull away.

He turned my shoulders to face him, running his hands up my arms until he'd buried them in my hair. Tugging gently till my head tipped back, he lowered his mouth to mine, and I opened for him, drinking in his taste.

"Been waitin' to do that since you curled around me."

I melted against him, my grandfather's betrayal forgotten in his strong arms. "You have?" I whispered.

"Oh, yeah."

"Devin?"

"Yeah, baby?"

"Maybe you should get a car instead of another bike."

"I'm a Harley guy."

"I still think it's a bad idea."

I couldn't get my grandfather's threat out of my head. Knowing that he tampered with Devin's brakes meant he was willing to do anything to get his way.

"It's a great fuckin' idea," Devin chuckled, then grabbed my hand and pulled me through the door of a Harley dealership.

"You just had an accident. Shouldn't you recover a few days before climbing back on one?"

"Nope."

"You're not the least bit apprehensive?"

"Nope. 'Get back in the saddle' my daddy always said."

"No mulling things over, considering every option?"

"Babe. I'm a man. Women mull things over, men act."

He had me there. I spent five minutes trying to decide what shade of lip-gloss to wear.

"I can act," I lied.

"Prove it."

"All right." I looked around the store at the shiny bikes then turned back to Devin and asked, "How, exactly, do you want me to act?"

"Pick out my next bike."

"Me?"

"You're gonna be spendin' time on it, aren't you?"

Lord, I hope so.

"But I don't know anything about bikes."

"Go with your gut. Which one calls to you?"

Which one calls to me?

I scanned the showroom and paused on a vintage-looking Harley in bubblegum pink. The body style appealed to me. It harkened back to the days of James Dean, when being cool meant everything.

"No," Devin mumbled in my ear. "You have excellent taste and it's a sweet ride, baby, but I'm not ridin' a pink bike, even for you."

"You wanted me to act," I giggled.

"We have that model in a gunmetal gray," a man called out from across the room.

I looked up at Devin and he mumbled, "Better. Can we see it?"

"Follow me," he instructed. "We just got it in."

We wound around to the back of the store then stepped into a stockroom, where several bikes were stored. The salesman pointed to the corner, and my breath caught. Everything about the bike looked like Devin. Solid, yet sleek, and the finish reminded me of the barrel of a gun.

Devin took my hand and led me to the beast, then cocked his leg over the bike before helping me climb on. We fit perfectly together on the seat. My front nestled firmly against his back the way I liked it, and neither one of us was crowded. It was as if the bike had been custom made to fit our bodies.

Devin checked the gauges, flipped switches, and checked the passenger footrests to make sure I was safe while riding.

"You like?" he asked.

I rolled my eyes.

"She likes it," he chuckled. "Price?"

"Just under twenty grand."

Devin didn't hesitate. "We'll take it."

"Just like that?" I asked.

"I need wheels, baby, and my other bike is totaled. I paid it off three years ago, and my replacement insurance will cover half the cost of this bike."

"Okay, but don't you need to test drive it first?"

"Babe, it's a hog," was his only answer.

All righty then.

An hour, two helmets, and one new bike payment later, we stood outside the dealership.

"Where are we headed?" I asked as Devin secured the helmet to my head.

"The open road and Tybee Island," he replied. "You wanna learn to *just be,* then there's nothin' like the wind in your hair to get you there."

"My aunts have a beach house there," I told him.

"You don't say?" He grinned, his eyes lighting from within, the blue almost glowing in the midday sun.

"Do you want to see it?"

His arm shot out and wrapped around my waist, tugging me into his body. "Forewarning," he mumbled low, his voice smooth like velvet. "When we get there, I'm gonna take my time making you come with my mouth. Then I'm gonna bury myself deep and make you come again."

My whole body trembled at the thought of his mouth and other parts of his anatomy making me come, and the smirk he'd been holding on to turned into a full-fledged, striking white smile. "Do *I* get to play?" I found myself saying.

His smile vanished instantly and his face grew dark and hungry. "Jesus," he mumbled, pulling me closer. "Jesus," he repeated.

"Is that a yes?" I questioned while staring at his lips.

"Thirty fuckin' years I waited for you thinkin' you didn't exist, so, yeah, that's definitely a yes."

Hearing that, I got on my toes and nipped his bottom lip then moved to his ear. I felt the same way. I hadn't known I was waiting for him until I saw him in the courtyard, but now I knew better. When he looked at me, I could see myself through his eyes and didn't feel scared or alone.

"Can we go now?" I breathed into his ear.

In answer, he grabbed a handful of my hair that was peeking out from underneath the helmet and tugged, his mouth finding mine for a deep, wet, thoroughly delicious kiss. "Get your ass on my bike," he growled when he ripped his mouth from mine.

I stumbled back when he let go then righted myself and reached out for his hand as he settled on the Harley.

"You'll need to take Islands Expressway and keep goin'," I told him. "It's about a thirty-minute drive."

He turned several switches then pushed one with his thumb, and the Harley roared to life. Devin revved the engine a few times then turned to me and grinned, stating, "I'll get us there in fifteen."

Ten

Free

TYBEE ISLAND IS THE epitome of rustic coastal life. Quaint wooden piers dot the sandy beaches, unspoiled by time and innovation. Just over three square miles, the island draws visitors and native coastal Georgians year-round. A favorite spot for beach weddings, we came across one as we pulled in next to my aunts' cottage.

Devin wasn't kidding when he said he'd get us here faster than the thirty minutes it normally took. He also wasn't lying when he said being on the back of his bike, with the wind whipping my hair around, would teach me to *just be*. And after a hellish morning, curled around his back, my chin resting on his shoulder as he opened the throttle, I finally relaxed. I put my grandfather and Maria's death out of my mind for the day, and focused on the man in front of me.

After removing our helmets, we sat silently on the bike and watched the couple. Their hands were intertwined as they faced each other. The bride wore a simple white dress and daisies in her hair. The groom, white slacks and a white shirt. Both were shoeless and wore matching smiles.

Devin reached back and pulled me to sit in front of him, wrapping his arms around my waist then resting his chin on my shoulder like I'd done on the trip up. I leaned into him and took a deep breath, letting it out slowly, never taking my eyes off the couple.

"They look so happy. So . . . content."

"That's what life's about," he mumbled in my ear. "Findin' someone who completes you then makin' 'em yours."

Turning to look at him, wondering if he would be the one who would finally complete me, I placed my hand on his cheek then brushed my lips across his.

He let go of my waist and cupped my face gently, then angled his head and took my mouth in a slow kiss that sparked the fires that had banked but never fully extinguished. When I moaned, he took the kiss deeper, running his hand to my ass and lifting me again until I straddled his lap. The pressure on my core ignited me further, and I ground myself against him.

Devin froze, ripping his mouth from mine, growling, "Which cottage?" as he stood from the bike, taking me with him.

I curled my legs around his waist and breathed out, "To your right," before burying my face in his neck and tasting the salt on his skin.

Now that the time had come, I realized I didn't want to play, didn't want to be slowly caressed, treated like cut glass. I wanted to be manhandled, wanted my hair pulled and to be taken in a way that I'd feel it for days to come. I wanted him to be a caveman. To bend me over a couch until I couldn't breathe for screaming his name.

Devin took the steps to the cottage in one stride, his boots pounding across the weathered porch. As he approached the front door, I licked my way up his neck and whispered, "Take me hard."

He hesitated for a brief moment, but didn't miss a step. Prowling up to the front door, he put a foot to it, splintering the doorjamb, and the door flew wide open. He stepped through, kicked the broken door closed, then moved to the dining room table.

My ass hit the tabletop, then his mouth was on me, his tongue thrusting as he popped the button on my slacks. Raising my hips, Devin pulled them from my body then tore my silk panties down and flipped me over.

His leather jacket hit the floor first then his shirt followed. I felt him working the button on his jeans as his other hand pinned my body to the table.

"You on the pill?" he asked as he kicked off his boots and his zipper came down.

I nodded, then a moment later, he raised my hips, ran the head of his cock across my swollen folds, and surged in.

I cried out at the intrusion. I hadn't had a man inside me in five years, and Devin was larger than any who came before him.

"You wanted it, you take it all," he growled.

I whimpered, but surged back, burying him to the root. A low moan spilled from his throat, so I rotated my hips slowly, causing a hiss to escape.

Reaching forward with both hands, Devin grabbed hold of my blouse, jerking until the buttons popped off, then pulled down my bra and found my nipples, rolling them as he pounded into me from behind. Each thrust was deep, hard, and the sweetest torment.

Pushing up with my hands, using my feet for support, I rammed back down on his upward thrust and cried out again. He was stretching me to my limit, reaching sensitive nerves that shot my desire to a heavenly level.

"Harder," I pleaded. I wanted to burn for him, wanted to feel the red-hot fire that took you over the edge into bliss.

On a grunt, Devin surged forward, pinning me to the table, one hand capturing mine so I couldn't move, then he pulled out slowly, caressing my walls until I panted with need.

"Please," I gasped, bucking my hips to take him deeper.

Devin wrapped my hair around his hand and tugged my head to the side, then planted himself full inside me before leaning down and taking my mouth. We exchanged air, breathing off the other while he devoured me.

The room spun, spiraling as needles of pleasure built to a boiling point. He wasn't moving, but his size stimulated nerves no one ever had, and my orgasm began to build. I squirmed as it started to crescendo, tightening around his length. Devin groaned, ripping his mouth from mine, then pulled out and slammed back in. I began chanting, "Oh, God," as he rotated his hips, then cried out in ecstasy when his hand moved between us and his thumb found my other entrance, an entrance I'd never considered sexual in my life, and he pressed in until his thumb was fully seated.

Heat scorched me from the added pressure, and I plunged headfirst into oblivion, screaming Devin's name as I bucked back against the onslaught of sensations.

Devin's passion for Calla was unparalleled, unlike anything he'd experienced before. Pulling her back to his front, he curled his hands around her shoulders and drove deep. She slumped against him, her climax having robbed her of strength.

Needing to feel her skin against his, he pulled her blouse from her body, then released the hooks of her bra and let it fall to the ground.

Devin captured a pebbled nipple then, pinching and tugging until she responded with a moan, her hips swiveled in arousal.

"Touch yourself," he grunted, as he felt the quickening in his loins. He was about to explode and wanted her with him for the ride.

She did as she was told then threw her head back against his shoulder. The curve of her neck called out to him, so he licked a trail down to her shoulder and sunk his teeth into the ivory skin. She bucked, cried out, and then clamped around his throbbing shaft. He thrust once more then buried his face in her neck and emptied his seed into her warm silken depths, a low groan spilling from his throat as she chanted his name.

A moment later, Calla's legs gave out, so he picked her up and carried her into one of the bedrooms. Pulling back the covers on the bed, he placed her on the crisp sheets, removed his jeans, and then followed, pulling her back into his body.

He lay there silently, running his hand up and down her spine as he came to grips with the unfamiliar feelings rioting for attention. Though he'd known her less than a week, the curve of her body, the scent of her hair, even the flecks of gray in her soft purple eyes all seemed familiar to him. He felt a soul-deep connection to her and knew without question that he was holding his future.

Calla quivered as she pressed her body to his, her exquisite scent of innocence and baby powder washing over Devin as her hair brushed his stomach.

Lifting her head, she placed wet kisses on his chest, her tongue darting out to taste his skin, and he grew hard again. Her soft hand drifted down to wrap around his shaft, and she lifted her eyes to him. The soft shade of her eyes had turned darker, hungry, and he growled, lifting her to straddle his waist then centered her above his now aching cock and surged up.

Her head dropped back as he filled her, pushing her full breasts toward his mouth. He latched on, nipping a bud as she rode him hard. She whimpered in anticipation, trying to find the release she was working toward, so Devin knifed up and flipped her to her back, sinking deeper inside her.

Her neck arched, the tendons stretched to their limit, then her mouth opened and a sweet mewling escaped.

Tipping her head down, she locked eyes with Devin, and he grunted to keep from spilling inside from the fucking beauty he saw.

Reaching for her hand, he placed it on their connection until she gripped him hard, then he found her clit and rolled it. She exploded around him, and he followed but kept his eyes on her until he was empty, not wanting to miss a single expression on her face.

When she fell slack, her chest rising and falling rapidly as she tried to draw in air, he fell to his side, taking her with him, but kept his hand on her ass to stay buried inside her as he took her mouth and drank in her sweet taste. Something primal in his DNA didn't want to lose the connection, didn't want his seed to escape her body, so he drew her leg over his hip and held her tight against him.

No words were needed after the way he'd taken her. She'd wanted him hard, rough, wanted to be claimed by him like an animal takes his mate, and he'd done just that, had claimed every inch of her with no regrets.

Her breathing evened out as he caressed her hip, and he knew he'd fucked her to exhaustion. Pulling her deeper into his body, Devin closed his eyes and let a contentment he'd never known, as well as the past two days of sleepless nights, pull him under.

A few hours later, a seagull squawking broke through his dreams and he opened his eyes to the fading light invading the cottage.

Devin rolled, pulling Calla with him, and listened to his surroundings. He could hear the high tide thunder, beckoning him to take a dip in the cool water. Running his hand up Calla's back, he tangled his fingers in her hair and tugged until he could reach her mouth.

He kept his eyes on hers as he kissed her awake, mumbling, "Hey," as her eyes opened.

When they'd cleared of sleep, a blush spread across her ivory skin, and she dipped her face to his neck, burying it there in embarrassment.

His little firecracker had a shy side.

"Hey," she whispered back.

Devin pulled her head from his neck, pushing the hair from her face. She darted her gaze to the headboard to avoid looking at him, so he mumbled, "Baby, look at me."

She obeyed, but bit her lip.

"What's runnin' through that head of yours?"

She hesitated for a half-second and then rushed out, "I have a bad feelin' I'm gonna turn into a wanton woman because of you."

Devin blinked, blinked hard again, then shoved his face into her neck and howled with laughter.

"Are you laughin' at me?" she asked snippily, which made him laugh harder.

Drawing a breath so he could speak, Devin choked out, "Baby, you gotta know, as long as it's with me, you can fall from grace any time you want."

He felt her warm breath on his neck as a giggle escaped, so he rolled her to her back and kissed his way to her mouth.

"You hungry?" he asked, brushing a kiss across her lips.

"Starving."

"This island have decent restaurants?"

"Mhm," she hummed, "especially if you like crab cakes. A-J's Dockside has the best in the south."

He'd rather stay in bed with her for a week, but with food being a necessity, he pushed up then grabbed her hand, pulling her from the bed.

Calla moved to the closet, mumbling, "I keep a change of clothes in here," then headed for the bathroom down the hall.

He threw on his jeans and headed to the dining room, where he'd left the rest of his clothes. By the time he was cleaned up and dressed, Calla came out wearing white shorts and a navy crop top that bared her sexy midriff. She wore flip-flops and her hair was pulled high on her head in a sexy ponytail.

His woman didn't take for-fucking-ever to change, thank Christ.

Flipping on the overhead light so he could get a better look, he grinned as he scanned her body. Then his mouth ran dry when a crystal of light glistened from her navel.

Jesus, she had a belly button piercing.

"Get over here," Devin growled.

At his tone, her eyes grew wide.

When she didn't move, he closed the distance in two steps and pulled her into his arms.

"What?" she gasped, dropping her head back to look at him.

He crushed his mouth to hers, growing harder by the second as he palmed her ass. Ripping his mouth from hers, he looked down into her lust-filled eyes and replied, "Just makin' sure you're real."

She blinked, caught off-guard, then answered breathlessly, "You keep kissin' me like that, you're gonna find out how wanton I can be."

His grin turned smug.

He let her go then pulled her to the door. He'd worked up an appetite and needed fuel for round three with his wanton woman.

"I'll secure that after we eat."

Calla looked at the door. The trim had popped off and the jamb was split down the center. When she pulled on the knob, the door popped open with little resistance.

"I don't think it locks now. In the future, there's a key under the turtle out front."

Devin wrapped his arms around her waist and pulled her back into his chest. "In the future, don't tell me to take you hard, and I won't kick the door in."

She tilted her head back and looked up at him. "Fair enough."

Feeling more relaxed than he had in years, Devin picked Calla up, stepped through the open door, and closed it, depositing her on the porch. He nipped her neck before taking her hand and dragging her to his bike.

A-J's Dockside was five minutes by bike in the evening traffic. They ordered crab cake sandwiches then sat on the dock and watched the fading sun kiss the horizon.

The sunset cast Calla in a warm glow, but he could see she wasn't watching God putting the world to bed.

"Talk to me," he said. "Penny for your thoughts."

She rolled her lips between her teeth then sighed and placed her sandwich on the handrail.

"I think my grandfather is the one who caused your accident today. Well, not him personally, it's more likely he had someone do it for him."

"Calla," he began. He needed to tread lightly. For one, he couldn't compromise Strawn's investigation. And secondly, he didn't understand what part she played in Maria's abduction and subsequent death, and he didn't want her blaming herself. "Tell me why you think that?"

"Before you arrived today, he insisted that I marry Bobby Jones to ensure the *family legacy* at Armstrong Shipping. When I refused, he told me if I didn't marry Bobby, he would destroy you."

An image of Calla on her knees after being struck burned in Devin's gut. "That's why he struck you, isn't it?"

She raised her hand to her cheek, and a fleeting look of pain crossed her face.

"Hey," he said gently, cupping his hand over hers. "He'll never lay a hand on you again. I promise you."

She looked into his eyes, and he saw the sparkle of tears she would not allow to fall. "I'm fine," she lied, "but knowin' what he's truly capable of got me thinkin' about my aunts."

"Thinkin' what?"

"Parents are supposed to protect their children, be the only people in the world you can trust without question. My aunts never had that from my grandparents. I have that from them, but those beautiful, amazing women have lived their entire lives knowin' that when push comes to shove, they have no one at their backs."

Devin drew her into his arms and placed his chin on top of her head. Rubbing his hand down her back, he bent to her ear and whispered, "You're wrong. They know if push comes to shove, the one person they can count on most in this world is the other. That's why they've remained so close."

She melted into him and nodded. "You're right," she admitted, looking up at him. "I never thought about it like that."

"We make our own family in this world," he continued, "with people we connect with. I'm closer to Nate and Megan than my own siblings. And though I'd do anything for them, I didn't hesitate to move away from them, because I knew I had another family here."

She thought about that a moment. "I can see Poppy and Sienna becoming my extended family."

Devin chuckled. "I'd say they already are. I've never met women as equally matched, and nuts, I might add, as you three."

She thought about that, too, and grinned. "You have a point."

"I'm never wrong," he added smugly, baiting her.

She scoffed. "Never?"

"Nope," he grinned. "Knew the minute I laid eyes on you you'd be a handful, and I was right."

"When have I been a handful?"

He cupped her ass and drew her firmly into his hips. "Good thing I like wanton women."

Shoving him away, Calla groaned, "I'm never sharing with you again," then turned to her sandwich and took a bite.

Devin smiled, glad he'd taken her mind off the asshole she called grandfather. He knew he couldn't delay much longer, knew he had to warn her of possible danger, but not tonight. He promised to teach her how to relax, to *just be,* and he was keeping his word.

✿ ✿ ✿

It was pitch black when we arrived back at the cottage to secure the door. Normally, the moon would have lit our way, but clouds had rolled in after sunset blocking the stars.

"I don't think you'll be able to fix it," I chuckled as we climbed the steps.

Throwing his arm around my neck, Devin pulled me in snug to his body and mumbled, "You doubt my ability to take care of your needs?"

A small grin pulled across my lips. "Needs, yes. Magically repair wood that needs to be replaced? I'll believe that when I see it."

A slight breeze kicked up as we approached the door and it swung inward.

"See," I laughed, pointing out the door. "You closed it before we left and it didn't hold."

Devin stepped in front of me, pushing me behind him, then reached in and flipped on the light.

"I left the dining room light on," he mumbled. "Someone's been here."

I peeked around his shoulder expecting to see the cottage tumbled like Maria's apartment, but it looked neat and tidy like always.

My aunts had gone with a nautical theme for the cottage. White clapboard walls were covered with lighthouse prints in every shape and size. Every nook and cranny held a miniature lighthouse they'd picked up on their travels. Over the rock fireplace hung a huge print of the Tybee Island lighthouse, which they'd centered the living room around. The kitchen was small, with pine cabinets that had been pickled white to match the rest of the cottage.

I could see all of those rooms in a single glance, and nothing looked out of place.

"The cottage looks fine to me. Maybe your cop's nose is working overtime?"

Devin looked down at me and cocked a brow. "My cop's nose?"

"Former cop's nose?"

He grinned. "I think you mean my instincts are tellin' me someone's been inside?"

"Those, too."

"If I ask you to wait here, will you listen?"

I wrinkled my nose and shook my head. "I think I've already established that I think the safest place for me is right behind you."

Devin rolled his lip between his teeth and glared.

I shrugged. "I can be headstrong."

"Don't I fuckin' know it," he sighed. "Keep right behind me, no rushin' off unless I tell you to run. I want you were I can reach you."

"Isn't this a little overboard? I mean, what's the worst we can find? That kids took advantage and tossed the place looking for valuables?"

"I don't have a clue, which means I want you where I can reach you."

I pushed him in the back to enter the cottage. "Fine, fine. Lead on, PI man."

Devin balked then looked down at me. "You're gonna be a pain in my ass, aren't you?"

I thought about it a moment. "Is that better or worse than borin'?" I asked, referring to our conversation the night before as Devin started heading for the bedrooms. I took hold of the back of his jacket and followed close. "Because I'll remind you that last night you said, and I quote, '*You're fearless, not borin'.*' If I'm to take that as a complement, then me bein' a pain in the ass must be, too."

Devin stopped outside the bedroom we'd vacated a little over an hour ago. As he reached through the doorway to turn on the light, he looked down at me and grinned. "Now you're bein' cute *and* a pain in the ass."

I rolled my eyes.

Grinning, he flipped on the light, and we both turned to look inside. Then I screamed.

Someone once said that a memory is like a scene from a movie, forever frozen in time. In the past, memories for me were like monsters hiding in closets, ready to strike without provocation. That closet just grew fuller.

In the middle of the bed we'd just made love in lay a man in his mid-forties with a knife driven deep into his chest. His eyes were open, blankly staring at the ceiling, as his blood saturated the mattress.

The metallic smell of blood seemed to permeate the air, saturating my senses until I gagged. Devin shoved me out of the doorway and then rushed me down the hall to the bathroom. Running inside, I hit my knees, wrapped my hands around the toilet bowl, and retched up my dinner.

I heard the faucet turn on and Devin's deep voice crooning, "Breathe, baby," as he placed a cold cloth on my neck.

He kneeled behind me, his strong hands coming to my shoulders to steady me as I sat back on my haunches and closed my eyes.

"I need to check the house," he whispered. "I'm gonna lock you in here. I don't want you to come out until I come get you."

Come out?

I was never leaving that bathroom.

I nodded, then lay down on the tile floor hoping the coolness would calm my stomach.

And here I thought I could waltz into that basement and ID Billy Ray. He'd been dead five days, so decomposition would have . . . *Great, now I have another monster in my closet to contend with.*

I heard the door open, so I turned my head and looked at him.

"Do you know that man?"

The muscles in his neck grew taut, and his blue eyes lit with fire. He nodded once.

"Who?"

216

"A reporter by the name of Charles Taft."

✿ ✿ ✿

"I don't understand why you have us in separate rooms?" I asked the sheriff's deputy standing guard.

In a flurry of lights, reminiscent of the day we found Maria, Devin and I were separated into the back of two patrol cars then whisked away to the Chatham County Sheriff's Office. I hadn't seen Devin since we arrived, and that was more than two hours ago.

I'd made the mistake of accepting coffee from an attentive officer, only to have it sitting like a lead weight in my empty stomach.

"It's standard in cases like these," the deputy answered.

"But we didn't see anything. I've told you this. We went for dinner then came back to find . . . that man."

Just saying the words brought the smell of blood bubbling to the surface.

I turned my head and looked at the two-way mirror. "We didn't kill that man," I bit out, talking to whoever was behind the glass.

Another ten minutes passed before the door opened and another officer strolled in carrying a file. He was older by about five years, with light blond hair and kind eyes with crinkles permanently etched in the side from either laughing too much or extreme stress. Considering his job, I went with stress.

I heard arguing in the hall and gasped.

My grandfather was in the hall.

I stood and headed for the door, but Officer Kind Eyes grabbed my arm.

"What is my granddaddy doin' here?" I hissed, yanking my arm away.

"You need to sit down, Ms. Armstrong."

"This is close to police harassment or, or, deputy harassment," I quibbled. "I haven't seen Devin in hours and, in case you didn't know, your coffee tastes like twiddle diddles."

The man blinked, then blinked again before a smile pulled across his mouth. "Twiddle diddles?"

"Scrotums. Stinky ones to boot."

At my explanation, the man threw his head back and laughed, and I knew then the crinkles were from laughing.

"Please," he said pointing to the chair, "have a seat, then we'll release you to your grandfather."

I moved to the chair, mumbling under my breath, "I'd rather be locked up."

"Sorry, did you say somethin'?"

"I said I'd rather be locked up, tortured with needles, or hung on a rack and stretched 'til my bones dislocate before I leave with that man."

Kind Eyes turned and looked at the other deputy when he grunted at my reply.

"I take it you're not close?" he asked, turning back to look at me.

I crossed my arms. "If by close you mean do I hate him, then the answer is yes."

He cocked his head and stared at me a moment.

"Ms. Armstrong," he began. "Your grandfather insists that Devin Hawthorne broke into his home this morning and abducted you. That he's dangerous and fully capable of killing Mr. Taft. He also said that you're engaged to a Mr. Jones, who is also waiting outside to take you home."

"He kidnapped me, not the other way around," I cried out.

"Pardon?"

"My granddaddy has some deluded idea that I have to run Armstrong Shippin' to ensure our family's legacy. So he kidnapped me this morning to force me to agree, and Devin came and rescued me."

The man looked shell-shocked.

"What's your name, Sir?" I asked.

"Justin Moore, Ma'am."

"Justin—may I call you that?"

"Yes, Ma'am."

"Justin, I was with Devin all evening. We went to have dinner, which any number of people will be able to verify, then went back to my aunts' cottage to fix the door before leavin'. Anyone could have entered while we were out, because the door was broken."

"How was the door damaged?"

Oh. Dear. Lord.

"Um, what did Devin say happened?"

He rolled his lips between his teeth and shook his head. "I'm not at liberty to say."

"Fine," I sighed. "We were otherwise engaged and he sort of . . ." I raised my hands and shrugged.

"He sort of what?"

Heat rushed to my face, but I knew I had to tell the truth. ". . . Kicked in the door in the heat of passion."

The other officer grunted again.

Justin tried hard not to smile.

Whatever. After what I'd been through that day, what did I care if they knew about my extracurricular activities?

Leaning in, I implored the man to listen. "Justin, there is no way Devin killed that man, no matter what my granddaddy says."

He leaned forward as well and opened his file. Picture after picture of Devin lying in the middle of the road, cars and trucks stopped inches from his head, spilled out.

I picked one up and grimaced.

"Who took these?"

"Charles Taft."

"The dead man?"

"The same. We found them scattered in his car parked across the street from your family's cottage."

I scanned through them all and came to one where Devin was looking directly into the camera as he moved toward it.

"He looks pissed, don't you think?"

"I'd be pissed, too, if someone cut my brake line hoping I would crash."

"Pissed enough to kill?"

I dropped the picture.

"The only way Devin could have killed that man is if I was involved, too, and I've been with him since this mornin'."

He leaned back and studied me.

"Well?"

"Well what?"

"Do I look like a killer to you?"

He studied me a moment longer then stood abruptly. Pulling out his wallet, he produced a business card. "Here's my card, Calla. Contact me if you have any questions . . . or need *anything* at all."

The officer in the corner grunted, then coughed to cover it.

I stood, too, shocked and relieved. "Thank you, Deputy Moore."

"Sheriff," he responded.

"You're the sheriff?"

"Yes, ma'am," he replied with a smile and then held the door open for me.

Maybe those crinkles *were* from stress?

I headed for the door, but the minute I walked through it, I stepped into a warzone.

Devin stood nose to nose—or nose to forehead since he was a good three inches taller—with Bobby when I stepped out, and Bo Strawn was close by, mumbling, "Use your head."

"Devin," I cried out, rushing to him before all hell broke loose.

He turned at my voice and headed for me, Bobby forgotten for the moment.

"Calla, we need to talk," my grandfather ordered, stepping in between Devin and me.

"You need to let Calla pass, Sir," Justin ordered my grandfather.

"Go to hell," I bit out and pushed past him.

"Is that any way for a lady to speak?" he growled, grabbing my arm. "One day with that man, and look what you've become."

My aunts materialized from around the corner and glared at their father.

"Get your hand off her," Devin hissed with a lethal edge.

Justin moved between Devin and my grandfather and with an equally murderous tone said, "Take your hands off Calla, or I'll lock you up."

When his grip loosened, I yanked my arm from his clutches and walked into Devin's waiting arms. "My apologies, Granddaddy," I snipped, turning in Devin's arms. "I should have said *go to hell, please.* How could I have forgotten my manners?"

Bernice beamed at me. "Pure southern smartass. I couldn't be prouder if you were my own daughter."

Justin looked between Devin and me. He held my eyes for a moment then turned to Devin and asked, "You got her?"

"*Always,*" Devin replied with a bite. "Don't let us keep you."

Justin studied Devin for a moment, then nodded and turned to my grandfather, glaring at him before heading down the hall.

For once, my grandfather was silent, but the color rushing to his face said he wouldn't stay that way.

Devin squeezed my shoulders and I looked up. "Let's go home," I whispered.

He gave me another squeeze, then jerked his head at Bo Strawn. "He's givin' us a ride back to my bike."

We made it two steps before my grandfather broke his silence, "If you walk out that door, Calla, I swear I'm cuttin' you out of the will."

"Same old, Daddy," Eunice hissed. "You think money and power are more important than your own family."

"This is none of your concern," he bit out. "You made your choice years ago, and I can see your flawed judgment rubbed off on my grandchild."

"How dare you," I shouted, ripping from Devin's embrace. "They were there for me when I lost my parents. Where were you?"

"Dealin' with the aftermath. You forget I lost *my* only son."

"And I lost *everything*," I cried out. "Momma, Daddy, Frankie. I was six years old and needed you. *I* NEEDED you, Granddaddy. To scare away the monsters, to hold me and tell me everything would be all right, to tell me you loved me and would always protect me. But you took advantage of my trust in you. You schemed and manipulated me for years for your own misguided end. You think our family's legacy to Savannah should be about power, but you're wrong. Our family's legacy should have been one of love, of compassion and loyalty to each other, but you're so power hungry you're blinded to anything else. So you can keep your money. I'd rather be poor with a good man who loves me, surrounded by children who will never know an unkind word, who will always know that family comes first, and that I would rather die than make them feel a single once of the pain you've caused my aunts and myself."

He didn't even blink. He was so consumed with his own immortality that he turned a deaf ear.

"This isn't over," he hissed, looking at Devin. "I'll not allow the likes of you to pollute this family."

Devin curled me into his side and looked down at me, ignoring the insult. "Fearless," he whispered then brushed a kiss across my lips.

"Guess I'm not borin' after all."

He grinned. "Thank Christ for that."

Devin turned us toward the exit, my grandfather forgotten.

"You're just lettin' her leave?" Bobby asked incredulously.

My grandfather ignored him and roared, "Calla!" as Devin opened the door.

I kept walking, shaking inside. All those years I'd prayed for that man to love me, and now I felt nothing for him. With the palm of his hand, he'd severed what thin line of family still remained between us, and now I was free.

Free to make my own way in life without the Armstrong noose around my neck.

Eleven

Evil is as Evil does

MIDNIGHT LOOMED WHEN DEVIN entered Jacobs' Ladder with Strawn in tow. Nate stood at the bar, his eyes on the two men as he opened a bottle of Jack.

He'd left Calla with her aunts and with a promise he'd take her to work in the morning, then he'd made a call to his old friend, Dane Parker, as they walked the few blocks to the bar.

Parker had been boarding a plane, so the call was brief. Devin gave him the rundown on Maria's murder and the possible involvement of Preston Armstrong and Bobby Jones. There'd been a pause before Parker had mumbled, "Christ."

Being a native of Savannah, Georgia, Parker knew exactly whom Devin was dealing with.

"You dig around in that man's business, and he'll cut you off at the knees," Parker said.

"I've felt the cut of the blade already," Devin growled.

"He made a move this soon?"

"Probable. But I need more information."

"Give me the details."

"I've got a dead woman who went lookin' for his granddaughter minutes before she disappeared. Calla is a fuckin' book editor, who's never gotten so much as a parkin' ticket. That puts the spotlight squarely on his shoulders, since he's the only person in her life who'd accumulate enemies. He's either involved, or someone associated with him is. I need information that only you can dig up."

Parker sighed, muttering, "Give me the names of the players, and I'll get back with you as soon as I land."

"Where you headed?"

"Alaska. Got a weddin' to attend."

"Who the hell do you know in Alaska?"

"You remember Jack Gunnison?"

"The sheriff in Colorado?"

"That's him. He pulled me in on a case a few months back, and the couple involved are tyin' the knot."

"Watch out for bears," Devin replied.

"Right." Parker chuckled, then signed off, "Later."

Strawn and Devin sidled up to the bar. Nate placed three shot glasses on the polished wood and poured the amber whiskey, ordering, "Lay it out for me."

Devin took his shot and threw it back, letting the burn steel his anger before he began.

"Taft was done in the cottage, which means he followed us to Tybee. He wasn't a small man, so it would take strength to subdue him. Jones is big enough, but he'd never get his hands dirty. And Armstrong's too old to handle Taft. That leaves the bodyguard."

"He was stone cold dazed when we left," Strawn put in, "but Taft could have been on the payroll and called in your location. And if Armstrong's involved in Maria's death, then he'd have no issues with killin' again."

"We need to find out what started this chain of events," Nate added. "What the hell did Maria see that had her lookin' for Calla, yet not skittish or afraid?"

"And," Strawn continued, "how do Stutter and Yoo figure into the equation?"

"That's the million-dollar question."

"Billion," Devin corrected. "Armstrong's worth billions."

Devin stood up and began pacing. He needed music to think, but pacing was the next best thing.

"Let's assume for a minute that Jones and Stutter have some sort of arrangement with Yoo. Maria overhears, and knowin' Calla is related to Armstrong, she goes looking for her. If she was followed by Stutter and didn't know it, then she wouldn't have been on guard. Which would explain her casual demeanor."

"Why'd they toss her apartment?" Nate asked.

Good question. A picture? No, a picture would be too easy to explain away unless it was of them dumping a body. In that case, Maria would have gone straight to the police. No, it had to be either written evidence or . . .

Devin turned to Strawn. "Did they find a cell phone in her possessions?"

"None on her body or in her apartment. We searched for it hopin' she might have made a call after her mother. We're still waitin' on a court order to subpoena her phone records."

"You think she recorded the conversation?" Nate asked.

"What's the first thing that happens nowadays when you come across an accident or police brutality?"

"He's right," Strawn said. "Everyone records shit these days."

"We know her apartment was secured the day after she disappeared, because Carmella went by. So they tossed her apartment lookin' for it after they killed her, which means it wasn't with her."

"That means whatever she heard has to be on that phone," Nate bit out. "We need to find it."

"It wasn't in her car. We found it parked down the street," Strawn replied.

There was silence for a moment then all three men started moving toward the door. "I'll call Calla," Devin said, pulling out his phone.

"She has keys to the buildin'."

"The Cartwright woman said Maria stayed behind near Calla's office," Strawn stated.

"Right, and if the lights go off while you're on a secret mission, you might just hide your evidence with the one person you're hopin' to help," Devin returned.

✿ ✿ ✿

Nate ginned at me as I unlocked the main entrance at Poe Publishing. I peeked a look at Devin and caught him glaring.

"It's company policy that all unauthorized personnel must be accompanied. I told you this," I stated, returning his glare. "The manuscripts are the authors' intellectual property. If anything happened to one, we could be sued. Besides that, you don't have a search warrant."

"You gave us permission to search your desk. We don't need one."

"Alexandra Poe doesn't care. She owns the buildin', which means she owns my desk. I explained all this to you after I called her."

"I'm still pissed that you called her. If you'd just given us the key, we wouldn't be havin' this discussion," he shot back.

"Well, if you'd explained to me why you think Maria hid somethin' in my desk, maybe I would have. But I don't like secrets."

"It's a hunch," Nate threw in, looking at Devin. "We know you were friendly with her, so she might have left evidence with someone she trusted."

Right. Not buying that for a second.

"I don't give a fuck about the rules," Devin interjected when I opened my mouth to say, *Maria was friendly with many people who worked there. So why, out of all of us, did they think it would be me?* "In one day, you were hauled off against your will and we found a dead man. The way the day's progressin', I don't want you anywhere near this shit when it goes down."

My lips twitched. "Duly noted," I replied, then pulled open the door. Who could argue with a man like Devin when he was beating his chest because he wanted to keep you safe?

"Why don't we stay in the lobby while they check," Nate suggested, taking my arm. "Police procedure and all, we might get in the way."

I don't think so.

They were playing at something, and my bullshit radar hit DEFCON 1.

"We aren't goin' another step until someone tells me what's goin' on. Clearly, you're protectin' me from somethin'."

Devin's jaw twitched, then he sighed and dropped his head back on his shoulders. "I didn't want to tell you this way."

"Just spit it out. I'm a big girl."

My heart began to pound when he stood there instead of answering immediately.

Raising his head, he muttered, "Christ," then began. "The reason Maria came here the day she disappeared is because of you."

"Me?" I cried out. "Why? How do you know this?"

"She ran into Jolene Cartwright," Strawn added. "Told her she was lookin' for you."

"I don't understand. Did she say why she wanted to speak with me?"

Devin shook his head. "That's all we know. We want to search your desk in case she left somethin' behind."

I started to relax then remembered our earlier conversation.

"But you told me today that you were gettin' closer. That you had a suspicion about who was involved. If that's so, then you must have an idea why she came here lookin' for me."

"That's true, but it's all conjecture. And I don't want to upset you if I'm wrong."

I looked at Strawn and then Nate. They both had their eyes cast down, and Strawn was rubbing the back of his neck. They wouldn't look at me, which meant they didn't believe it was conjecture.

Who did I know who was capable of murder?

Oh. My. God.

"It's my grandfather, isn't it?"

"We don't know anything right now. That's why we're here."

OhGodohGodohGod.

I began to pace, trying to wrap my head around this news. My heart slammed a mile a minute as I tried to come up with some other reason Maria would have come to see me. I couldn't.

My grandfather was hateful and vindictive, but a killer? I couldn't see it. Didn't want to see, if truth be told. And it became apparent in that moment, even after everything he'd done, that I still held out hope he would change before he died. But if he murdered Maria?

"This will destroy my aunts," I cried out.

"Baby, we don't know anything for sure," Devin said, grabbing my arm to stop me.

No, we didn't, but there was one way to know for certain.

"Then let's find out," I said, pulling away from him, heading to the bank of elevators.

We rode in tense silence to the third floor. Devin took my hand and squeezed it, but it didn't help. I was on the verge of throwing up for the second time in one day.

When the elevator opened, I took off running around the corner to my desk.

I used my computer for everything. I didn't even open my drawers on a daily basis, so it was possible the key to her murder had been in my desk all along.

Pulling the middle drawer open, I began digging through my scrap paper and notes.

"Move aside," Strawn said. "I can't have you touchin' anything."

Devin pulled me back and sat me in a chair a few feet away. Running his hand through my hair, he whispered, "Stay here, okay?"

I nodded in quick succession as my foot began to tap out a rapid beat. Then my nails took the brunt of my anxiety as I watched Strawn methodically empty each drawer, then pull it out and look at the bottom. In the second to last drawer, he paused and looked up at Devin. I stood and asked, "What?"

His glove-covered hand pulled out what looked to be a white phone wrapped in a sheet of my pink notepad paper.

He folded back the paper, his eyes scanning it, then he read out loud, "Ms. Armstrong. I need to speak with you as soon as—" he ended abruptly.

"Is that it?" I blurted out.

He looked at me and nodded. "We need a phone charger."

I dropped my bag and began digging. "I have one."

I handed it to Devin then held my breath as he plugged it in and turned the phone on. It took a lifetime to boot up. When he tried to swipe it open, Strawn said, "It's password protected. I'll need to get this to the tech boys."

I was desperate to know the truth. I couldn't wait the time it would take for the tech boys to get around to hacking the phone.

"Do you know her birthdate?"

Devin turned and looked at me. "Why?"

"Because every woman I know uses their birth month and day as their four digit code."

"It'll be in her file," Strawn said, putting down the phone.

He'd brought the file with him, so he opened it and flipped through the pages. When he found what he needed, he picked up the phone and punched in the number. The screen opened, and he looked me. "You want a job?"

I shook my head. I couldn't joke at a time like this. "Just look, please."

His eyes softened before he flipped through apps.

"Got it," he mumbled, looking up at me with concern.

"Just play it. I have to know."

Devin curled me into his body and held on tight. "No matter what we hear, this isn't a reflection on you or your aunts."

I said nothing, because it was a lie. If my grandfather had murdered Maria, it changed everything. We couldn't bring her back, and I'd never be able to live with myself knowing my family had brought that kind of pain to her family.

"Ready?" Strawn asked.

"Ready," I lied.

He punched play, and the tiny screen jumped to life.

"You've said that every time we've met. I'm tired of waitin' for you to get married," Billy Ray Stutter replied casually.

"Billy Ray," I said.

"We no wait aroun'. If you wan in, it has be now," a woman said in broken English. She sounded Asian, but I couldn't be certain since she wasn't in the screen shot.

"Who is that?"

"My money's on Fang Yoo," Nate bit out.

"I'll have the money as soon as I convince Calla to marry me, I've told you this. Tell the buyers to give us a few more months," Bobby Jones' unmistakable voice rang out, and I closed my eyes and started shaking. "Oh my God, that's Bobby."

"How much is she due to inherit?" Billy Ray asked.

"Millions. The old man kept pushin' me to marry her, so I went diggin' to see why he was hell-bent on seein' it happen. Turns out she inherited her father's shares when he died, and Preston doesn't want anyone he doesn't deem worthy of his 'family' to get their hands on it."

I stepped forward and tried to grab the phone. "What's he talkin' about? My grandfather owns all the family's shares of Armstrong

Shippin'."

Strawn jerked the phone away and then paused the video. "You can't touch it. It's evidence."

Devin grabbed my arm and pulled me back, growling, "Finish it."

Strawn pressed *Play* again, and I held my breath, chanting in my head, *please don't incriminate my grandfather, please don't incriminate my grandfather.*

"How many shares did she get?" Billy Ray asked.

"Her great-grandfather was pissed at Preston, so, as a lesson, he left half his shares to her father and half to her grandfather."

"And the little bookworm doesn't have a clue?"

"Nope. Her father had a trust, leavin' the care of his children to his sisters, but the management of his finances to his father. Preston kept it hidden from her and the aunts to keep them under his thumb."

"All right. But how does knowin' that get you wed to her?"

"I've got the grandfather on my side. I just have to convince her. If that doesn't work, I'll take the drastic measures all men take when negotiating with wealthy women."

"You're gonna finesse your way into her panties and knock her up so she has to marry you?"

"That's the idea," Bobby chuckled. *"She's got the looks, so it won't be a hardship. But she's distant, a bit of a cold fish if you get my meanin', so I'm not expectin' a hellcat in the sack."*

"Video ends here," Strawn announced, and my legs gave out in relief.

"So, it was Bobby, not my grandfather?" I asked hopefully as I sat down.

"Probable," Strawn answered. "But we'll have to prove it. Any chance he's left-handed?"

I shook my head no. "No, he's right-handed. Why?"

Strawn stared at me for a beat then asked hesitantly, "Is your grandfather left-handed?"

"No. Why are you askin' this?"

Devin turned to look at me. "Whoever killed Billy Ray was left-handed. If Bobby wasn't, then we've got a third man involved."

"This is hard to wrap my head around," I mumbled. "So what you're sayin' is Maria overheard Bobby say he was gonna marry me for my money and she came here to warn me, but was murdered instead?"

"She must have thought she got away clean," Nate said.

"Probably left after she stopped recordin', but they saw her and followed."

Devin crouched in front of me and took my hands. "This wasn't your fault. Or your grandfather's fault."

I nodded. "Poor Maria. She must have been so scared."

"We'll make this right, baby. I promise you that."

If the fire in his eyes was any indication I'd say Bobby was looking at thirty-five to life.

"What happens next?"

"Next? We fillet open his life and see what falls out until we find this third man and what they were attemptin' to buy."

The mention of filleting made me think of Taft laid out on my aunts' bed, his blood soaking the sheets.

"If Bobby had Maria killed, then it's likely he had Taft killed as well," I murmured, as the realization of all he'd been involved with sunk in. "I've known him my whole life, Devin. How could I not see the evil inside him?"

"You wouldn't have, baby. Evil will do anything to protect its perfect image. It isn't until it's exposed to the daylight that it's unleashed."

I thought about my grandfather. He didn't hide his contempt for others; it was sown into the very fabric of his being, free for anyone to see.

"I think," I began, searching for the right words, "that my

grandfather isn't truly evil, just set in his ways. Until today, I didn't see the difference."

He pulled me forward and wrapped his big frame around me, holding me secure. "Somethin' like that," he sighed.

"Can we go home now?"

I was exhausted. The day's events had worn me down, and my soul hurt at the thought of what Maria must have gone through in her last moments. I wanted to wash away the day in Devin's arms. Wanted to feel his strength and know I was safe.

He stood, dragging me with him. "I'm takin' Calla home. We'll reconvene in the a.m. after I update Parker."

"I'll call the Chatham County Sheriff and give him an update."

"His name is Justin Moore," I supplied as I picked up my bag. "He gave me his card and told me to call if I needed anything at all. Do you want it?"

"The sheriff?" Strawn asked.

"Yes. Justin Moore. Did you meet him last night? He's the man who tried to step in between my grandfather and me. He's very nice, and what my aunts would call a gentleman, even if he asked the most embarrassin' questions."

Strawn looked at Devin and smiled. "I'll bet he did. So he gave you his card in case you needed anything at all?"

"Yes. Is that unusual?"

Devin started pulling me toward the elevators, barking out, "Later," as I tried to keep up. When we were out of Strawn and Nate's earshot, he growled, "What kind of questions did he ask?" in a deep, surly voice.

"Why are you growlin'?"

"What. Kind. Of questions?" he bit out again, jabbing the elevator button repeatedly.

"I don't know. If I remember correctly, he didn't know what twiddle diddles were, so I had to explain."

He blinked, then narrowed his eyes. "I don't even know what the fuck twiddle diddles are, for Christ's sake."

"Why are you shoutin'?"

"I don't know," he shouted back.

Is he jealous?

Blazing eyes. Check.

Jaw like granite. Check.

Looking down, I saw his hands were balled into fists. Check.

Moving closer until his lips were an inch away from mine, I whispered, "I also had to explain that you kicked in my aunts' door in the heat of the moment, because we were anxious to get inside and rip each other's clothes off."

Blazing eyes turned smoldering as the elevator opened. He ignored it and leaned down, whispering back, "Did you tell him I fucked you on the table 'til you screamed my name?"

"I think he got the picture," I answered.

He drew in air deeply through his nose then let it out slowly. "Fuck, but you drive me crazy," he growled, then captured my mouth for a heated kiss. When I moaned, he broke from my mouth and asked, "Baby, what the fuck are twiddle diddles?"

I reached down and cupped his crotch, rubbing my hand down the inseam of his jeans until he hissed.

"Family jewels. Bollocks. Testicles."

Devin grunted, then backed me into the wall and punched the *down* button again, muttering, "Keep it up, and they'll be called blue balls."

✿ ✿ ✿

Prowling after Calla as they headed for his bike, Devin's breath caught when she looked back at him and cast an impish smile. Hearing that Moore had made a subtle advance toward his woman,

Devin itched to possess her body again, to let her know exactly whom she belonged to. He didn't give a fuck if she was still reeling from Jones' betrayal. In his mind, there was no better way to deal with heartache than to feel alive—wanted. And he wanted her with the force of an invading army.

Reaching out her hand as she walked backward, Calla crooked her finger at him as she went. He saw a blush warm her cheeks and he grinned. His Southern belle was playing at something, and he couldn't wait to find out.

She stopped at his bike and looked back at him. The moonlight danced off her eyes as she bit her lip and straddled his bike, raising a brow at him as she sat in front.

He started to say *hell no*, but an idea formed and he grinned, his eyes hooding in anticipation.

He sacrificed their helmets since it was two a.m. and the ride home was less than a mile. For what he had in mind, the helmets would be a deterrent. Climbing on the back, he pulled her in close, so they fit on the seat. The bike wasn't safe to ride in this position, but he didn't give a shit. He'd risk the consequences.

Pointing to a control in the middle of the gas tank, he leaned in and mumbled, his gravelly voice an octave deeper for effect, "Turn that to on."

She glanced up at him to see if he was joking and then turned the control to *on* as he indicated.

"Always make sure you're in neutral before starting the bike." Placing his left hand over hers, he lifted it to the clutch. "Pull that in, and hold it," he instructed in a low whisper, then ran his hand down her silky leg until he'd positioned her foot on the shifter.

"Kick it down until it won't click anymore." Again, she did as instructed. "Now, gently lift the shifter with your toes until you see that green light go on." He pointed to the neutral indicator then nipped her neck.

"I've got it," she answered breathlessly.

"Good girl. Now let go of the clutch and flip this switch to *run*," he added in a velvet purr, his hot breath caressing her neck, "and push *start*."

The engine roared to life with a growl. "Now, we give her a moment to warm up."

Dazed and on fire for his touch, Calla swallowed hard and mumbled, "She already is."

"Let's get her hotter then," he returned, tilting her head back for a kiss.

Calla tried to turn on the seat, but he stayed her with his hands, pulling her ass to his crotch so she could feel what she did to him.

Leaning the bike to its center of gravity, he raised the kickstand, lifted her legs to wrap around his thighs for support and protection from the hot pipes, and then gave it gas, going slow because of their dangerous position.

Savannah was deserted, the streets dark if not for the glowing streetlights casting shadows. Devin used this to his advantage.

Sliding his hand up her leg, he cupped her sex, rubbing the seam of her shorts. When her hips shifted, pressing into his palm, he slipped his hand inside one leg of her shorts until he reached her lace panties and then pulled them to the side. When he entered her wet heat, he groaned. She was drenched, ready for him.

The illicit dance upped the heat factor as she tried to hold still, and within a quarter mile of River Street, her head slammed into his shoulder and she cried out softly. He knew then he'd lose control of the bike if he didn't stop, so he pulled into a shadowed corner and parked.

Pulling his hand out of her shorts, he dove back in the front and gave her the attention she needed. One finger joined the first as his thumb rolled her clit, and she ground down on his hand. Her breath caught when he increased his pace, and she rolled her hips, looking for her climax.

Claiming her mouth to cover her cries of pleasure, his free hand found a pebbled nipple, and he rolled it, pinching hard. She bucked, grinding down on his fingers. He pulled her shirt up so he was skin to skin with her breast, and continued his attentions to the swollen tip. She moaned at the contact of his warm touch, and her legs spread wider for his driving fingers.

"When I get you home," he gritted out, "I'm gonna taste that sweet pussy of yours, and I don't want you to move a muscle. If you do, I won't give you what you want."

Calla whimpered, then arched her back, shuddering as she tightened around his fingers, milking them like it was his cock, and he groaned low in his throat.

He kept working her as she rode out her orgasm, taking her mouth again to avoid detection. She finally slumped against his arm and opened her eyes. Her hair was a sexy mess, a look he was beginning to realize was just her, and she had a dreamy quality about her face. When she reached up and ran her delicate hand across his face, he couldn't help but whisper, "Christ, you're beautiful."

Her hand paused on his cheek then she turned on the seat so they were facing each other. "I've never been called beautiful before," she answered scanning his face. "I like that the first time I hear those words, they're coming from you."

He leaned in and nipped her lip. "You're beautiful, kind, and a million other qualities that drive me wild."

"Ditto," she answered. "But your soul—she placed her hand over his heart—"attracts me the most. You're gorgeous on the outside, but your inside is blinding in its beauty."

He wrapped his hand in her hair and yanked her head back. "You can't say that shit to me while we're out on the street when all I want to do is bury myself inside you."

She licked her lips. "Then take me home. I promise not to move."

Growling, he took her mouth again, then ordered, "Climb on behind me," when he was done.

She did as she was told, snuggling in close to his back as he fired up the Harley.

Devin pushed the speed limit getting home, impatient to get his hands on Calla. A half a block from Bay Street, a car appeared out of nowhere from a back alley as they passed. He gunned the engine, avoiding being clipped on the back end by inches. He felt Calla turn and look behind them as he took a left on Bay and headed for the ramp that would take them down to their building on River Street.

In the historic district, with its short streets and back alleys, it wasn't uncommon to have near-misses with cars as tourists tried to navigate back to their hotel. But the raised hair on the back of his neck told Devin it wasn't a tourist.

Did Armstrong try twice in one day?

But why come at him with Calla on the bike?

Morning came quickly after little sleep, thanks to Devin and his insatiable appetite for my body.

He'd dropped me off at work with a promise to pick me up when I was done and strict orders not to leave the building without him. He was being overprotective considering everything that happened the day before. Normally, I would have balked at the idea of being ordered around by anyone, but deathly images of Maria and Taft invaded what sleep I'd had, so I didn't argue.

I made it to my desk before Poppy and Sienna arrived at work, so I grabbed my mug and headed for the break room, in need of caffeine. I'd missed work the day before and half a day on Monday cleaning for Carmella. I was behind and needed to up my game that day if I wanted to get through several chapters of *The Way to a Man's*

Heart is Through His Dick.

As I stirred sugar into my coffee, Jolene walked in with her own mug.

"You get your family emergency sorted yesterday?"

She was referring to the excuse I'd given when I called in to work on the way to my grandfather's house.

"Not really. Some new developments have arisen," I yawned.

"Do tell," she grinned. "Your granddaddy is a cantankerous old man. I can only imagine what it's like dealin' with him, sugar."

She filled her mug then turned to walk out with me. "Granddaddy is a complicated man. I bore the brunt of that yesterday, but I think I understand him better, if that's possible."

"You ever decide to write a book instead of editin', you should use him as an antagonist. The man would be solid gold as a villain."

"Me? What about you? Have you ever thought of writin' one?"

"I have ten started," she chuckled. "None of them call to me, so I keep on editin' until the right plot forms."

The elevator opened as we stood there, and Poppy and Sienna poured out, deep in conversation as they walked up.

"That's why the city has signs posted about panhandlers, Poppy. Just keep walkin' next time."

"But he looked awful, Sienna. He was just standin' there starin' at the buildin' like a ghost or somethin'."

"Yeah, and the ghost hissed at you when you offered to buy him breakfast. Next time, keep goin' and don't look back."

"Hey," I called out. "What's goin' on?"

Both of them startled at my question, then came at me with questions flying.

"Some friend you are," Poppy accused. "Not one word from you yesterday, and we must have left twenty messages."

"I—"

"You were kidnapped, and you didn't think we'd be worried?"

"Well, you see—" I tried again.

"New rule," Poppy bit out. "When you hook up with the guy you're lustin' after and then get kidnapped, a phone call fillin' us in is at the top of your list."

Jolene moved to stand in front of me, grinning. "Sugar, you don't need to write a novel, your autobiography would be a best seller."

"Whatever," I responded.

"Not whatever," Sienna quipped. "Wallflowers don't keep shit from each other. I'd press you for more information, but I have to get up to Alexandra, so we're discussin' this over lunch. And when we do, don't even consider leavin' a single detail out," she ordered, pointing a finger in my face.

I was beginning to feel guilty. My friendship with them had become important, and I didn't want to mess it up.

"I'm sorry I didn't call, but we found a dead man yesterday and were interrogated for hours. By the time we got home, it was close to midnight. Then Devin figured out what happened to Maria and we had to come here to get the evidence. I'm dealin' with a grandfather who slapped me then kicked me out of the family for choosin' Devin over him, all while lyin' to me about my inheritance. And, on top of that, I think I'm already in love with Devin and it's only been a few days." I left out the part about Bobby, because they hadn't proved it yet, and Savannah being Savannah, rumors flew like bees to flowers, and I didn't want him skipping town.

All three blinked. Then blinked again. Then they opened their mouths, but nothing came out.

I shrugged, because what else was there to say? My life was a damn suspense novel.

"Screw Alexandra," Poppy finally mumbled. "Break room, now."

"Normally, I would be appalled by that statement," Alexandra Poe stated. I turned slowly at her voice and found her leaning against a wall near the entrance to our floor. The Grand Dame of Poe

Publishing was seventy, but she looked closer to sixty. She had a shock of white hair in a short, stylish bob and sharp eyes that missed nothing. And apparently the hearing of an elephant.

She pushed off the wall, clasping her fire-engine red-tipped fingers in front of her and started moving toward us.

Poppy moaned softly and took a step behind Sienna, pushing her forward.

Alexandra raised a brow at Poppy and chuckled. "I said *normally* I would be appalled. I'm inclined to let it go considerin' I just got off the phone with Preston, and the arrogant asshole had the gall to ask me to fire Calla."

"What?" I gasped.

"You heard me correctly. The man's insufferable."

"Alexandra," I began, stepping forward, "please don't listen to him. I love my job."

"Listen to him?" she scoffed. "I told him to take a hike; that you were one of my finest employees and it would be a cold day in Hell before I let you go. But after hearin' what I just heard, I wish I'd told him what I really thought of him."

"I can handle him," I told her.

"You don't handle men like Preston Armstrong, you cut them off at the knees. If you give me the word, Cali, I'll slice them off without a second thought."

She could, too. My grandfather may have been the biggest employer in Savannah, but Alexandra was up there and had connections all over the world. With a single phone call, she could reduce our export production. With several phone calls, Armstrong Shipping would be hurting. But those who would be affected most were the employees who counted on their paychecks to support their family, not my grandfather who had more money than a king.

"That won't be necessary. I'm fine. But thank you for, um, bein' willin' to cut off his legs."

She watched me for a moment like a bug under a microscope then nodded, looking almost disappointed I didn't give her the green light to cut my grandfather off at the knees. Then she turned to Sienna and raised a regal brow, who then moved immediately to follow her. As they turned the corner to her office, Sienna looked back at me and bugged out her eyes, then pointed at me and mouthed "Lunch."

"Weeellll," Jolene drawled dramatically, "A good chewin' on from Alexandra is one way to get your juices flowin'."

"I'd rather do it the old-fashioned way," I mumbled.

"Oh? And how's that?"

I turned and grinned at her. "Editin' a well-written steamy sex scene usually does it."

"Sugar, from what I just heard, you don't need fiction to help you in that department."

She wasn't wrong.

"You wanna know somethin'?" I asked.

"If it requires details about your sex life, then by all means, share."

Poppy and Jolene both leaned in, their focus centered on my answer.

"You know how we always say that men in books are better than real life?"

They both nodded. Riveted to my answer.

"It's all lies. All of it. Real men are way better."

"That's it?" Jolene replied disgruntled. "Sugar, I could have told you that."

"You could have?" Poppy and I both replied.

"Of course. They're just words on a page. Real men come with baggage you gotta fix. Muscles that keep you safe. And hearts that beat only for you. Not to mention a little somethin' between the legs that'll send you straight to heaven and back. Repeatedly, if you give them time to recover."

I looked around to make sure no one else was listening.

"Sometimes they don't even need time to recover."

"Now, that's more like it." Jolene smiled.

Poppy threw her hands up and started backing to the exit. "Say no more. If I have to be around this man, I don't need to know this." Then she paused in her tracks. "Really? No recovery time at all?"

"Not so far," I answered.

"God, you suck. First time out of the gate, and you land Superman," she grumbled then turned and left, hollering, "Lunch," as she went.

Jolene raised a brow at me in question.

"She has daddy issues."

"Aww, that explains it. But don't we all, sugar?" she questioned before turning to leave.

She was wrong and she was right, of course. Some of us, unfortunately, had grandfather issues instead.

Twelve

What's my Job?

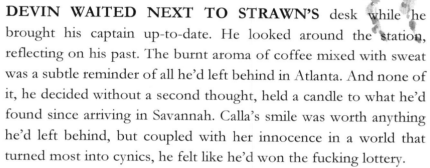

DEVIN WAITED NEXT TO STRAWN'S desk while he brought his captain up-to-date. He looked around the station, reflecting on his past. The burnt aroma of coffee mixed with sweat was a subtle reminder of all he'd left behind in Atlanta. And none of it, he decided without a second thought, held a candle to what he'd found since arriving in Savannah. Calla's smile was worth anything he'd left behind, but coupled with her innocence in a world that turned most into cynics, he felt like he'd won the fucking lottery.

Rising when Strawn exited his captain's office in a rush, he fell into step with him as he headed for the elevator.

"Captain said it isn't enough for a warrant," Strawn mumbled low. "Jones may not be Armstrong, but he's Armstrong's right hand, so he needs more proof before goin' to the DA."

Disgusted, Devin growled, "And you wonder why I left the force?"

"I know exactly why you left," Strawn agreed. "Don't tempt me."

"All right. We can discuss it *after* we find Maria's killer."

"Deal," Strawn answered. "Until then, we need to find a way to prove that Jones was involved, so let's run it down."

"Fact," Devin started, all business. "We know Jones is right-handed, so he didn't kill Billy Ray. At most, he's an accessory."

"What about that giant of a bodyguard Armstrong employs?"

Devin shook his head. "He led with his right when he came at me."

Punching the *down* button, Strawn bit out, "Then who the fuck are we lookin' for?"

"All this ties to Jones needin' money for a shipment. We need to follow Stutter's money to the seller."

"Can Parker do that without compromisin' his position?"

"Only one way to find out," Devin said, pulling out his phone.

The call went to voicemail, so he left a message. They exited the station each heading for their vehicle. As Devin neared his bike, he began scanning it. He'd never ride again without first checking his brakes.

"What about Yoo?" Strawn said.

"I haven't caught up with her. She's been AWOL at her office when I've gone past."

"Feel like takin' a ride now?" Strawn asked.

"No time like the present."

"I'll follow you," Strawn stated, climbing inside his truck.

Devin led him into the heart of Savannah. The striking difference between old Savannah and the rest of the city still amazed him. It was as if time stood still within the three-and-a-half mile historic district, yet the rest of the city was forgotten. Streets filled with rundown businesses and homes, housing panhandlers from all walks of life, were all within a block of million-dollar brownstones. Yoo's business' headquarters was on a similar rundown street.

The homeless watched as they drove up, their curiosity piqued, so Devin parked his bike where he could see it. Losing two bikes in two days would be a bitter pill to swallow, one he didn't think his insurance company would believe.

Strawn knocked on the wrought iron security door, pulling his badge out as they waited. They heard the sound of footsteps inside, but they seemed to be heading toward the back instead of the front.

"We've got a runner," Strawn bit out, peeling off for the back of the building.

Unholstering his 9mm, Devin stepped back and sighted the front door. If they doubled back in an attempt to outsmart Strawn, he'd be ready.

Moments passed, but there was no movement at the front door. Then Devin heard shrieking from the rear of the building. He took off, putting a hand to the metal railing in his path. He cleared it without missing a beat and headed for the back. When he rounded the corner, he found Strawn on the ground wrestling with an Asian woman who had to be six-feet tall and built like a tank.

"You need help?" Devin asked, smiling.

"Get my fuckin' cuffs," Strawn growled, grappling with her hands as she tried to claw his face.

She wrestled one free and drew back her hand, screaming, "You no take me to jail," before she clocked Strawn in the jaw. His head snapped back, and he lost control of the second hand, giving her the opportunity she needed. She bucked her huge frame and rolled until she was on top of Strawn. That's when Devin stopped laughing. He charged whom he decided was Yoo, and slammed into her, taking her back to the ground and off Strawn before she smothered him. When he slid off her in an attempt to subdue her hands, she got in a left hook, and Devin saw stars.

"It's harder than it looks," Strawn bit out as he got to his knees, his breath punching from his lungs like a racehorse. "Who's laughin' now, Hawthorne?"

Devin blocked another left-handed punch, his muscles straining against the weight, then he barked back, "She's left-handed."

"I noticed that when she punched me the first time."

Strawn took his time pulling the cuffs from his pocket, enjoying the show now that he wasn't on the receiving end.

"If she'd been in the video last night, instead of a voice in the background, I might have come here sooner."

She rolled again, half-smothering Devin, so he put his forearm to her throat and pressed hard against it, hoping the loss of oxygen would slow her down.

"Word to the wise," Strawn said. "If you cut off her air, she'll pass out on top on you."

"Fang Ken Yoo no go to jail," Yoo shrieked, rolling away from Devin.

"I think she told you to fuck off," Strawn grinned.

Devin dodged her fist, replying, "Nope. It's her name."

"Interestin'. She's surprisingly strong, don't you think?" Strawn added. "You want some help?"

"Take a seat. I'll be done in a minute," Devin growled, rolling with Yoo, ready to put her in a choke hold if he had to. "I wasn't raised to hit a lady, Ms. Yoo, so please don't tempt me."

She tried to get to her knees, but Strawn was ready with the cuffs. He slapped one onto her left wrist then twisted her arm until it was behind her back. When she tried to roll again, Devin dove for her other arm and pulled it behind her back. Off balance and without the use of her hands, Yoo pitched forward, taking both men with her as she landed on her face.

Both Strawn and Devin were panting when they finally rose from the ground. As they stood, brushing grass from their jeans, a cheer erupted around them. Devin turned and found a crowd of homeless men and women, all with matching smiles.

"Christ," Strawn snapped. "What are the odds this stays quiet?"

"Slim," Devin scoffed. "Not with the way the streets talk. First patrolman they see will hear about it."

"Fuck," Strawn bit out.

"Not Fuck," Devin grinned, his lips twitching, "Fang Ken Yoo."

"Wait, so you're sayin' that Bobby Jones either killed Maria or was there when she died?" Sienna asked.

I looked around the outdoor patio at Huey's on River Street to make sure no one was listening. We'd left Poe to eat lunch so we could have privacy. Devin had ordered me to stay in the building, but the break room was always filled with employees with big ears and bigger mouths.

"Devin said whoever killed Billy Ray was left-handed and Bobby isn't, so there's no way to know. I suppose it's possible he wasn't there and this other person orchestrated everything. We'll just have to wait and see, but one thing's for sure, Bobby knows somethin' even if he wasn't there, and he didn't come forward. Not to mention, he was plottin' to get me pregnant so he could marry me for my money."

"Have you asked your aunts about these supposed shares?"

"Yeah. They said any money left to me was put into a trust that my grandfather controlled until I turned twenty-five. They didn't know I owned half the family's shares, and I never asked about the money, because I was saving it for my future children."

"Wouldn't you have seen the amount on your tax return?" Poppy asked.

"If I did my own. The company's accountant always does them for me at my grandfather's insistence, and if I owed anything, he cut a check for me. I've never bought a car or house, so I've had no need for a copy. When I went to college, his accountant sent the checks and forwarded any paperwork they needed. I've been pretty blind to a lot of things it seems."

Sienna shook her head. "Yep. You really did have your head in the sand."

"I figured that out last night. Granddaddy's held his money over my head my entire life, and it turns out I'm as rich as him. That bein' said, I'm relieved beyond words he wasn't involved with Maria's death. I despise him for so many things, but this? I don't think I could have handled knowin' that my flesh and blood committed such a heinous crime."

"What are you gonna do? Will you confront him about the money? About his lies?" Poppy asked.

"Nothin'."

"Nothin'?"

"It changes nothin' except I know my future children can go to any college they choose, and I'll be able to take care of my aunts 'til the end of their days in a way they should have been taken care of all along."

"Cali?" Sienna said, "It's obvious your grandfather was all bluster last night when he said he would cut you off from his money. Clearly, he knew he couldn't, so is it possible that he uses threats to get what he wants, but never actually executes those threats?"

"You mean, did he actually cut my aunts from his will?"

She nodded.

"I suppose it's possible," I answered, wondering if it was true. Did he try to manipulate them the way he did me, only to lie about cutting them out? If that was true, that would mean he wasn't as heartless as he appeared and there was still hope he'd change his ways.

"Enough about your grandfather," Poppy said, smiling. "Tell us all about devilish Devin."

Leaning back in my seat, I sighed dreamily. "He's perfect."

Sienna began grinning as well, and said, "Do tell."

"Nothin' to tell, he's just perfect."

"Rose-colored glasses," Poppy mumbled. "No man is that perfect," she answered looking over my shoulder.

"I don't mean he's perfect, perfect, just that he's perfect for me."

The hair on the side of my neck was swept away, followed by warm lips. "You think I'm perfect?" Devin purred in my ear. "But not perfect enough to follow my orders to stay inside, I see."

Instead of feeling embarrassed at having been overheard, I raised my hand and buried it in his hair. "I do, and I'm not alone, so I'm not disobeying technically," I whispered, turning my head. "What are you doin' here? I thought you were with Detective Strawn huntin' bad guys."

He took the chair next to me and sat down, throwing his arm around my shoulders until I was tucked in tight against his side. Then he picked up one of my hands and started to fiddle with a ring on my index finger.

"Bad woman," he finally answered.

"Pardon?"

"We were huntin' a bad woman, not a bad guy."

"You've lost me," I answered.

"We went to interview Fang Yoo. She ran, and we had to subdue her. She's in lockup now waitin' to be interrogated."

I turned and looked at him in shock and noticed he had a bruise under his right eye that was beginning to swell.

Did she punch him?

Images of Devin chasing a tiny Asian woman around her yard as she ran for her freedom filled my head, and I had to bite my lips to keep from laughing. But I had to know if this big, bad, tough guy had been clocked by a woman, so I raised my hand to his cheek and asked on a choked laugh, "Did she punch you?"

His jaw tightened.

I snorted then covered my mouth.

"With her *left* hand," he bit out, and all humor faded away.

"Yoo is left-handed?" I gasped.

"Yeah."

"Are you sayin' that you think Yoo killed Billy Ray?"

"Yeah."

"And Maria?"

251

"Jury's still out on that. She was strangled, so it could have been either one."

"What about Taft? Did she kill him as well?"

Devin looked at Poppy and Sienna then looked back at me. "Angle of the wound suggests a right-handed person. He was lyin' down on the bed when the deathblow came."

"So it wasn't Yoo," I mumbled.

"Unlikely."

"So Bobby killed Taft?"

His jaw grew tighter.

"I found out right before I came here that his whereabouts are accounted for during the time of the murder."

"Are you sayin' there's a fourth person involved?"

"No. I'm sayin' Jones' whereabouts have been accounted for by a witness. We have to prove otherwise."

A lightbulb went off, and the bottom dropped out of my stomach. "He was with my grandfather last night. He's—he's Bobby's alibi, isn't he?"

He nodded slowly, watching me closely.

"That means if Bobby killed Taft, then my grandfather knows," I whisper-shouted.

I'd had waking nightmares about Maria running for her life, and Taft laid open like a fish, wondering what kind of person could do such a thing. Now evidence *again* pointed to the fact that my grandfather was involved.

My heart started pounding, and I stood abruptly, threading my hands through my hair. "I've gotta get back to work," I said for an excuse to leave.

What I needed was to run, to burn off the adrenaline coursing through my body making my heart race.

Devin stood and tried to take my hand, but I pulled back. "I can't do this right now."

Poppy and Sienna stood, too, and made their way around the table. When they started to reach out to me, I stepped back from them, as well. I didn't want to be touched. I didn't want them to comfort me. I didn't want . . . to tarnish any of them with my fucked-up family.

"I have to go," I mumbled then grabbed my purse. I made it two steps before Devin grabbed my arm and started steering me in the direction of Frock You and my apartment.

"I need to be alone," I begged.

"That's the last thing you fuckin' need."

"He's involved, Devin. He's evil, just like Bobby."

"If he is, then we'll deal with it."

Deal with it? How do you deal with a grandfather who's a murderer? How do you deal with the fact that an innocent young woman was dead because of your family? How do you fall in love with someone and sentence them to a life of being with the granddaughter of a killer? A man like Devin, who stood for truth and justice, deserved better.

I began to shake, the need to run overwhelming.

Ripping my arm from his grasp, I took three steps back and put my hand up to stop him from following. "You need to stay away from me. I knew this thing between us would end eventually, so I'm savin' us both the heartache of becomin' attached and you the stress of defendin' my family when this all comes out."

He looked shell-shocked.

"I don't know where the fuck this is comin' from, but if you think I'm lettin' you walk away from me, think again," Devin growled.

"I think you don't have a choice," I answered.

I would save him from my family even if he wouldn't.

Devin took a step toward me, but I backed up further. One of the haunted Savannah trolleys was heading in our direction, so I waited a second more then said, "Good-bye, Devin," and ran across the street just in front of the trolley so he couldn't follow. Ducking, I jumped into the back of the Trolley and plastered myself to the wall. The man at the front narrowed his eyes at me, and I mouthed, "Please," as tears began to fall. He ducked and looked out the back when I heard Devin shout, "Calla?" He looked back at me and nodded. I don't know if he thought I was running from an abusive boyfriend, and I really didn't care. I just need space to think.

After we'd gone a fair distance, I peeked over the railing to see if I'd made a clean getaway. Devin was running in the opposite direction, pushing through the crowd, and my heart sank a little.

"You hidin' from somethin'?" an elderly woman asked from the seat in front of me.

"Yeah."

"Can I ask what?"

I thought about that a moment. "My past, my future, what could have been but can never be."

"You've got a lot of baggage."

I nodded. "I do."

"Maybe you should unload some of it and move on?"

"I hear Florida is nice," I answered jokingly.

"Not *move*, let it go." I looked over the railing again and saw Devin standing in the street; he was turning in circles trying to get a lock on my location. The trolley had stopped for traffic, and he glanced at it and then started moving in our direction.

I slid down the wall with my back resting against it, praying the traffic would clear.

"Well?" the old woman asked.

"Well what?"

"Are you gonna let the past dictate your future?"

I looked at her. "My past and future are rolled together, held hostage by an evil man."

"And?"

"And? Explain, how can I have a future when anyone I invite into my life will be touched by that evil?"

"So you choose to be a martyr to your own happiness?"

"No, that's not what I'm doin'. Simply put, I don't want anyone to suffer because of me."

"And walkin' away from them isn't makin' them suffer?" she tsked. "My momma used to tell me that every action in this life touches someone. How we choose to live our lives is the difference between touchin' someone with the hand of God or the hand of the devil. I'd say walkin' away from someone you care about is about as far away from God's love as one can go."

The trolley rocked forward, heading down the street again as I digested the old woman's wisdom.

"What exactly are you plannin' to do if you escape?" she asked, looking over my shoulder at the road behind us.

"Rightin' a wrong done to an innocent woman."

"And then?"

I shook my head and looked down. I didn't know what I was doing anymore.

"Well, you got about fifty feet to decide, and I'm thinkin' if you don't shit and get off the pot now, then your future will be decided for you."

I snorted at her colloquialism. This sweet old lady with her words of wisdom had a potty mouth. "Why do you say that?"

"That way leads to evil, does is not?" she pointed in front of her. "And that way leads to God's grace, where you can touch lives with light, so they'll forget about the darkness." She pointed in Devin's direction. "So what's it gonna be? Follow the path into darkness and sacrifice a part of your soul in the process, or take a leap of faith that God will work his grace inside of you?"

Turning in circles, Devin had a sinking feeling he couldn't shake. Calla was slipping away from him like tiny grains of sand through his fingers, and he knew in his bones if he didn't find her now, she would do something stupid. Something she'd never recover from.

Though their paths had only crossed a few days before, set on a collision course that neither one of them could stop, he felt like he'd known her his whole life. In a short amount of time, she'd become his other half—his fucking heart. Serendipity, as she'd said that first night, had played a hand in bringing them together, and now that he'd found his heart, he wasn't about to let her go.

As he scanned the street, his heart raced to a thunderous beat, but his gut burned with hatred for her grandfather. He was slowly piecing together that both grandparents withheld affection during her upbringing. Used manipulation instead of love to bully a woman so full of love and compassion that she'd sacrifice what she wanted just to spare him from her grandfather's own brand of evil.

Panic began to set in as seconds ticked by without locating her. He'd never felt this helpless. A bruiser of a man didn't faze him. Death barely touched him now, but this half-pint of a woman with lavender eyes that reached into his soul would be his undoing.

Where the fuck are you?

He caught sight of the trolley she'd ducked behind and took off running. It was the only place he hadn't looked. It was two blocks ahead and ready to turn off of River Street for the rest of its tour.

One block away.

He pushed his legs faster.

Half a block away.

It turned the corner.

"Stop!" he roared, pushing through tourists as they ambled slowly down the cobblestone street.

He rounded the corner, but he was too late. The trolley was gone, heading to some unknown graveyard to captivate the masses.

He put his hands on his knees to catch his breath while he formulated a plan. She wouldn't allow her grandfather to get away with murder, so he'd check there first. If she wasn't at his home, then he'd check at Jones' house. He knew his betrayal was eating at her as well. She'd called him her friend, like an annoying older brother you couldn't stand, but you loved anyway because they were family. She'd told him softly, in the dead of night while he held her, that if he'd asked, she would have done anything for him within reason.

Yet another person in her life who had used and manipulated her for their own end.

When he found Calla, he was tempted to keep right on going out of town. They couldn't hurt her if they couldn't find her. Then again, if what he suspected was true, she wouldn't be seeing them anyway. Not unless she felt like making a drive to the maximum-security prison on the other side of the state.

Pushing off his thighs, Devin turned to head back to his bike. Then he stopped in his tracks. Calla stood five feet behind him. Her head was bowed, her eyes cast toward the road, and he could see tears dripping from her cheeks.

"I'm sorry," she whispered.

He couldn't move, unable to bridge the gap between them for fear she would turn tail and run again. He could see it in her rigid lines and curled palms; she would bolt at the slightest provocation. She may have come back, but she wasn't a hundred percent committed to the decision. No, he couldn't take the first step. She had to come to him of her own free will; it had to be her decision to take the first step, or she'd balk and he'd lose her forever.

"Talk to me," Devin muttered cautiously.

She chanced a guarded glance at him before she began.

"You need to understand that I've been lonely my whole life. Even with Bernice and Eunice showering me with love, I was still hollow—empty inside. Then you showed up like a force of nature and life had color. Instead of hollow, I felt full. You have me off-balance. Every moment around you feels like ridin' a rollercoaster. When you say my name or call me baby, my head spins in circles. I've never had that, and I don't want to lose it. But I've lost everything I've ever loved in the past, and because of that, it taught me to protect myself by leavin' first. That's what I did today."

She wasn't the only one spinning like a wheel. Every shy smile and touch of her hand distracted him like nothing had in his life.

"Baby—" he started to reassure her that he wasn't the type of man who walked away. That when he committed to something, he saw it through until evidence suggested it was time for a new course of action. And the evidence in front of him told him he was looking at his future wife, but she raised her hand and stopped him before he could explain.

"There's more," she said. ". . . My whole life my family's history, their legacy to this city has been retold like Scripture from the Bible, and it's a deep part of who I am. I can't run from that, from my roots, or my responsibility to honor my ancestors, no matter what my grandfather has done. It's my cross to bear, not yours or the girls'. That's also why I ran. I wanted to protect you from the weight of it."

She stopped for a moment, looking around the street as if searching for an answer, so he held his tongue, praying she'd find the right answer for both of them.

When she turned back to him, a decision clear in her eyes, he took a deep breath and waited. "I need your help. I don't know how to do *this*, Devin." She motioned with her hand between them both. "I don't know how to protect you from who I am, protect my own heart, and keep you at the same time."

"You don't," he answered, relieved, able to take a breath that didn't feel like his last. "That's *my* job."

Her brows pulled together in confusion. "I don't understand."

"Calla, it's *my* job to protect *you*, not the other way around. To make sure you're happy, that you feel full instead of hollow, and it's *my* fuckin' job to make sure you never feel lonely again."

"Then what's *my* job?"

"To *love* me." Her lips began to tremble, and it took sheer strength of will not to reach out and crush her to him. But he continued instead. "To crave my touch, to trust me with your whole heart. To fix me when I need fixin', to lay your troubles on my shoulders so you don't have to carry them. To need me more than air. To just fuckin' *love me*."

"That's it?" she asked around a restrained sob. "That's all I have to do?"

Devin chanced a step forward and put out his hand. She looked at it, then up at his face. His eyes begged her to reach out and take his hand, to reach out and choose him.

"It's fuckin' everything to me," he growled, but the words caught midway out, broken with his unspoken plea.

A small sob escaped her lips, and she looked at his outstretched hand again, but she didn't move.

"You have to come to me," he explained. "It has to be your decision. But understand, if you take my hand, that's it. No more runnin' from me. No more tryin' to protect me from your family. You'll be mine. Completely. And baby, if you haven't already clued in, I take that *very* seriously."

She raised her hand then hesitated.

Searching his face again, she looked deeply into his eyes and asked, "You promise?"

He wasn't sure what she was asking him to promise, but he had a good idea. She'd been left behind by the death of her family, unloved except for her aunts, manipulated by a grandfather who should have protected her, and used as an excuse to murder a woman by a man she considered a friend. She was asking him to guard her heart, not to leave her behind, and not to trample over the gift she was giving him—her love.

"I promise," he vowed, the words ripping from his mouth with force.

She didn't take his hand when he answered. Instead, she took a step and threw herself into his arms then buried her head in his neck and wept, words of sorrow for Maria, her mother, what it would do to her aunts when they found out, all mixed together.

When she slumped against him, Devin went to his knees and pulled her in tighter, holding on while she let go. Cars passed by, tourists, too, all staring at them as they headed for Bay Street to escape the heat in one of the local bars. And still he held her while she emptied years of loneliness, disappointment, of self-inflicted solitude onto his shirt.

Once the tide of emotion ebbed, Devin stood slowly and helped Calla to her feet. When she looked up at him, he tried to wipe the slowing river of black from beneath her eyes.

"Let's get you home," he whispered, then brushed a kiss across her mouth. But as he did, the bricks beside him exploded and mortar peppered the air, blinding him for an instant. On instinct, he picked Calla up at her waist and took off down the sidewalk.

"What just happened?" she cried.

Devin ignored her and pushed through the crowd before he put her down and grabbed her hand, taking off at a run. He hadn't heard the report of a gun, but he'd been in enough firefights to know when a bullet had just missed his head and buried itself into the brick and mortar. If he hadn't leaned down and kissed Calla when he did, he'd be dead right now.

Devin stormed into the detectives' division looking for Strawn. He'd left Calla at her aunts' with strict instructions to stay inside. She'd agreed, but they'd kept what happened to themselves to keep from upsetting Bernice and Eunice. She'd told them she had a headache and Devin had brought her home from work so she could rest. They believed it, and started making her tea as he'd said good-bye to her in Frock You's kitchen.

Strawn looked up as he entered and motioned to him with a jerk of his head to an empty interrogation room.

Devin followed, holding his tongue until the door was closed behind him.

"Tell me you got that viper to talk," he bit out. "Calla and I just got shot at in broad daylight with tourists everywhere. I want Jones and Armstrong off the street. If they're willin' to risk Calla as collateral damage in their quest to save themselves, then they're willin' to do anything."

When he was done, Strawn took the floor out from underneath him.

"We confirmed not an hour ago that Armstrong, Jones, and his giant of a bodyguard were in Savannah at a business meetin' when Taft was done."

Devin closed his eyes and dropped his head, then his hand came to his face and he pinched the bridge of his nose to control his temper.

"You're tellin' me that Armstrong may be innocent of any wrongdoin' concernin' Maria Espinoza and Charles Taft?"

After what Calla just went through, he wanted to kill someone. He thought he was protecting her, giving her time to ease into the idea that he may be involved, that's why he'd told her about her grandfather being Jones' alibi. He'd put her through hell for nothing.

"That's what I'm tellin' you. We've got thirty men who will testify in court that Armstrong and Jones were in a meetin' and couldn't have been on Tybee Island. And not only that, their own drivers confirmed the giant didn't leave the parkin' garage."

Devin turned and put his fist through sheetrock. It didn't ease the rage boiling under his skin, so he punched it again. Then again.

"You feel better?" Strawn asked as he waved off a patrolman who'd opened the door to check on Strawn.

"Not in the fuckin' least," he growled. "My woman just emptied her soul on my shoulder because I told her that her grandfather might be coverin' for Jones last night. That's what *we* believed when I left here, so I tried to ease her into the idea, and she handled it about as well as a kitten bein' thrown into the river. So until I know exactly what the hell is goin' on, I'm not gonna tell her otherwise and get her hopes up, yet again."

"Jesus," Strawn replied.

"You don't know the fuckin' half of it, my friend, so lay this out for me one more time before I rip that old man's head off. Because someone, I'll repeat, just took a shot at me and Calla on the fuckin' street."

"All right, let's start at the beginnin'. Maria overhears Jones talkin' about marryin' Calla, and she's followed by at least Stutter and Yoo. Jones could have been there, but we don't know."

"Taft is outside the buildin' when Stutter is brought out, askin' me questions. Bein' a typical reporter."

"Your apartment was broken into, and your computer searched, so we'll assume that was Taft diggin' for a story."

"Or he was keepin' tabs on me for Armstrong."

"Doesn't fit. You hadn't made your move yet."

"Not true. It was crystal clear to her aunts I was interested that first night, which they relayed to Eunice's boyfriend. Calla told me Armstrong had been blackmailin' him to keep an eye on things, so Armstrong knew about me before we ever found Stutter."

"So he sends Taft to follow you around, and he watches from a distance, sees what's clear to anyone watchin' that you're drawn to each other."

"Right," Devin said, and he began to pace. "Armstrong orders Taft to keep an eye on us, probably follows me hopin' to get pictures he can use to discredit me in Calla's eyes. By now he knows we're together, because Jones is there when I come home and he threatens me."

"So Armstrong has your brake lines cut by Taft to get rid of you, and then what?"

"Jones probably confided in his mentor about Maria, so Armstrong reached out to Yoo to get rid of Taft while he and Jones were in a meetin' lookin' innocent as a newborn babe."

Strawn grinned. "It fits."

"Yeah, it fits.

"We'll know for sure within the hour. Tech guys are viewin' the footage from the parkin' garage and inside the hotel. Bad news is, Armstrong is now aware that we're lookin' at him and Jones for Taft. His attorney is on the phone right now with my captain, so if the footage doesn't show anything, we've got nothin' unless Yoo talks."

"Then break her," Devin bit out.

"She won't say a word. Asked for an attorney, and we're still waitin' for him to arrive."

"Bo, I need somethin' to go on. I can't protect Calla if I don't know where the threat is comin' from. If her grandfather is innocent and this is all on Jones, I can live with that, but you've got to break that woman now."

"Agreed. But my hands are tied until her attorney arrives."

"Play her the tape," Devin said. "Play it then tell her you're bringin' Jones in."

"Before her attorney gets here? I need this case ironclad tight."

"Then take the phone in with you and lay it on the table where she can see it. Let her own imagination takeover."

Strawn held Devin's glare for a moment then replied, "Fine, but you're stayin' clear of the room. I don't need any more holes in walls."

Devin looked at the wall and sighed. "Tell your captain I'll fix the damn wall when these assholes are behind bars."

Strawn clapped him on the arm and they exited the room. Devin waited at Strawn's desk while he retrieved the phone from evidence. Ten minutes later, he watched as Strawn escorted Yoo into an interrogation room, and it was the first time since he'd left the force that he wished he still had his badge. He would have given anything to be in that room.

Five minutes passed into thirty while Devin drank old coffee and paced. An older man in a cheap suit arrived while he waited, asking to see Yoo, so he stopped pacing and watched as he entered the interrogation room.

Showtime. The public defender had finally arrived. He'd give it fifteen minutes tops before Strawn came out with an arrest warrant for Jones and Armstrong. Yoo was too emotional to keep quiet. The minute she thought she was going down, her attorney wouldn't be able to stop her from running off at the mouth.

Like clockwork, thirteen minutes later the door opened and Strawn exited. But the look on his face spelled trouble.

"What?" Devin asked as he approached.

"Tech boys called, and the footage confirms both Armstrong and Jones were in Savannah. They couldn't have done Taft."

"And Yoo? What does she have to say?"

"She's singing like a canary. Jones' goose is cooked. She did Billy Ray and he handled Maria. They finished him off when Maria stabbed him in self-defense. They knew the only way to keep Maria quiet was to kill her, and with arms dealers involved they didn't want loose ends."

"So it's like we thought. They were runnin' guns?"

"Yeah. Just as we thought. These guys are bad news according to Yoo, so that's why they finished off Stutter. They weren't sure he was gonna make it and didn't want to chance him talkin' while under the influence of medication, so they took the decision out of God's hands if he lived or died."

"So she did Taft for Armstrong to cover his tracks?"

Strawn waited a beat then dropped the bomb.

"Yoo insists she doesn't have a clue who Taft is or who killed him. Insists she's never had contact with Preston Armstrong and wouldn't have dealt with Jones if Stutter hadn't brought him in. And the fuck of it is, I believe her."

"Then who the fuck killed Taft?" Devin hissed.

"My guess? Whoever's usin' you for target practice."

Thirteen

The End is Nigh

SIX DAYS AGO, I had a normal yet admittedly boring life. Six days ago, I had a job I loved, a home that was just the way I wanted it, and grandparents, admittedly not your typical grandparents, who I foolishly thought gave a damn about me. Six days ago, I was also oblivious to the kind of evil that lurked in the hearts of others. But all that had changed.

Five days ago, I'd *seized the day* and allowed fate to lead me rather than close myself off from love and friendship. I'd grabbed hold with both hands to a future I desperately wanted, determined to navigate this new life as I stepped from the ruins of my past.

They say the grass is always greener on the other side, but when you get there, you'll find that your own grass was just as vibrant if not more so than what you strove to find.

They're wrong.

Sometimes the grass *is* greener, the flowers sweeter, and the hearth brighter than anything you could have imagined, and your heart truly beats with wild abandon for the first time in your life.

I'd found that by stepping out of my comfort zone and into the arms of a man who made me feel emotions I never had, made me want things I never had, made me want *him* in a way that scared me— and someone was trying to kill him.

And that someone might be my grandfather.

Pretending to have a headache, I went upstairs after Devin left. I couldn't stop thinking about the bricks exploding beside his head and knew I would break down in front of my aunts if I didn't hide.

Wearing a path in my carpet, I replayed the moment mortar burst into dust, filling my eyes with the debris. If Devin hadn't leaned down to kiss me . . . I shuddered at the thought and wrapped my arms around my body.

"How do I stop him?" I mumbled, pacing back and forth. "I can't lose Devin. He's mine. I won't allow anyone to take him from me."

Pounding on my door stopped me in my tracks, and I called out, "I'm fine, Aunties. I just need to rest."

I couldn't talk to them now. I was too upset and afraid I'd let slip what happened. As much as Eunice and Bernice loathed their father, I knew that, just like me, they had held out hope he might change. Knowing what he was truly capable of would kill them.

"Cali, it's Poppy and Sienna."

I rushed to the door and unlocked it, throwing it open. "What are you doin' here?" I asked as the tears I'd been holding onto began to fall. I'd left them on the street, walked away from them just like I had Devin. I thought they'd gone back to work.

They stepped forward and drew me into a group hug. "Wallflowers stick together through thick and thin and never leave a Wallflower behind," Poppy whispered. "We watched to make sure Devin found you and then saw him bring you back here."

"My life's a mess," I hiccupped. "My grandfather is more than likely involved in Maria's murder, which will kill my aunts; and someone took a shot at Devin while we were on the street, and I'm afraid that was my grandfather, too. I have to figure out how to stop him before somethin' happens to Devin. I can't lose him."

Sienna took my hand and led me to my couch, while Poppy went to my kitchen, grabbed a glass from the cabinet, and filled it with water. She was halfway to me, the drink sloshing in her hand, when she stopped short and gasped. "Holy cow, you really are Honoria."

"That was fiction, this is not. Real life doesn't always have a Happily Ever After."

"Yeah, but think about it for a minute. If your grandfather *is* behind this, then set a trap for him."

It hit me then what she meant.

"I doubt my grandfather is the one actually pullin' the trigger," I pointed out. "If he's involved, then it's more likely Jessie is the shooter."

"It still works, Cali. You could tell your grandfather you and Devin are goin' someplace or let slip that Devin is somewhere he isn't, and we could watch from a distance and see who shows up. If no one shows, then you'll know that it isn't your grandfather."

I bit my lip and looked at Sienna to see what she thought.

She thought we were nuts.

"You're both nuts!" she bit out. "There is someone shootin' at people, and you want to draw him out and put a target on your own head?"

I looked at Poppy. "She kinda has a point."

Poppy sighed, walked over to my bookshelf, and started rifling through the titles. "There ought to be some way to use all these books we read to our advantage."

She started pulling out one book after another.

"Deception?"

"Too messy," I pointed out.

"Raven's Song." She held it up.

"Do you own a sabre?" Sienna asked.

"Good point," she mumbled.

Pulling another book from the shelf, she turned to us with enthusiasm, "To Lie To Cheat To Steal?" She looked hopefully at us both.

"Possible," I said, "if it weren't for the fact that I'd have to *seduce*

Jessie to get a confession out of him."

"Another excellent point."

"Tryin' to catch them in a scheme is too complicated. Why don't you ask your grandparents' housekeeper? They know everything that's goin' on inside a house. Why not call her and ask if Jessie was at home at the time of the shootin'?" Sienna threw out.

I jumped from the couch. "You're a genius," I cried out and dashed for my phone.

Douglas picked up on the second ring, and I asked to speak to Debra, the current housekeeper. She was a middle-aged woman who'd been with my grandparents for five years, and baked the best oatmeal cookies I'd ever tasted.

"Miss Calla?" she answered.

"Debra, I don't have much time, so I'm gonna be direct. Has Jessie been with my grandfather all day?"

"Yes. He's in the driveway now polishin' the limo."

Hope surged at the possibility.

"Did they leave at any time today?"

"No, miss. Your grandfather's been here all day." She paused for a moment, then whispered, "His attorney came here early this mornin' and told him he had to prove his whereabouts last night. Somethin' about a man who was murdered. Your grandfather was in such a fit, he hasn't left his office since."

I sank to my couch in relief. "Thank you, Debra. You don't know . . . you don't know how much this means to me."

I hung up and looked at the girls.

"Well?" Poppy asked.

"He's been home all mornin'. Jessie, too. They couldn't have been the ones who shot at Devin."

My bottom lip began to tremble. My grandfather was at least a known enemy. How do you stop someone when you have no clue who they are?

"This is good news, isn't it?"

I nodded. "Yes. But that still leaves the question, who is shooting at Devin?"

"Right," Poppy mumbled. "There is that."

Sienna stood and grabbed my hand, pulling me from the couch. "What we need is coffee and fresh air so we can think."

"I promised Devin I wouldn't leave."

"The courtyard is fresh air. That wouldn't be leavin'."

"Good point. We can get coffee in the store."

We headed downstairs and waved at my aunts as we walked into the kitchen. The pot was empty, so I pulled out a filter and began making a new one.

"This will only take a minute. Go on to the courtyard, and I'll bring the coffee out when it's done."

Poppy snagged a biscone on her way out, then stopped and grabbed another with a grin, while I pulled down mugs then headed to the front to check on my aunts.

"The girls and I are havin' coffee out in the courtyard. Do you want any?"

Eunice was up on a ladder changing out a mannequin, and she shook her head no. "I won't sleep tonight if I drink it after three. Is your headache better, butterbean?"

"Yeah, I'm much better now."

Better because my grandfather wasn't a killer.

"Where's Bernice?"

"She went out front mumblin' somethin' about trollops in high heels."

I moved to the front window and looked out. Bernice wasn't anywhere to be seen.

"Did she say where?"

"I didn't ask, she didn't say. She just mumbled somethin' about trollops and 'not on my watch.'"

I opened the door and stepped out. Tourists were everywhere, but no Bernice. I started to turn to head back inside when I noticed the door to Devin's office wasn't completely closed. I moved to it and pushed it open, assuming Bernice had gone inside.

My eyes had to adjust in the dark room, but when they did, I gasped and ran forward, falling to my knees next to my aunt's lifeless body.

"Bernice!" I cried out as I rolled her to her side. She had a knot on her forehead and blood seeped from a wound. I started to get to my feet, needing my phone so I could call 911, when pain exploded at the back of my head. I dropped to my knees, grabbing my head, and felt someone move in behind me.

"Pity," a woman's voice whispered. "I had no intention of killin' *you*, only Devin."

Fear slithered down my spine, and I slowly turned my head and looked up into brown eyes I knew. Eyes that now held a hint of evil.

"Gayla? You're the shooter?"

Gayla Brown was one of Poe's copy editors and a woman most likely to die of a sexual disease. Her tales about her sexual conquests were legendary around the office. She dressed to be noticed and she was. She had long, blonde hair, a tiny waist, and breasts that pushed the limits of any blouse she wore. And apparently, she was just this side of crazy.

"You know, I find it ironic that when Poppy and Sienna came to me for advice on what to wear for a night out huntin' men, I unknowingly dressed you to catch the one man who destroyed my life."

What the hell?

"I don't understand? How do you even know Devin?" I asked.

She actually pulled up a chair and sat down on it, crossing her legs and adjusting her short skirt as if she had all the time in the world.

I looked at the door to see if I could reach it before she got to me, but the gun she picked up from Devin's desk and pointed at me scratched that idea off my list.

"I was a beat reporter in Atlanta. A damn good one, too," she began as if retelling a fond memory. "I met Devin on a murder investigation. He gave me that look that said he wanted to do more than be interviewed and I, of course, was more than willing to . . . partake in the fruits of his loins."

My stomach recoiled at the thought of Devin in this woman's bed.

"Anyhow, I played the coy game that women and men play, even wrote a sterling op-ed on him to further his career, but he played hard to get. After a time, I got tired of the games, so I waited for him to come home one night, and do you know what he did?"

I shook my head.

"He had me arrested."

I waited for the punch line, the heinous act Devin had committed, but she just sat there, her head cocked at an angle, and her eyes were just this side of wild, like she was waiting for my response. And since she was nuts and holding a gun, I said, "I'm sorry. He shouldn't have done that."

"I lost everything because of him. My job, my reputation. I had to change my name just to get a job. Then I wake up Monday morning and there he was splashed across the front page like a conquering hero. I can't even use my real name because of him."

She was getting more worked up as she spoke, waving the gun around like an extension of her hand, so I looked around for something to use as a weapon.

"He wanted me," she hissed, continuing with her tirade. "I could see it in his eyes."

I felt something move across my leg as she carried on about how they were meant to be together, so I chanced a glance at Bernice and saw that her eyes were open. They darted down toward my leg, so I followed their path and saw her cell phone. I shook my head slightly, telling her not to move. In the dim light, Gayla would see the glow, and I couldn't risk it. Not with a gun in her hand.

"So now what?" I asked to distract her from Bernice. "Are we gonna sit here until Devin comes back so you can shoot him?"

Please say yes. We just needed time for one of the girls to come looking for us. They'd call Devin, and then he'd ride in on his Harley and kick her ass.

"Wait? No, I don't think so," she replied, and my heart plummeted. "Now that I've had my trip down memory lane, I have a *much* better idea. He took my life from me, so it's tit for tat. Get to your feet," she ordered, standing herself, pointing the gun at my head.

I looked down at Bernice then back at Gayla. "Why? What are you gonna do?"

"It occurred to me that livin' the rest of his life knowin' he's the reason you died is a much better punishment. He'll be in a prison cell of his own makin', and know what it's like to be me."

✿ ✿ ✿

Poppy and Sienna headed inside Frock You looking for Calla. When they didn't find her in the kitchen, they headed out into the front of the store.

Seeing only Eunice as they scanned the room, Sienna called out, "Where's Cali?"

"Out front lookin' for Bernice, I think."

Poppy walked to the door and pulled it open then stepped out onto the sidewalk and scanned the street.

"They aren't out here," she called over her shoulder. "Maybe they went for ice cream," she mumbled. "Ice cream always helps me think."

She started to re-enter Frock You, but she paused when she heard a muted cry for help.

"Did y'all hear that?"

"Hear what?" Eunice called out.

Turning, Poppy headed in the direction of the voice then stopped and listened again.

"My niece has been taken by a madwoman."

Recognizing Bernice's voice, Poppy pushed open the door, flipped on the light, and found her lying on the floor in a puddle of blood, a phone pressed to her ear.

Poppy shouted, "Bernice!"

"Out the back door," Bernice cried out. "She took my baby out the back door."

Sienna and Eunice entered the room in a rush, and Poppy headed for the back of the office. Finding a door wide open, she ran out into the back alley and caught sight of Cali being forced into a red SUV.

She cried out, "Stop," and started to run toward them, but a woman who looked just like Gayla Brown raised a gun and pulled the trigger. A bullet whipped past Poppy's head, burying itself in the old bricks behind her, so she dove back through the door.

"Was that a gunshot?" Sienna shouted as she made her way back to Poppy.

"She shot at me," Poppy cried out.

"Who? Calla?"

"Gayla Brown."

"What is goin' on?" Sienna shouted. "Why is Gayla Brown shootin' at you?"

"I just saw Gayla Brown shove Cali into a SUV. She had a gun, and she shot at me."

"She's gonna kill my girl," Bernice shouted, "to punish Devin."

The girls looked at each, their eyes wide in shock, and cried out, "She's the shooter," in unison.

Sienna pulled keys from her pocket and grabbed Poppy's hand. "Come on," she bit out as she dragged Poppy out the back door and down the alley to her car.

As they climbed in, they heard the squeal of tires and looked up the ramp to see a red SUV hang a left on Bay Street and then accelerate.

"That's her," Poppy called out, pointing.

"Call the police and ask for Detective Strawn," Sienna ordered as she threw her car into reverse.

She took the ramp up to Bay Street and ran the red light as she exited the parking area, barely missing cars as they drove through the intersection. Then she pushed the gas to the floor and headed in the direction of the SUV.

Bay Street turned into Islands Expressway, the scenic, winding road that led to Tybee Island. The SUV had had enough of a head start that they could have pulled off without them knowing and headed into town. This was Sienna's worry and she kept pushing the speed limit, but after ten miles, just as Sienna thought they'd lost Calla, Poppy shouted, "There."

"Why is it taking so long to track Strawn down?"

"They keep puttin' me on hold. I don't think they understand what 'life or death' means."

"Call them back and tell them you're his girlfriend and that his house is on fire."

Poppy did as she said and repeated the message, and low and behold, he finally answered.

"This is Strawn," a deep voice echoed in her ear.

"Thank you, God. This is Poppy Gentry, one of the Wallflowers. A woman by the name of Gayla Brown, who works with us at Poe Publishing, has taken Calla Armstrong against her will. We are currently in pursuit on Island Expressway. Can you send backup?"

There was a pause on the other end, then Strawn growled, "You wanna run that past me one more time?"

"Calla. Kidnapped. Red SUV. Island Expressway headed toward Tybee Island. Send backup."

There was a muffled sound like a hand being placed over the receiver, then she heard Devin in the background thunder, "WHAT?" then he started barking orders. "You, get me a unit who can keep up with a bike, and you, find out who the fuck Gayla Brown is."

Whoever he was shouting at must not have moved, because Strawn bit out, "Do as he says. I'll pull her identification," then she heard clicking on a keyboard for a moment. Devin started answering, "No. Not her. Next," then shouted, "Stop! . . . Kendall Brown, I will rip your fuckin' head off."

"Does Gayla go by the name Kendall?" Poppy asked.

Sienna didn't take her eyes off the road, her attention was zeroed in on the back of the red SUV, but she shook her head slightly and shrugged.

"Poppy, this is a dangerous situation. We don't know what this woman is capable of," Strawn bit out. "You need—'"

"She's capable of shootin' at me," Poppy interrupted a tad hysterically. "I know how dangerous this situation is. Please, just help Calla."

He was quiet for a moment then in a calm, gentle voice, said, "Tell me where you are, sugar, and I'll make sure everyone comes home safe."

"We're in Sienna's car in hot pursuit. We're safe, just worried about Calla."

" . . . Poppy," Strawn said in a stilted tone.

"Yeah?"

"*Where*. On. The road. Your present location."

She looked around for a mile marker and saw a sign for Tybee Island.

"Ten miles from Tybee Island."

"Got it. Now pull off the road and let us handle this. I'll call Chatham County and hopefully head them off before they get to the Island."

"No way," Poppy answered. "Wallflowers *do not* leave a woman behind."

"Damn, Skippy," Sienna muttered, pushing the pedal to the floor.

"Pull over, dammit," Strawn ordered.

"Sorry, it's not happenin'. Until we see sirens, we're stickin' to them like glue."

"Poppy, technically you can't see sirens, you can only hear them," Sienna pointed out.

Poppy rolled her eyes. "I assure you he caught my meanin'."

"If you don't pull over, I'm gonna arrest you for endangerin' the public," Strawn threatened.

"Is he shoutin' at you? What's he sayin'?" Sienna asked.

"He says if you don't pull over, he's gonna arrest you for endangerin' the public."

She scoffed. "Bite me, lawman," Sienna shouted at the phone. "Would *you* leave a friend behind?"

There was static on the end of the line, so Poppy asked, "You still there, Detective?"

" . . . Did she just say *bite me?*"

"She did. And she meant it."

" . . . Tell Sienna I'm givin' her fair warnin'."

"What warnin' is that?"

"That when Calla is safe," he growled low—she looked at Sienna and swallowed hard. His tone brokered no arguments, and she decided they'd pushed him too far—"to hide."

Gayla crept, obeying all speed limits once we passed over the bridge into Tybee Island. I would have made a run for it in the slower-moving traffic if it weren't for the barrel of a gun pressed into my side. As it was, I kept still like a statue, terrified the slightest movement would cause her to fire.

"Why Tybee?" I asked, my voice shaking.

With stone-cold anger, she answered. "Last place the two of you fucked like dogs. I'm hoping the image of you dead in the last place he had you will push him over the edge."

I'd had my suspicions that she had been behind Taft's death, but her admission that she knew Devin and I had been there the night before sealed it.

"Why did you kill Charles Taft?"

Her jaw tightened. "He was there when I messed with Devin's brake lines. I didn't see him until he followed Devin and took pictures of his crash. I had to get my hands on his memory card."

"So you followed him while he was followin' us?"

"He was easy pickin's. I made sure he saw me walk up to the cottage, and when he came to investigate, I promised to screw him if he gave me the pictures he took. Good thing I did, too, or your pale ass would be all over the Internet by now. I'm pretty sure your grandfather wasn't payin' him to keep that close a watch on you and Devin."

"He took pictures of . . ."

"Oh, yeah. He was watchin' you from the window the whole time. The perv went back to his car when you were done and jacked off, too."

My stomach dropped, and I knew I was gonna throw up.

"You look green," she chuckled.

"Bein' held at gunpoint will do that to you," I mumbled, trying to breathe in through my nose and out through my mouth to avoiding puking all over myself.

The wind kicked up, and the skies had turned darker as we made our way to my aunts' cottage. The hurricane brewing off the coast was sending rain in our direction. It seemed fitting that the day I might die would turn gray.

When she pulled up in front of my aunts', parking so the SUV was hidden by the cottage and the sea, the skies opened up and cried, and I mimicked them.

This was it. This was where it all ended. I'd never see my aunts again, never feel Devin's lips on mine or his arms holding me tight until I felt safe.

"Out. Hands where I can see them," Gayla ordered.

She stood with the driver's side door open, motioning for me to crawl to her.

I didn't want to die, and I knew if I did as she asked, she would walk me into the cottage and pull the trigger. I was dead either way, so I decided it was now or never.

Crawling across the seat, I waited until I had a foot firmly on the ground and then I lunged at her, putting my head into her gut. Gayla stumbled in her stilettoes and landed on her ass, so I made a run for it out onto the beach, hoping she wouldn't want to draw attention to herself.

I was wrong.

Bullets bit the sand next to me as I ran full steam for the waves crashing in front of me. The storm had kicked up the sea, and only a strong swimmer would be able to survive it. After spending my childhood in these waters, I was as strong as they came, so I decided to risk it. At least if I drowned, I would die on my terms and not at her hand.

There was a pier about fifty yards away, so I angled my dive into the cool Atlantic. Waves pummeled me, so I dove under them, only coming up for air when my lungs burned to avoid being shot.

The tide would take me out then a wave would send me forward.

I was getting nowhere and fading fast, so after five minutes of fighting the current, I decided to tread water for a moment and looked back the way I came. I froze, wiping salt water from my eyes to make sure I wasn't hallucinating.

Poppy and Sienna were on the beach shouting at me, and Gayla was on the ground not moving.

I don't know where they came from, but hope surged, and I started kicking for the shore. But for every stroke, the current took me back two.

The pier was my only hope.

With renewed determination, I swam sideways against the current, kicking and pulling at the water. Twenty feet. Ten feet. Then five. A wave thrust me toward a leg, and I grabbed hold, wrapping my arms and legs around the pole.

Maneuvering so I could see the shore, I was overjoyed to find bright lights from emergency vehicles dressing the beach like Christmas lights. And in the pouring rain, surrounded by the black water of the Atlantic, I could see Poppy and Sienna pointing toward me as Devin sprinted across the sand, pulling his shirt from his body before diving into the ocean and swimming in my direction.

I smiled even though I was freezing. Not because Devin was about to save me or because Gayla was being hauled away in cuffs. No, I was smiling because I'd been saved by two women, who had proven in five short days that they were my friends, my equals, my Wallflowers. And, as they'd said: Wallflowers are for life. Wallflowers always stick together, and Wallflowers never leave a woman behind.

When Devin reached me, I dove into his arms.

"I love you," I cried out. "I don't care if it's only been five days. I love you, and I want you to know it."

Clutching me to his body, Devin grabbed hold of the pier and then growled in my ear, "What'd I say about tellin' me shit like that when we're in public?"

I smiled into his neck.

"Then take me home and punish me."

The thundering of feet could be heard from the pier above us, then someone hollered, "Hold on! We've got a harness coming," but Devin didn't respond. He was too busy kissing me senseless as waves crashed around us.

Five days was all it took for me to find my Happily Ever After.

Now, it was Poppy and Sienna's turn.

Epilogue

Three days later . . .

JACOBS' LADDER WAS RELATIVELY quiet for a Saturday afternoon, which worked for Devin. After a week one could only describe as heaven *and* hell, he needed quiet.

Taking the last pull from his beer, he jerked his head at Nate and held the bottle up, indicating he needed another. Laughter broke the air above him, and he looked up and smiled. His Wallflower and her friends were sitting at the same table as the week before. The same table on the same day he'd looked into those lavender eyes and fell helplessly down the rabbit hole.

Nate headed over with a fresh beer and then popped the metal top off below the bar, all while looking up at Calla and her friends.

"Still can't believe those two women attacked that bitch with driftwood. Takes courage," he remarked. "A lesser man would have waited for the cops."

Devin looked up at the Wallflowers. Lesser man or not, there weren't many men or women period who would have chanced getting shot for a friend.

"They're special, that's for sure," Devin stated.

"Yeah, special," Nate echoed absentmindedly, his eyes locked on Poppy.

"Dilligaf," Devin murmured.

"What?" Nate asked.

"Nothin'," he returned and smiled around his beer.

Pulling his eyes from Poppy, Nate grabbed a towel and began wiping down the bar.

"How's Bernice?"

"Stitches to her forehead, but other than that she's rarin' to go."

"And Eunice? She let Odis Lee back in?"

"Nope. Flower delivery comes every day, and she takes it with a smile."

"Earnin' his way back in," Nate stated.

"He's lucky she talks to him at all."

"I wouldn't trust him."

"Good thing he's not in love with you then." Devin grinned.

"What about Armstrong? Now that Jones is in jail, has he reached out to Calla?"

Devin's jaw ticked at hearing the old man's name.

"He called."

"And?"

"He thanked me for savin' his granddaughter."

Nate's brows shot to his forehead. "That's surprisin'," he replied.

Devin smiled. "Manners are somethin' you don't forget in the Armstrong family. Even if the one you're thankin' is a low-life PI."

"Still doesn't want you with Calla?"

Devin took a pull from his beer and swallowed. "I asked him that, and his reply surprised me."

"What'd he say?"

"He said no one is good enough for his granddaughter."

"That's tellin'."

"Yeah, it is. He's got a fucked-up way of showin' it, though."

"You tell Calla?"

He shook his head. "She's resolved to the fact of who he is. If he wants to make amends, it's up to him."

The girls cackled louder, and Nate looked up again, pausing as he wiped down the bar. Devin watched as Nate's eyes grew lazy with interest. He knew that look. He also knew Nate wouldn't act on it yet. Nate was married to his bar, and it would take a certain type of woman who could handle his commitment—and Gertrude. Nate knew it, so he'd avoided committed relationships. Devin figured for the right woman, anything was possible, once he pulled his head out of his ass and admitted he was standing at the edge of the same rabbit hole, that is.

"You missed a spot," Devin mumbled to pull Nate's attention away from Poppy.

Looking down at the bar, Nate frowned and swiped at the imaginary spot. Shaking his head, Devin looked up and saw Poppy staring at Nate, and chuckled softly.

"You ever hear from Parker?" Nate asked, laying a bowl of peanuts in front of Devin.

"Last night," Devin answered, grabbing a nut. "Seems the reception up in Alaska is sketchy. He was stayin' in a cabin and couldn't get a signal out. He's lookin' into Armstrong for me just so I can lay that beast to rest, once and for all."

"And Jones? Now that he's behind bars, is he sharin' about the arms dealers?"

"Nope. He and Yoo are tight-lipped. Seems they'd rather die in prison than name names."

"You gonna follow up?"

Devin raised a brow. "What do you think?"

"Exactly that." Nate grinned. "Let me know if you need help."

The bar door opened and Bo Strawn walked in. He held up one finger, and Nate turned and grabbed another frosted bottle from the cooler.

As he made his way over to Devin, the girls kicked up their noise again, and he looked up. Then he scowled.

Devin turned to their table and watched as Sienna narrowed her eyes at Strawn, then stuck out her tongue.

Strawn had been fit to be tied by the time he arrived on scene. Poppy had kept him on the phone until Gayla had pulled in front of the cottage. He'd ordered them to stay in the car, but thank Christ they hadn't listened. When he arrived at the cottage, he'd gotten into both their faces, went as far as dragging Sienna off to the side and chewed on her until she exploded. She'd never backed down from her position that she was right, had argued he would have done the same thing if it was his friend, and that had frustrated Strawn into silence because it was true.

Strawn peeled his eyes off Sienna and slid up to the bar.

"I pity the man who takes her on," he growled.

"Would need to be a strong one, that's for sure," Devin agreed.

"He'd have to lock her up to keep her out of trouble," Strawn went on.

"Heard stories about a Sheriff who did just that in Colorado," Devin replied, picking up his beer.

"How'd it turn out for him?"

He looked at Strawn and smiled. "He married her."

Strawn murmured, "Jesus," then grabbed his beer and took a long pull before he pulled a memory card from his pocket.

"For you," he murmured. "I deleted the pics off the one in evidence before anyone saw them. We didn't need them after she gave a full confession."

Devin looked at the memory card.

"So you saw them?" he hissed.

Strawn grinned. "Fuckin' cowboy."

"Bite me," Devin answered, deciding to let it go. He figured at most, the way he'd covered Calla's body, his ass was on display.

Strawn's jaw grew tight at being reminded of Sienna's sharp tongue.

The girls burst out laughing again, diverting both men's attention, and Strawn shook his head. "What's so fuckin' funny?"

Nate grinned. "Hot Cop versus the Asian Giant."

Strawn's eyes shot to Devin. "Jesus."

"Get used to 'Hot Cop.'" Devin chuckled low, clapping his friend on the back.

"Laugh it up, 'Dashing Detective,'" Strawn returned.

The video of them both wrestling with Yoo had hit the Internet about three hours after their confrontation with her. They'd both been too busy rescuing Calla to know about it until they made it back to the station.

"You boys should take your show on the road," a waitress called out.

Devin heard Calla shout, "That's my man," and he looked up. The light from above cast a halo around her head again.

Part angel, part wanton woman.

As if he called to her, Calla turned her head and their eyes locked. Her light purple eyes shone bright as she looked at him, then hooded in response when he flashed her a sinister smile.

Picking up his beer, Devin remembered a conversation they'd had about how she watched him that first night. Specifically about being fascinated with his neck when he took a drink.

To crave my touch whispered through his mind, so he tilted his head back and took a long swallow. When he righted the beer, he glanced back at her, and she appeared dazed.

He lifted a brow in response, and Calla looked away, then she leaned forward and said something to the girls before standing up.

"I need the key to your office," Devin told Nate.

Nate turned and looked at him, saw his eyes were on Calla and that she was descending the stairs with the same heated look.

Nate dug his keys out and tossed them to his friend. Devin snagged them out of the air as Calla approached, then he grabbed her hand and pulled her toward the office.

Strawn watched as the two disappeared behind the door. "Worth lyin', stealin', or killin' for."

"Yep, he always was a lucky bastard," Nate replied.

"Not that lucky," Strawn said. "They go where it's headed, he'll have Preston Armstrong for a grandfather-in-law."

Nate grinned. "Solace."

"Can't win them all."

Nate caught movement up above as he chuckled, and looked up. Then he frowned.

"Does Sienna look like she's just seen a ghost?"

Strawn turned and followed his eyes.

Poppy and Sienna were both standing, but Sienna was locked in place, her face void of color, as a man talked to her. When he reached out a hand and touched her arm, she jumped, then her eyes softened. As they spoke, the man pulled out his wallet and handed her a card, then hesitantly leaned in and brushed a kiss across her cheek before turning and heading down the stairs.

Strawn peeled his burning eyes off the man and looked up at Sienna. Her cheeks were flushed, and her eyes followed the man as he headed for the door.

Standing from his stool, never taking his eyes off Sienna, Strawn growled, "Catch you later," then stormed off toward the exit.

Nate watched as he left, and then grinned.

He figured it would take Strawn about a day to make his move, whether he was ready to or not.

The End

About the Author

CP Smith lives in Oklahoma with her husband and five children. She loves football, reading, and card games. Writing for her is about escape. She writes what she loves to read, and leaves the rest to those with better imaginations.

You can reach Ms. Smith at:

cpsmith74135@gmail.com

Made in the USA
Columbia, SC
19 April 2017